Praise for *Michelle Marcos* on

WHEN A LADY MISBEHAVES

"Her heroine is a spunky delight, and her dark, hostile hero is an ideal foil...Marcos displays talents that are sure to grow with each new title." —*Romantic Times*

"The first in a bold and original new series by a bold and creative new voice in the romance world. Michelle Marcos is impressive in her debut. The characters in *When a Lady Misbehaves* are complex and immensely fascinating, the story is imaginative, and the plotting is excellent. Ms. Marcos makes some clever twists on the traditional romance...Marcos is an author to take note of." —*Romance Reviews Today*

"This rags-to-riches story by debut author [Marcos] absolutely sizzles. *When a Lady Misbehaves* is beautifully done and I highly recommend it." —*Fresh Fiction*

"*When a Lady Misbehaves* is loaded with smolder and charm...It was a joy to read this inventive, sexy, and ultimately moving story. When I want a great historical romance, I'll reach for anything by Michelle Marcos!"
—Lisa Kleypas, bestselling author of
Mine Till Midnight

ST. MARTIN'S PAPERBACKS TITLES BY

MICHELLE MARCOS

Gentlemen Behaving Badly

When a Lady Misbehaves

Gentlemen
Behaving Badly

Michelle Marcos

St. Martin's Paperbacks

For God

GENTLEMEN BEHAVING BADLY

Copyright © 2008 by Michelle Marcos.
Excerpt from *Wickedly Ever After* copyright © 2008 by Michelle Marcos.

ISBN: 0-312-94850-6
EAN: 978-0-312-94850-4

Printed in the United States of America

St. Martin's Paperbacks edition / July 2008

St. Martin's Paperbacks are published by St. Martin's Press, 175 Fifth Avenue, New York, NY 10010.

10 9 8 7 6 5 4 3 2 1

Gentlemen
Behaving Badly

Chapter One

My dear Lord Prescott,

It has taken me a long time to find the courage to write this letter. I beg your forgiveness for corresponding with you without first having made our acquaintance, but this is a matter of greatest urgency. To put it plainly, I need you.

You see, as a lady of leisure in the employ of Madame Fynch, proprietress of the Pleasure Emporium, it is my duty to provide entertainment for the members of our exclusive club for gentlemen. The Madame has told me that I am idle and do not try hard enough. It is my belief that the ardor of my gentleman callers is evidence of my work, and I told her so. She was furious with my impertinent response and forced me to find a gentleman who would implement a course in humiliation under which I would learn to treat better those charges which she appoints me.

I know I've been very naughty in the past, but the Madame says this time she is prepared to discharge me for my insolence. She has given my performance here bottom marks, and she says that my only hope of reprieve is to have an impartial observer judge my innocence or guilt in the matter. I therefore come to you. If found guilty in your eyes, I am to submit to whatever *brand and expression of discipline you see fit, even if it means you must give me "bottom marks" as well. Between us, sir, I will do anything—anything at all—to be able to remain here. Please come at once, and exercise your ruling. You have only to decree how grateful I should be.*

> *Yours completely,*
> *Lollie*

Mina Halliday smirked wickedly as she folded the stiff blue paper. Whetting a man's appetite for sex was so very easy, especially when you knew precisely what form his appetites took. And at this incendiary invitation, this particular man would certainly come. She'd stake her entire collection of erotica on it.

With a practiced hand, she tilted her candle over the flap, and the red wax pooled into the shape of a heart. She glanced at the shelf above her writing desk, where a row of monogrammed seals sat like tiny soldiers awaiting orders. She ran her finger down the line until she found the right one, and then she pressed it firmly into the warm wax—*L.*

With customary neglect of the rules of propriety, Lollie flung open Mina's bedroom door, carrying two cups. "Ye didn't come down for tea, so nice as I am, I brought it up for you."

Mina smiled broadly. "I've got a good one for you, Lollie," she said, the gleam in her eye intensifying as she waved the letter at her. "And this quill is very special indeed. To both of us."

Lollie pursed her generous lips as she snatched the letter from Mina's hands and sat down on her bed. " 'Lord Roderick Prescott.' Never 'eard of 'im."

"You'll meet him soon enough, if my letter does what it's supposed to. I can promise you that he's got pots and pots of money. You want to take your time with this one, Loll. In fact, I wouldn't doubt it if he brought you a shiny bauble or two to relieve your discomfort."

"Relieve my—" Lollie's expression dissolved from puzzlement to dismay. "Oh, no . . . not another spanker!"

Mina held up her hands to calm her. "He's very rich, and—"

Lollie jumped off the bed, her pretty blond curls bouncing against her shoulders. "No! I told you I don't want them kind o' quills. Give 'im to Serafina. She goes in for all the harsh ones."

Disappointment contorted Mina's features as she grabbed Lollie's skirt. "Please, Lollie. It's got to be you."

Lollie pinned a fist to her hip, broadcasting her blatant irritation. "Why?"

"Because . . . because . . ." Mina fumbled for a coherent order to express all her pent-up emotions. "Because I think this may have been the man who had my father arrested."

"What?"

Mina sat Lollie next to her on the bed and leaned forward conspiratorially. "First, you've got to swear to me you won't breathe a word of this to the Madame."

Lollie's graceful eyebrows drew together in concern. " 'Course I won't."

Mina glanced at the door. Though the other courtesans would be dressing for the evening, the Madame often made her rounds of the house to make sure all was ready for the arriving gentlemen. "Before I came to work here, my father was a jeweler on Fulsom Street. One day, a man came to his shop and brought with him a tiara. It was a lovely thing, lots of diamonds and a great big sapphire in it—I saw it later when Papa was working on it. Well, this man asked Papa to replace the expensive jewels in it with semiprecious stones. It was a curious thing to ask, devaluing such a fine article. But he paid well for the job—in advance—so Papa thought nothing of it. When he had finished the job, Papa turned over the tiara and the precious gems. The man left, pleased with my father's work. A few hours later, the constabulary came to the shop and arrested my father, saying that one of his clients had brought a tiara in for cleaning and it was returned to him with substandard jewels in it. Within four days, my father was convicted of thievery and fraud—and shipped to Australia's penal colony."

"The crooked sod! Who was he?"

Mina's eyebrows rose. "I don't know. I never saw him. I wasn't even at the shop when Papa was arrested. And none of the authorities would tell me the name of the man who accused him. The clerks at the Old Bailey all tell me the same incredible thing . . . the case is a matter of national security and they can reveal nothing about it. National security! They won't even tell me where I can write to him! It's been three months since he was arrested, three months since I've laid eyes on him. I don't even know if he survived the voyage."

"Poor duck," she said, placing her hand on Mina's

shoulder. "And you think this Prescott bloke is the one what turned yer father in?"

"That's what I want to find out. The man who accused him had to have had some political influence. No one gets sentenced so quickly. And to have a closed-door trial, where even I'm not allowed to testify on my father's behalf? Who can arrange that quick a conviction? It has to be someone high up in government."

"How do you know it was Prescott?"

"Well, I don't. Not for sure. But Papa had only a handful of clients with so much power. In fact, only two men that I know of. The only thing I know about Mr. Tiara is his predilection for aggression, because he had been bragging to Papa about a woman he had taught a lesson to the night before he came to the store. So I have to find out for certain which of these two men is the one who ruined my father."

Lollie blinked her large blue eyes. "What are you going to do if it's 'im?"

The question hung in the air as Mina's anger filled the room. "Ruin him back."

Lollie's porcelain features twisted into a grimace. "So what do you want me to do?"

"You have to find a way to get him to admit to it. Talk to him. All night if you have to."

She harrumphed. "I can see you've never been with a quill, 'specially not a spanker. Believe me, you don't want to entertain them all night. You'll be wanting them in and done with . . . right quick."

Mina shoved a lock of her straight brown hair behind one ear. "No. I mean, keep him in the salon. Sit at the bar, talk to him. I'll keep plying him with drinks. This way, I can listen in on your conversation."

"What am I supposed to do? Ask him if he had the owner of Halliday's jewelry shop arrested? He's not going to confess something like that to the likes of me."

"Of course he would. One of the most astonishing things I've seen since I started working here is how incredibly talkative these quills are with you girls. Men talk to courtesans as if you were the most discreet and sympathetic of confidantes. They share things with you they would never tell a father confessor, or even their own spouses. They brag about even the most depraved and wicked things they've done, because they think you've no right to judge them. I'm sure you can get something out of Lord Prescott. All you need to do is get him to talk about jewelry. Show him your necklace. Ask him what he thinks about it, or how much he thinks it may be worth. We'll see whether he brings up my father's name or his shop."

Lollie shook her head. "I don't know, Mina. If this is so important to you, why don't you take this quill yourself?"

Mina backed away, her expression sobering with unspoken emotion. "You know that's impossible." Mina had long since accepted that she was no beauty. Of the dozen courtesans in the Madame's employ, none was less than flawless. With such a dazzling array of gorgeous women to satisfy the lust of a man's eyes, no one paid any attention to Mina. She might as well be part of the furniture. "Please, Lollie. This is important to me. I'll give you a week's wages if you do this for me. A month's. Anything you ask. Please."

Lollie sighed noisily, her petulance only adding to her charm. "All right. But this better be the last perverted quill you get for me. The next one better be a good-looking prince eager to marry a Covent Garden trollop."

Mina exhaled her relief. "I'll start making inquiries right away."

⨍THAT EVENING, MINA WENT downstairs to the Pleasure Emporium's main salon. On Saturdays, clients filled the salon early.

Madame Fynch strode up to Mina as her foot hit the last step on the staircase. "How many?" The Madame was a tall woman. Her dark hair had blanched to gray, and she wore it neatly tied in a chignon. Pale, flaccid skin draped over a skeletal face. Her eyes were tiny gray dots, and wrinkles cut into her thin lips. Her gauntness and conservative dress, which seemed so austere and forbidding to all of her girls, lent her a certain stateliness and respectability that clients never challenged. Her bearing spoke of a person who was pragmatic and worldly, and there was no trace of judgment in her voice when she conversed with men. But when she spoke to the girls, her voice was sharp enough to skewer meat.

Mina quickly reached into the pocket of her pinafore. "Twelve, Madame. One for each girl." She placed the letters into the Madame's outstretched hand.

"Hmm. Impressive. You've been prolific today."

Mina beamed. It was nearly impossible to please the Madame, and a compliment from her was a rare token of esteem. Still, Mina had much to be grateful for.

When her father was arrested and his jewelry shop seized, Mina was out of house, family, and prospects. Her father's life was not the only one ruined. When she came to the doorstep of the Pleasure Emporium looking for work, the Madame could have easily turned her down. After all, Mina lacked both the beauty and the experience to be one of the Madame's courtesans. But Mina offered the only thing she did have—her writing ability and her naughty imagination—and it seemed to have paid off.

The Madame placed the sealed letters inside the portfolio in the crook of her arm. "Now . . . explain your tardiness."

"Madame?"

"You're late to the bar tonight. Clients have been here for fifteen minutes, and Charlotte has had to pour them drinks. I don't want a courtesan to serve drinks like a common barmaid. It diminishes their value to the gentlemen. Is that clear?"

"Yes, Madame," she replied, silently piqued by the insult. She might not be the most valuable employee at the Pleasure Emporium, but her success at bringing in clients lent her some worth, too.

"Now, prepare two whiskeys for Evie and Sir Horace. Then bring a bottle of champagne for Serafina and Lord Fewell. Look smart about it."

"Yes, Madame." Mina dashed across the salon to the far end and ducked behind the bar to prepare the drinks, grateful to be free of Madame Fynch.

The Madame walked across the room to welcome a visiting gentleman. Enfolded in her left arm were two things: a ledger of the clients' accounts, and a black portfolio that she called "La Carte." On it was printed, in gold lettering, the menu of her ladies' services. Whenever a new client came to the bordello, the Madame would escort the gentleman to her office and explain what the poetic euphemisms in the booklet were. She would describe, in a detached and unemotional way, what manner of fellatio was offered in the Fire and Ice, the Waterloo, and the Turkish Bath. Men who liked to watch sexual acts would be offered one woman, the Lonely Maiden, or two women, the Errant Schoolmisses. If a man desired variety—and had the wherewithal to pay for it—he could choose the Persian Harem, in which several ladies would join him in his bed. Men loved these terms, collecting each adventure like rare coins they would later brag about and exchange among themselves. Madame Fynch exuded the air of an architect as she elaborated to the client in detailed terms how she intended to build the cathedral of his fantasy. It was widely rumored that after hearing the selections from La Carte, no gentleman ever prevaricated about opening an account on the spot.

Madame Fynch had a practiced mind for business. She had managed her husband's finances and supervised his legal staff when he was too drunk to do it. When he passed away, his law practice went with him, but he had left her a somewhat substantial inheritance and the freedom to manage her own money. She invested part of her remaining wealth in purchasing a dilapidated brothel, which had achieved some notoriety thanks to a scandal two years before involving a scullery maid who had married a marquis. It had remained an establishment of some curiosity among the *ton,* so she decided to capitalize on its fame. She took over the tobacconist's shop that once stood next door and remodeled them both into a single beautiful *maison,* serving only the wealthy and the fashionable.

To the casual observer, the parlor, card room, and conservatory looked respectable enough, like most others of their kind in any house of means. In the salon, a large chandelier dripping with crystals hung from a large white medallion. The candles in them projected their light onto cornflower-blue walls. Upholstered chairs in brocades and striped fabrics were clustered around the expansive room. It was a place where a man of wealth and breeding would feel right at home.

But the real Pleasure Emporium was a flight up the stairs. The bedrooms.

The Madame had personally decorated each room to offer a different experience for her clientele. For those with a taste for the exotic, there was the Pasha's Bedchamber, a room draped with curtains and lined with silk cushions; for those of a primitive bent, there was the Grotto, a cavelike dwelling where food was served on the floor; and the piquant could enjoy the accoutrements of the Stable, a place filled with leather implements and a saddle with a protruding pommel. Fantasies of every kind were dutifully tended to and celebrated.

Despite the meticulous attention she'd given to enhancing the erotic ambience of the upper floors, Madame Fynch's courtesans were so skilled that they actually spent very little time in the bedchambers. It was a testament to their seductive talents that they could so enrage a man's passions through conversation and touch, by the time they escorted a gentleman to the rooms, he required little more stimulation to make him climax.

Nevertheless, the rooms would be filled tonight, Mina noted. The salon began to swell with the regular clientele, plus one or two new faces. Mina bustled about, filling glasses, lighting cigars, and taking gentlemen's hats and walking sticks when they came to the door.

"Good evening, Your Grace," she heard the Madame say as she walked up to the white-haired man who leaned heavily on his cane. "I daresay we haven't seen you in over a month. I do hope you haven't tired of playing our little games."

"Not at all," he responded, his full voice belying his advanced years. "I just got back into London, and was looking for some jovial company."

"Shall I see if Cordelia is in?"

"No, by Jove, I don't think I could manage her tonight. I was thinking of some redheaded spice to flavor my tea."

"I know just the girl. Let me show you to the salon. Mina, a glass of Madeira for our guest."

Mina went to the bar to fetch the drink. She watched as Charlotte slithered over to the duke wearing a clinging dress of sheer muslin. There was a grace and ease about her movements, acquired over years of practice. Her auburn hair was lush and silky, the best feature among her many beautiful qualities. She curtsied low before the duke, making sure he could see well down the front of her dress. Charlotte was mesmerizing. It was like watching a skilled artisan ply her craft. The duke seemed well pleased with his companion.

The courtesans rarely failed to please even the most jaded palates. The ladies were beautiful, of manner refined, and dressed to the height of fashion—if that fashion allowed for a touch of the risqué with a splash of brazenness. The Madame had had the foresight to build the business as a place of refinement and welcome for the noble elite, and only men of the higher echelons of Society could afford to frequent the bordello. Here, the wealthy and titled could enjoy a lady's company without having to consort with others of an inferior class. A far cry from the hundreds of other such places throughout London, the Madame's establishment was clean, elegant, and more exclusive than many of the social clubs. Gentlemen paid well for the satisfaction of knowing that the women they selected had not been enjoyed by their valets the night before.

From across the room, the Madame beckoned Mina.

"Yes, Madame?" she asked, coming to a halt in front of Lollie and a rather rotund man.

"Mr. Hargreaves would like a savory. Please ask Cook to prepare him something to eat."

The man fiddled with his cravat. "Much obliged, Madame Fynch. In the meantime, I wonder if you could point me to the, er, cloakroom?"

"Certainly, Mr. Hargreaves, it's right through that door."

"Don't be long, now, Perceval," Lollie said.

"I'm already long, Lollie," he said, tweaking her cheek. "And when I'm around you, I get longer and longer."

Lollie laughed at his retreating back. When the door

clicked shut, her smile disappeared. "That's what 'e thinks. The old sod barely even wrinkles the sheets."

"Lollie!" admonished the Madame. Her voice fell to a forced whisper. "I will not have you talk about a client in a derogatory manner within earshot of others. Is that clear?"

"Yes, Madame."

"That's the second time in as many days I've mentioned that to you. I won't need to repeat myself, will I?"

"Naow, Madame."

Madame Fynch rolled her eyes. "And work on shedding that deplorable Cockney accent. You sound like a cat with a cold."

"Yes, Madame," Lollie said, biting the retort that formed on her lips. "You needn't worry about Mr. Hargreaves, though. He likes 'em common. Like that other bloke what keeps coming round."

The Madame shook her head. *"Who."*

"I can't remember 'is name, Madame."

"No, I mean '*who* keeps coming round.' "

"I told you, I don't know."

Madame Fynch heaved an exasperated sigh and walked away.

Mina chuckled. "You know, Lollie, you can be pretty thick sometimes."

"Naow, I know what she means. I just like getting up 'er nose." Lollie winked a sparkling blue eye and Mina giggled.

Lollie had been a street corner prostitute before the Madame picked her up for her uncommon beauty. She had the rarest quality of hair—blond, almost white strands that curled in soft, wispy whorls. Her face was exquisitely featured with high cheekbones, voluptuous lips, and eyelashes thick as sparrow's feathers. With her snowy loveliness, she might have easily passed for queen of a Danish empire or a Norwegian princess.

Until she opened her mouth.

Much to the Madame's consternation, the Cockney in Lollie was as indomitable as the law of gravity. And though Madame Fynch had managed to coerce Lollie into speaking more genteelly around the clients, it proved impossible to fully leach out the taint of the street from her manner. As the saying went, you could take the girl out of Covent Garden, but you couldn't take the Covent Garden out of the girl.

The other women weren't as common as Lollie. Madeleine was the bastard daughter of a French courtier; everyone called her "the Countess" because she never let anyone forget she descended from royal blood. Serafina was a Spanish noblewoman who, though married, had pursued a man to England where he promptly discarded her. Evie and Charlotte, who had become very close friends, were scandalously divorced from their aristocratic husbands. And the rest had their own stories to tell.

Mina headed toward the kitchens to pass on Madame Fynch's message. On the way, she passed the front door, where the Madame was placing her letters in the hands of a messenger. Blood raced through her veins as she contemplated the significance of that one letter, the one addressed to Lord Roderick Prescott. Unbidden images flashed in her mind of her father enduring hard labor under the lash of a merciless prison guard, and her heart twisted. She had to find out who the conniving bastard was who had consigned her father to a hell on earth. If he had done the damage, he could undo it. Or at the very least, let her get in contact with her father. All her hopes were pinned to that one missive.

There was no room for failure. At all costs, she simply had to get Lord Prescott to come.

Chapter Two

Salter Lambrick leaned over the body of the dead man to get a look at his face. There was no mistaking it. Lord Prescott was no more.

Salter rubbed the thick black stubble on his own face, a gesture that reminded him of the haste of the call. He stood up to get a better perspective of the murder scene, but was disappointed—not at what he saw, but at what he *didn't* see. Whoever had met Prescott here was careful not to leave any evidence of his presence.

Salter walked around the room slowly, allowing the alchemy of all his senses to paint a picture of what had happened last night. The victim and the murderer had met here in Lord Prescott's study. Prescott had been sitting at his desk, and at some point, the murderer came round behind him and strangled him with a garrote. Prescott was wrestled to the floor, where he fell facedown. Once in the superior position, the murderer leveraged his weight to hold Prescott down as he tightened the cord around the man's neck. From the boot scuffs on the marble floor, Salter could tell that Prescott had thrashed a good deal. But with a man kneeling on his back, Prescott had no way of defending himself.

Salter's black leather boots creaked as he crouched down. With a loud grunt, he heaved the stiffened body over, and it rocked into a square of sunlight beaming from the window. Prescott's face was waxy and pallid, and his tongue spilled over his blue lips. It was a hideous death mask, but Salter had shed the horror of death long ago on the battlefield. He lifted the man's chin to get a closer look at the murder weapon. The crease between Salter's thick brows deepened as he untwisted the cord embedded in the dead man's neck. It was not a garrote at all, but a leather whip. Not a long one, like the kind used on carriage horses, nor even a bullwhip like the kind used on insubordinate soldiers. This was a peculiar instrument, with a sturdy handle and a thong about three feet long. Like the kind they used to chastise schoolboys.

Brackets appeared on the sides of his mouth, the creases accentuated by the dark shadow of the emerging beard. Why would a murderer bring an object like this to kill someone? If the murderer wanted to do Prescott in quietly, surely he would have brought a dagger or some poison, or at the very least, a better-fashioned garrote than a whip.

Salter let the leather cord slither from his large hands. Perhaps the murderer wanted to sneak it in without detection. Or maybe the whip belonged to Prescott, and the murderer obtained it here. The answer to that question would explain whether the murder was planned—or the tragic result of a vehement quarrel.

Salter fished around in Lord Prescott's pockets. He found the man's untouched billfold in his coat pocket.

Evidently, robbery was not the motive. In his other breast pocket, Salter found two items: a folded piece of paper, and a leather tawse. Salter unfolded the piece of paper, and what he saw astonished him.

My dear Lord Prescott,
   It has taken me a long time to find the courage to write this letter.

As he read the rest of the missive, Salter had to smile. So that's where Prescott was headed with all these implements of torture . . . a bordello! If the letter was to be believed, Prescott seemed to have a peculiar affinity for dominating women.

Salter shook his head at the writer's lewdness. He had never made use of a bordello, but had the letter been addressed to him, he just might have been tempted enough to try it.

Salter refolded the blue parchment, a frown casting a shadow over his features. Come to think of it, there might be more to this letter than a sexual proposition. What if Prescott's murderer was someone at this bordello? An irate madam to whom he owed money? Another customer, jealous over his chosen courtesan? Or maybe even the very woman who wrote this letter . . .

"Alcott," he called out.

A young constable wearing a weathered brown coat came to the door. "Yes, sir?"

"Have you met with all the servants?"

"Yes, sir," he said, thumbing through his notepad. "Their statements ring true. None of 'em seemed to have any knowledge of the murder. After they retired for the night, no one 'eard a sound till this mornin' when the butler raised the alarm. Frankly," he said, lowering his voice, "I don't think any of 'em *could* do it. Cook's a frail woman, the maids are little things no bigger'n me sister, and the butler's older than the Lord Almighty."

Salter chuckled. "Fine. You can release them to their duties. Tell them that with their master gone, they should start looking for employment elsewhere."

"Right you are." Chase Alcott jerked his head toward the body. "So whatchu reckon, Chief Constable?"

Salter put the letter in his coat pocket. "I think that this case isn't going to be easy. Lord Prescott was senior aide to the Lord Mayor of London. And the Lord Mayor is *not* going to like the scandal this will stir up. Besides, as the Chief Magistrate of London, his office will be placed under a great deal of scrutiny. I think we had better be prepared for the pressure to solve this case quickly and quietly."

"Any ideas who done it?"

"Not yet, but I've got a lead to track down. Ask that butler fellow to get me one of Prescott's coats. I'm going to do a bit of impersonating." He glanced down at the tawse in his hand, its supple leather strap split into two pain-inflicting tails. Whoever wrote that letter had some explaining to do.

Chapter Three

It was a brisk Wednesday evening at the Pleasure Emporium. Four girls were already ensconced in the bedrooms, and six were still chatting up their clients in the grand salon. A trio of blindfolded musicians played soft music in the center of the salon. Lollie had just finished with her last appointment, and, after freshening up, was taking a rest at the bar. Mina surreptitiously poured her a small glass of ale, Lollie's favorite drink.

"I'm going to need a lot more than that tonight," Lollie said, folding her pale yellow dress into the chair. The Grecian coif and frock seemed to have been invented just for someone with her fair hair and generous bosom. She looked especially ravishing tonight. Of all the girls, it was Lollie Mina liked—and envied—the most.

Lollie gulped it down, and Mina poured her another. "You'll want to take it easy with that. And make sure the Madame doesn't see you."

Lollie rolled her eyes. "I know, I know. 'Lollie,'" she began, imitating the Madame's reproving voice. "'Ladies do not drink beer. I'll not have you burp in a gentleman's face.' Bugger. If he can cream in mine, why can't I burp in his?"

Mina had to laugh at Lollie's tart tongue. Though common, Lollie was one of the most sought-after girls at the bordello. As for Mina, even if she hadn't been dressed as a servant, she'd still be invisible to a man's eyes. As she quietly served wine and port, no one even glanced at her face.

There was a sharp rap at the door. Mina heard one of the upstairs parlor maids answer it. The maid then entered the salon and knocked on the door to the Madame's study. "There's a Lord Prescott here to see you, Madame."

Mina, who had been polishing the crystal goblets, nearly dropped one. She turned to look.

And froze.

A man's darkened form filled the doorway. Broad of shoulder, narrow of hip, long of leg. Certainly not the silhouette of the older, fatter, goutier men who made up most of the Madame's clientele.

What she saw was more than a man . . . it was an attitude. Confidence swirled around him like steam from melting ice. The military bearing was unmistakable, and he seemed far too virile a presence for his refined clothes. He was all hard lines and rough edges. Though his navy blue coat and gold brocade waistcoat seemed of the very highest quality, they utterly failed to civilize him.

Perhaps it was the expression he wore, as if he had just stepped out of a dagger fight. Or his severe black hair and swarthy complexion, which gave him a piratical air. Perhaps it was the ruthless hazel eyes, which bespoke a life accustomed to aggression. But something about this man shook Mina to the core, and she was paralyzed by her conflicting emotions. Here was a man who might very well be the bastard that stole away her father, her security, her happiness—and changed the course of her life. And yet a gust of heat rushed through her body, coloring her face.

"That's him," she whispered to Lollie. "That's the man I wrote to the other day for you."

Lollie turned to look. "The spanker?"

Mina nodded. They turned to watch as Madame Fynch escorted him to her study to open an account. Money never changed hands in the Pleasure Emporium; it was all part of the exclusivity of the establishment. The door closed behind them.

"Ooh, blimey, sod that." Lollie finished her drink in one gulp and stood.

"Lollie? Where are you going?"

"Count me out."

Mina's chest caved. "You can't back out on me now!"

"Did you see the size of him? I'm not going in to get beat upon by a man like that."

"Oh, please, Lollie, don't do this to me. He's just a quill. Just get him to talk to you, like you do with every other man."

"Yeah, but every other man don't look like they'd rather hear you scream than moan."

"Don't be ridiculous. You're letting your imagination run away with you."

"That's not all that wants to run away."

"You only have to make him talk."

"Well, what if he don't want to talk, eh? What if he just wants to go in the Stable Room and tie me to the hitching posts?"

"We won't let him. I'll keep serving him drinks. Don't worry."

But it was she who was worried . . . worried that her resolve would weaken. She had set things in motion, and whatever the cost, she must see them through. She had mapped out a plan for retribution, and by God, she had better follow it. True, the man seemed far more cruel and unassailable than she originally imagined. But she would make sure she had the upper hand before she struck.

Madame Fynch emerged from the study, followed by Lord Prescott. She glided over to Lollie, who stiffened in her chair.

"Lollie," she began, "may I present Lord Roderick Prescott. Lord Prescott, this is Lollie."

Lollie held out her hand, a courteous smile broadening her full lips. "I'm extremely pleased to meet you."

His eyes softened as they raked appreciatively over Lollie's beautiful face and form. "So this is the provocateur? Impressive. I received your letter, Miss Lollie, and I should like to have a word in private with you, if you please." His tone suggested he was accustomed to giving orders.

"Yes, sir." Lollie momentarily glowered at Mina before preceding him to one end of the salon, to an alcove obscured by palms and ferns.

Mina silently thanked Lollie for having such forethought. The alcove offered space where Mina could eavesdrop unnoticed.

Eyes darting toward the alcove, Mina hurriedly poured wine into two crystal glasses. *No!* her frenzied mind screamed. Smaller glasses, so she could refill them more frequently. She filled snifters instead, placing them and a decanter on a silver salver before racing to the alcove.

". . . a most indiscreet letter, young woman."

"I wanted to meet you," countered Lollie. "I would have said anything to get you to *come*."

"And you have a most indiscreet tongue."

"So I've been told."

Mina appeared next to them with the salver. Like every other man, Lord Prescott didn't even look at Mina's face as she lowered the tray. But for once, she was grateful for her invisibility.

"Have you also been told that I severely punish those with wayward tongues?"

"Yes, sir. A little birdie told me." There was a barb in Lollie's statement, and it flew right to Mina. Mina withdrew quietly, but instead of returning to the bar, she crouched behind the potted palms.

"So . . . you are a student of flagellation."

"I beg your pardon?"

"I said, you're a student of flagellation."

"Oh, no. I've never been to school a day in my life." Mina cringed.

"I see," replied Lord Prescott. "That's fascinating, considering how erudite your letter was. Tell me, what prompted you to write to me?"

Oh, no, Mina thought. This interview was not going well at all. *Change the subject, Lollie!*

"That's not important, Lord Prescott. What I want to know is what I can do to please—"

"*I'll* decide what is important. Answer my question. Why did you decide to write to me?"

"I—I just did. I had heard what a handsome man you are, and I can see now that those reports were completely true."

"Don't try to seduce me yet, young woman. I will tell you when you may have that privilege. From whom did you hear such reports?"

"From lots of people."

"Did the Madame tell you about me?"

"No, sir."

"Another client?"

"No, sir."

"Clearly you are not wanting for companionship. There seem to be gentlemen aplenty here for one such as yourself. So I want to know why, of all the gentlemen in London, it was my acquaintance you wanted to make."

"I—I can't remember."

After a brief silence, Lord Prescott said, "You didn't write this letter, did you?"

Do something! Mina thought frantically. She rose, the decanter balanced on her salver, and came to the table. "May I offer you another drink?"

Lollie breathed a sigh of relief at the interruption. "Yes, please."

Lord Prescott's eyes remained fixed on Lollie as Mina tilted the decanter over his empty glass. "Here's one for you as well, sir."

Suddenly, a large hand shot out and seized her wrist. Mina jumped, nearly dropping the etched-glass decanter. For the first time ever, a quill's gaze swung to her face and his eyes locked with hers. Mina shrank from the intensity of his stare, but the strength of his grip held her in place.

"There are ink stains on your fingers."

Instinctively, Mina shook her head, but the evidence belied her.

He rose to his full height, towering over her. His fingers tightened on her wrist. "Young woman, are you the one who sent for me?"

Mina was transfixed by his gaze. His hazel eyes narrowed, and fear crawled up her arms.

"I asked you a question."

Mina said the only thing that came to her flustered mind. "It was a mistake."

He raised a determined finger at her. "Wait here," he commanded, and strode off toward the Madame, who was talking quietly with one of the musicians.

"Cor, what the hell happened?" said Lollie.

Mina's heart was beating so fast, she could barely speak. At the other end of the salon, with his arms folded in front of him, Lord Prescott spoke solemnly to Madame Fynch, who merely nodded her head.

"Oh, Lollie, what have I done? I'm going to get the sack now."

"Better to *get* the sack than be *in* the sack with the likes of him."

The Madame left Lord Prescott behind and strode up to the pair of them.

"Mina, Lord Prescott has expressed an interest in you. Please accompany him to your room."

"That's impossible. I'm not . . . what about Lollie?"

The Madame's face bore no expression. "He doesn't want her. He wants you."

Blood drained from Mina's face. Men didn't ask for her. They didn't even *notice* her. "What am I to do with him?"

Stoically, the Madame responded, "Whatever he asks."

"But I can't—"

"He has started a very generous charge account. You'll be amply remunerated."

This was all going horribly wrong. She looked apprehensively at Lord Prescott, who was scowling from a distance. He looked so large and so forbidding. Mina contemplated all she had written in the letter.

"I can't," she admitted weakly.

"Mina," said the Madame in a tone she rarely had to use. "You will take this gentleman up to your room, and you will entertain him. If it's talk he wants, give him talk. If it's sex, give him that, too. You are in control of what you choose to give, but whatever you do, make certain that he leaves happy and willing to return. Is that clear?"

Distraught, Mina turned to Lollie.

"Go on, Mina," she said. "Talk to him. Now you can ask him whatever you want to know."

There was hope in that. Talk. Yes, she needed to get him to talk. She just wished that she had had more time to prepare what she was going to say.

She stepped out from the relative safety of their group and walked haltingly toward the man. He loomed larger as she drew nearer. She couldn't even look him in the eyes for fear that he might see her ulterior motives . . . or worse, her withered heart.

She walked past him and toward the staircase up to

the rooms. Lord Prescott walked closely behind her.
He was so tall, so substantial, that her shadow on the
floor in front of her was completely engulfed by his.
She sensed danger in his presence, as if an armed gun-
man walked behind her.

When they finally reached the attic floor where her
bedroom was, they could no longer hear the musicians
downstairs or the buzz of conversation. She was all alone
with a stranger she wanted to hate but could only fear.

She opened the door to her room and flew to the
desk, where she furiously lit all four stems of a candelabra. Somehow, the light made her feel safer.

She flattened herself against the wall as he silently
walked round her room, the sound of his boots like a
heartbeat on the wooden floorboards. Her bedroom had
always exuded the comfortable smell of old books and
wood. Now there was a foreign presence, a smell of san-
dalwood and sun, and she couldn't reconcile the two.

She watched him as he inspected her washstand, her
window, her bed. "You don't entertain much in here."
It was not a question.

"I'm a servant," she replied, hating the tremble in
her voice. "I don't entertain customers."

He came closer to her, and leaned over the desk.
"Serving spirits does not seem to be your only office
here." He picked up a sheet of blue parchment. "You
also seem to be the correspondence secretary."

"I write a lot of letters."

He picked up the stack of seven sealed and addressed envelopes she had written to prospective
clients that afternoon and glanced through them. "Are
these gentlemen friends or family?"

She grew indignant at his brazenness. She snatched the letters out of his hands, hoping he didn't see the name on the topmost letter. It was that of Frederick Stratton . . . the second of her father's potential enemies. "Why are you here?" she demanded.

"Why should that surprise you?" he asked, pulling a letter on blue parchment out of his coat pocket and tossing it on the bed. "I came at *your* invitation."

She glanced at the envelope bearing her handwriting, and bit her lip. "You are not for me. You came for Lollie."

"It was your lascivious challenge that drew me here, your . . . tempting words that lured me to you."

Mina scoured her mind for a plausible justification. "No, it wasn't me. It's just that I . . . I have good penmanship. The girls tell me what to say. I write it."

"Young woman," he began as he sat on her bed and drew the leather tawse out of his pocket. "I do not suffer liars gladly. You brought me here under false pretenses. That was your first lie. You told me that you do not write these letters. That was your second. See to it that there isn't a third."

Blood thrummed in her ears as she stared at the wicked-looking strap. His eyes were fixed upon her— unflinching, unblinking—and she momentarily felt paralyzed. A hard vertical line was etched above his nose, setting his black eyebrows in a permanent scowl. It suddenly hit her that he was far, far stronger than she, and she was far, far away from anyone who might hear her scream.

"I write the letters," she whispered.

"Why?"

"To bring gentlemen to the club. Men who can afford it."

"How do you know these men?"

She went to a small dresser near the window and slid out a drawer. She pulled out a book and handed it to him.

He glanced at the spine. "*DeBrett's Peerage, 1813.* This is a directory of noblemen and gentlemen. What do you do . . . write to all these men, one by one?"

She nodded. "I'm up to H."

A smile touched his lips, and it softened the hardness of his face in an unexpected way. "I see. So men whose names begin with the letters I through Z can retain their moral purity for now."

She grew annoyed. "I only ask them here. I don't make them come."

He chuckled. "No. Presumably, you leave that duty to the other ladies." The bed made a creaking sound as he stood up. She darted against the wall.

He strode to the spot she had just vacated and drew open the drawer again.

Don't look in there. She wanted to stop him or push him away, but that would require touching him.

His eyebrows lifted in surprise as he peered over the titles of her secret books. "The *Satyricon.*" He stared at her, as if trying to gauge her reaction. She tried to appear nonchalant, but her erratic breathing betrayed her. "*Fanny Hill . . . Ars Amatoria.*" He picked up a volume that no longer had a cover and looked inside. "*Memoirs of a French Lover.*"

She could no longer withstand his intrusion into her private collection of erotica, particularly that one. "May I have my book back, please?"

"In a moment." He took it over to the desk upon which the candelabra stood, and sat on her chair. "Interesting."

A whole minute passed. "May I have it now?"

He gave her a sideways glance, and returned his attention to the book. "You may have it back when I'm through and not a moment before."

She swallowed hard. It was agony watching a strange man thumb through her favorite naughty book. This humiliation was worse than the one she endured from the smirking bookseller she had bought it from so long ago. She remembered the day she brought it home, delirious at finding this erotic treasure, and at the same time quaking at the mere possibility of someone finding it. She ripped off its cover and slipped the bare book inside a cover she tore from *A Proper Lady's Guide to Household Management.* There, in the back room of her father's jewelry shop, she read the steamy pages, savoring each image and turn of phrase like drops of honey. When she became too aroused to sit still, she would lock herself in the water closet, the only truly private place, and give her body its release.

"What are all these marks in the margins?"

Oh, no. He saw them.

He continued. "These little hearts beside some of the paragraphs. What do they signify?"

The truth buzzed in her head like angry hornets. She warred with the impulse to lie again, but the threat in his dark gaze drowned it out. Even so, the truth was not easy to confess.

"Things I'd like to try," she muttered.

He regarded her for a long moment, amusement and

curiosity playing on his handsome face. "I see. Why don't you?"

Mina sensed danger. Not the physical danger of having a sadistic man within arm's reach, but a more threatening sort, the kind brought on by an intuitive man who has assumed the authority to probe her heart.

He closed the book. "I doubt the Madame would mind. On the contrary, I think she'd encourage it. Why haven't you brought men up here to satisfy your curiosity?"

She took a deep breath. "I'm a servant. I don't entertain customers."

"This is a brothel, not a cloister. What's preventing you?"

Isn't it obvious? Why must you make me say it? "May I have my book back now?" She held out her hand, her eyes glued to the nondescript cover. But when he made no move, she looked at his face.

And wished she hadn't. There was a look of such profound understanding that she nearly crumbled in humiliation.

If he said anything nice to her, she'd scream. She didn't want to be pitied. She wanted to be adored, treasured, sought after. She wanted men to pursue her, write love letters to her . . . not the other way round.

After a moment, he said, " 'Prescott' is quite a jump ahead of H. Why did you send for me so soon?"

The dark cloud around her heart shifted. "I—" She remembered her mission, to get him to talk about his dealings with Halliday's of Fulsom Street, but the words eluded her. How on earth could she disarm him if she herself was so ill at ease? "I—" This was torture.

She couldn't be honest, and she couldn't lie. So she said the only thing she knew to be true. "I wish you would go."

The silence stretched between them. He just stared at her, expressionless. She had offended him, made him angry. The Madame would hear of his unpleasant experience. There would be reprisals.

"Very well." He stood and walked over to her pillow, where he had laid his tawse. He picked up the leather instrument, and Mina's heart skipped a beat. "I'll go. For now."

Mina puzzled over the uncertain victory.

"But you and I have some unfinished business. You will come to my residence tomorrow evening at seven. We shall continue our interview in significantly more comfort. For me, anyway," he said as he pocketed the strap.

Her heart plummeted. "But . . . wouldn't you prefer Lollie? Or Charlotte or Evie?"

He smiled crookedly. "As a matter of fact, I want no one *but* you."

She froze, unable to comprehend his meaning. Why would he want her over the much more beautiful and more experienced ladies? Those were the very words she had hoped all her life to hear a man say. And yet now that she had, all she felt was cold dread.

"Here is my card. I will make the arrangements with Madame Fynch to have you delivered promptly at seven. As for this," he said, holding up her book, "I trust you won't mind if I borrow it."

Her eyes bulged. "Actually, I do mind." Letting him read that particular book with all her markings in it was tantamount to showing him her diary. It was out of the question.

"Well, given that our meeting tonight was less than . . . conclusive, I had hoped you wouldn't mind if I found my case in the comfort of these pages. Unless, of course, you'd prefer to demonstrate your favorite passages on me tonight?"

She shook her head.

"Very well," he said. "You may have it back tomorrow. Seven o'clock. Do not disappoint me."

Mina was awash in relief that he was finally leaving. But he didn't move. She looked up at him in puzzlement. Those dark green eyes, needled with chestnut brown, continued to stare down at her. Then he did something that took her completely by surprise. He smiled a crooked smile, cupped the side of her face, and let his thumb brush her cheek.

The tender intimacy of his gesture provoked an astounding sensation within her. It was as if he could see past every barrier she had erected against others, and with only one touch made them all collapse. Something was being born within her, something she couldn't name. It was a sensation she hadn't experienced in a long time. Hope.

And with that, he was gone.

Chapter Four

"You can't wear that!" exclaimed Lollie in horror, her mouth full of food.

Mina continued to tie her pinafore around her waist. "I'm not going."

"Ye what?"

"You heard me," she said, shoving her limp brown hair into her mobcap. "I won't be coerced into this. Madame Fynch can send someone else." Mina had had all morning and afternoon to think about it. It was foolish to believe that this was going to work. She wasn't going to get any information from Lord Prescott. The man knew her weaknesses, and she was simply outmatched.

"Don't be such a frightened ninny. He's just a quill."

She pulled out a chair at the dining room table and sat opposite Lollie. "You take him, then."

"He don't want me, do he? He wants you."

It was beyond Mina's comprehension. With so many tempting morsels on the Madame's menu of beautiful women, she could not understand why he would choose her. "I don't care. I refuse to take part in this."

"Mina, you pick a fight with a bloke like Lord Prescott, there's only one way it's going to turn out. And anyways, I thought you wanted to get him to talk about his dealings with your father."

"I do. But I can't manage it. I'm not . . . capable."

"Nonsense. You can get a quill to do anything you like. He's a man, ain't he? There's a point where he would do anything you ask."

"I haven't the faintest idea how to seduce a man, Lollie."

Evie walked into the room, followed by the rest of the girls for their five o'clock supper, on the tail end of Mina's remark. "Ha! That's the simplest thing in the world."

"Mina, don't be ridiculous," scolded Charlotte, attired in a wisp of a dress that seemed to be made of air. "What about all those books you read? You probably know more about seduction than we do."

"Not from those books. The men in them are uncomplicated. All they have to do is look at the females and they're inflamed with lust. Some old vicar whispers a few bawdy words in a milkmaid's ear, they have a jolly good run round an oak tree, and then they fall behind some bush or other. They don't exactly require too much convincing."

"Well, if you didn't know how to seduce a man," countered Evie, "we wouldn't have so many customers walking through that door." The others voiced their assent.

"That's different."

"How?" Evie asked.

"I don't know. It just is." Mina struggled to make sense of her thoughts. "It's just that . . . when I'm sitting there at the desk, I can . . . I don't know . . . create a fantasy. I can make up a story that he can be a part of."

"That's all seduction really is," said Charlotte,

breaking off a piece of bread. "Making up a story of love."

Evie shook her head, laying a napkin on her lap. "There's more to it than that, Charlotte. You've got to make the story come true."

"She's right," interrupted Mina. "Setting it up is just the beginning. That's the easy part. The hard part is actually making it happen. The man becomes the variable. He's the mysterious element. You don't know what he's going to do or say, or how he's going to react."

Charlotte leaned forward, her rouged nipples showing prominently through the transparent robe. "But you are in control. Remember, the man wants to be a part of an adventure. If you drive the fantasy, he is free to enjoy it."

Mina shook her head. "I don't think that applies to this man. I think this Lord Prescott wants to drive. He seems to like being the one in control."

Charlotte smiled. "That's because you gave him that fantasy. You're letting him take charge. What you need to do is give him a different fantasy. One that will make him completely forget the last one."

"Like what?"

"Well, what if you cut right to the chase? Take over. Be that brazen milkmaid you read about. Get right down to business. Once a man has had his go, there's no need for fantasies. He's through with you. He won't even want to look at you anymore."

"I can't have that either," she said in horror. The whole point of this exercise was to get him to open up to her. "Lollie, you said that there was a point when I could get a quill to do anything I want. What is that point?"

They answered in unison. "Just before he puts it in."

"Yeah," said Lollie. "The Point of Surrender, I calls it. Once he's got it nice and hard, and you're still resisting, he'll become desperate. At that point, he will do or say or give anything you like, just so long as you open your legs."

"Get him nice and hard . . ." Mina repeated thoughtfully. "How do I do that?"

Lollie rolled her eyes. "Blimey, girl, just show up!"

"That's easy for you to say," Mina responded. "You're stunning. You could arouse a man just by looking sidewise at him."

"Well, then," Lollie said, removing Mina's mobcap. "We'll just have to make you stunning, then, won't we?"

Riding on a current of female enthusiasm, Mina let Evie, Charlotte, and Lollie whisk her away to the bath chamber, where they began her transformation. They chatted gaily among themselves, hardly involving her, treating her like a live doll. Three Graces playing with a simple mortal.

Mina admitted that it felt wonderful to be pampered in this fashion. After bathing her in scented water, they ushered her into Lollie's bedchamber. They flounced about her, applying creams to her hands and feet, powder on her face and chest, and a swath of rouge on her cheeks. She slipped on perfumed stockings and a brand-new chemise. Mina's corset was dingy and worn, so Evie, who was as slender as she was, gave her one of her more ornate ones. One of Evie's opera dresses, an elegant Grecian creation in ivory, was slipped over Mina's head. Curling her lifeless mousy-brown hair with irons proved impossible, so they looped it up and set it with pins capped with amber-hued jewels.

The final touch was a dab of red beet juice on her lips, which Lollie applied. "Like me mum used to tell me: a woman without paint is like food without salt."

They brought her to the dressing mirror, and Mina gasped. Staring at her from the glass was a different person, a woman so unlike her that it stole her breath away. Her skin was radiant and pale, contrasting sharply with her lively brown eyes. Her lips achieved fullness from the blush of the paint. Her brown hair was no longer dull; instead, her elegant new coiffure sparkled with the jeweled pins. Her breasts mounded over the cut of the dress, and her long neck rose gracefully from a simple chain. The underdress was far too tight for her, accentuating her hips and bottom, but the transparent flowing overdress obscured the immodesty.

"Mina, you're lovely," gushed Lollie.

Mina smiled tremulously at the reflection. She was far from being a swan, but at least the ugly duckling had sprouted some pretty feathers. The three Graces had imbued her with confidence and temporary beauty, and had given her the charge to bring a man to his knees. She wasn't sure if she could do it, but now she was willing to try.

◦"I'M TRYING, SIR," SAID Chase Alcott from behind the pile of papers he'd gutted from the desk. "I've turned the whole bloody house upside down for the key. It's nowhere."

"Well, try harder." Salter was growing impatient at

his inability to identify the murderer. The longer it took, the colder the trail became. It wasn't until Salter discovered Lord Prescott's strongbox, an iron cabinet hidden within the ornate base of a wooden column, that he found a lead in what appeared to be an unsolvable murder. Whatever was in that strongbox might tell him why Prescott was killed. And if he knew why, he might just be able to deduce who.

"You know," Alcott said, scratching his head, further disheveling his blond locks, "we could get Master Jack. He could crack 'er open in no time."

Salter rubbed his face. He was reluctant to use criminals to solve crimes. Then again, the criminal is the mirror image of the lawman. They each see an object from opposite perspectives: one bent on destroying, the other on protecting. But if a man was smart enough, he could use his adversary's perspective against him. "Know your enemy well," his old field marshal used to tell him. "If you know both yourself and your enemy, each battle will end in a victory."

That's why he had recruited Chase Alcott. Chase had been nothing but a skinny thief, picking unsuspecting pockets and swiping merchandise from shop shelves. His mother and sisters were poor and he provided for them, but he had chosen to do it by pursuing a life of crime rather than through respectable employment. It was only after Salter had rescued him from a merciless beating by an irate shopowner that Chase had had a change of heart. Salter sensed that Chase didn't have a mean streak in him, and took a chance on reeducating him.

Now, at twenty-one, Chase was the best young constable on the force. Nerve and guts, tempered with common sense and heart. Knew his way around the city, and knew his way around people. Fine-looking boy too, with tousled blond hair and a square jaw shimmering with a day or two's growth of beard. He never dressed to a style he could afford; it was his contention that if he looked more genteel, he'd lose the pulse of the London underground. Plus, he'd joke, his mates would call him a mincer and kick his arse.

"No," Salter answered, "let's leave Master Jack out of this tonight. I've got another engagement."

"Engagement, sir?"

"Yes. So pack up and go. I need to talk to the servants. She'll be here any minute."

"She, sir?" A mischievous smile pulled on Chase's lips.

Salter stiffened. "Not that I'm under any obligation to tell you, but she's a lead. She might have some knowledge of Prescott that may be useful to me."

" 'Course, sir. Whatever you say," said Chase, carelessly stuffing papers back into empty desk drawers.

Salter glanced balefully at the strongbox, gray and cold and silent. He wanted to do it the easy way, but if necessary, he'd resort to brute strength to get it open. He couldn't do that with the girl from the bordello. The key to her seemed infinitely more complicated than that of the confounding locked box. What an unusual creature she was. Eyes bright with intelligence, a mouth begging to be kissed, and yet . . . there was a sadness in her aspect that hinted at years of pain.

"Alcott, you've got sisters, haven't you?"

"Too many, sir. How many would you like?"

Salter smiled. "Just tell me something. How can

they . . . ?" He shook his head. "I'm not sure how to ask this. How do they know to feel confident? Is that something that's inborn, or is that something they pick up along the way?"

Alcott's eyebrows rose. "Well, I don't pretend to be an expert on women, mind, but I do know that most of 'em start out feeling just fine about themselves. They're naturally confident creatures, women are. Too confident, if you ask me. Some grow into that confidence. Others get the confidence beat out of 'em. You know, by the circumstances of life and all. But once they get it in their heads how much we men need 'em, ha, the game's won and not by us."

Salter nodded pensively. He found himself intrigued by this girl. He wondered what circumstances could have hammered such a mortifying lack of pride into her. Then again, it was not his mission to fix her. In fact, it were probably better she remain that way. Women were far too full of themselves as it was. Perhaps if more women were like this girl, they might not tend to be so promiscuous. He rubbed his forehead. He knew of one in particular who could benefit from such modesty.

Still, it was astonishing that in the midst of so much licentiousness, she should remain such an innocent. It was a matter that warranted looking into. Then he remembered . . . it was his job to find out more about her.

And not in the way he wanted.

ᴄᴘMINA'S CARRIAGE PULLED UP to the sprawling town house on High Oak Drive. She gave the driver a coin after he helped her alight from the cab, and watched him drive away. She stood at the entrance to Lord Prescott's door, battling the urge to run. She envisioned her father's face and the harsh circumstances he must be facing in an Australian prison, and she steeled herself. She would get as much information from Lord Prescott as she could, for her father's sake. Even if it cost her her virginity, it would be a small price to pay for finding out who had had her father arrested and seeing to it that he was safely returned. The thought of the violation sent a chill through her body.

She was reluctant to subject herself to Lord Prescott's insightful gaze. But there was another fear, one that seemed to sting more than she cared to admit. It was the fear of rejection, of being found unappealing . . . or worse, just plain repulsive. Despite her trepidation, Lord Prescott had touched her, physically and deliberately, and it had given her an unearthly pleasure. She dared not reveal how much that simple caress had meant.

She groaned. She was afraid of his ardor; she was afraid of his indifference. It was making her crazy. She stomped a foot impatiently to shake loose all her fears and banged the knocker on the door.

A leathery old butler opened the door. "Good evening, miss. Do come in. The master is in his study, but he will join you in the drawing room presently."

Mina looked around the house. The décor was refined but wholly unsentimental, making it seem pretentious and sterile. Once in the drawing room, she removed her hat and placed it beside her on the settee. She waited in the silent space, the ticking of a mantel clock her only distraction. After a few minutes, she heard heavy footsteps coming down the hall. She rose from the couch, her body tense.

The door opened. Lord Prescott froze mid-step.

He was dressed in a hunter-green coat that matched his eyes. The ivory cravat contrasted sharply with his bronze skin and his hair, which was black as a raven's wing. Fawn-colored breeches stretched over the sinews of his thighs, ending where his gleaming Hessian boots began. She didn't remember him being so well formed.

Her hopes for a compliment were deferred as his eyes danced around her face and body, seeming more surprised than pleased. "You look like a courtesan."

Her heart lifted, and then just as quickly sank. His meaning was unclear. The courtesans at Madame Fynch's possessed an unearthly beauty, but on his lips the word seemed almost disappointed.

"And you look like a man who would purchase such a one. Now that we've sorted that out, shall we sit down?" Without waiting for his assent, she sat on the settee and removed her gloves.

He sighed indulgently. "By all means. What will you have to drink? Sherry?"

"Port."

He glanced at her, puzzled by her audacious request. Port was enjoyed after dinner, and never by ladies. "Very well."

Now she felt better. Fear had ebbed, and anger had taken root. This evening would go according to *her* plans, not the other way round.

"The Madame needn't have packaged you this way for me. Or is this standard practice?"

"Your home is lovely."

He turned to her from the drinks table. "That was a very evasive answer."

Her eyes flashed a challenge at him. "It was a very indiscreet question."

"Sorry," he said, and handed her the glass.

When she took it from him, she glanced at his hand. "That's an impressive ring you're wearing, Lord Prescott. A ruby, I daresay. Did you know that rubies and sapphires are actually the very same substance? The only distinguishing characteristic is their color."

"No, I didn't know that," he said, settling into the couch opposite her. "The only thing I know about rubies is their extraordinary price."

"Then perhaps you also didn't know that some rubies are actually imposters. They are merely spinels posing as rubies. Might you have been duped into purchasing an impostor?"

He peered at her over the rim of his glass. "I hope not. I paid enough for the real thing."

"May I see it?"

There was amusement in his eye as he slipped the ring off and handed it to her.

She studied it. "You were not deceived. Tell me, wherever did you obtain such a fine gem?"

"I can't remember."

"Pity. I'm somewhat of a jewel fancier, and I've rarely seen such sparkle in so red a stone. Would it have been here in London?"

"No doubt."

"Then I beg you to recall where you purchased it. Could it have been at Halliday's on Fulsom Street?"

"It's possible."

She held the ring closer to the candle on the table, trying to see beyond the face of the gem. "Curious. Halliday is renowned for the cut of his precious stones. Are you familiar with his work?"

A smirk touched his lips. "I'll tell you what's curious. Your interest in my ring."

Mina stiffened. "I don't intend to steal it, if that's what worrying you."

"And your knowledge of London's jewelers."

She harrumphed, and handed his ring back. "I fail to see why you should become so alarmed over such a trifle. I only asked if you've ever patronized Mr. Halliday's establishment."

"Surely on a servant's wages you are not in a position to be such a connoisseur of gemstones."

"Being a servant does not equate to being a dullard. Just because I cannot buy them does not mean I cannot appreciate them."

"Point taken."

"Besides, even servants can be enthusiasts and even experts on a great many subjects, so it should not surprise you that I am knowledgeable in a great deal more than you believe."

"Including erotica."

The word banished all train of thought.

"I happen to know that the books you keep so carefully hidden in your drawer are illicit. They've been banned in this country and are prohibited from distribution, especially to ladies . . . even servant girls. The one now in my possession, *Memoirs of a French Lover,* is contraband. I daresay you must be the only authority in all of England on this particular subject matter."

"Now you are mocking me."

"Not in the least. Sex does not begin between the legs, but in the mind. And if such is the case," he continued, "then I believe I may be in the company of the most fascinating woman in all the land."

She might have laughed if she wasn't so flattered. But this worked in her favor. If he thought her so knowledgeable, it would be that much easier to get him to the Point of Surrender.

"Thank you."

"Therefore, I should like your earnest opinion of page twenty-seven."

She blinked in surprise. "I beg your pardon?"

"In your book, *Memoirs of a French Lover* . . . there are little marks there. Frankly, I'm partial to the activities on page forty-nine, but I'm intrigued by your interest in page twenty-seven."

Mina's heart started thumping. She didn't remember precisely what was on page twenty-seven, but whatever it was, she knew it must be extremely naughty.

"I think it utterly indecent of you to have read that book."

He threw back his head and laughed heartily. "I'm indecent? So the corkscrew finds me crooked."

"What I meant was," she said, curbing her indignation, "I consider it most ungentlemanly of you to have read that book after you knew I specifically wished you not to."

His mirth faded to an amused grin. "Ungentlemanly,

am I? A strange accusation from one with such unlady-like reading habits. One book, by chance, or perhaps even two—but an entire collection of erotic novels speaks to a reprobate and perverse nature. You're a wicked, wicked girl, and you ought not to point fingers."

Her gaze sank to the floor. "May I have my book back now, please?"

Candlelight danced in his eyes as he regarded her intently. "Certainly." He stood up and went to a shelf against the far wall, pulled it down, and handed it to her. "Read it to me."

"Excuse me?"

"I said, 'read it to me.' I enjoy dirty books—and letters—so entertain me once more with your corrupt words." He sat in the long settee, threw a booted foot atop the tea table, and crossed his legs at the ankle. With his hands clasped behind his head, his muscular body was stretched out to its full length.

Mina stared at the naked book in her hand. She didn't know when it had happened, but once more, Lord Prescott had taken control of his own fantasy. He wanted to humiliate her, and he was doing a damn fine job of it. She had to take the reins back from him. She had to steer the fantasy herself, or she would never get what she wanted out of him.

"I've got a better idea. Let's just see if we can't write our own story of love."

His smile broadened quizzically. "How do you mean?"

She got up and sat beside him. "Page one." She put her hand upon him, and stroked the expanse of his chest, her touch making him inhale sharply. The amusement fled from his face, and he sat up properly. She slipped her hand underneath the lapel of his coat, and let her hand slide over the silk waistcoat infused with his heat. "Page two."

Her hand went up to his shoulder, and her bare fingers delighted in the sensations of muscle. It was so incredibly warm under his coat, and it seemed to be growing warmer by the second. Absently, she found herself wishing she could slip her whole body into the crevice between his waistcoat and coat.

He bent his head to kiss her, and she stopped him. "Not yet. I'm writing this story." Her fingers nearly cried out when they left the delicious comfort of his chest, but she gave them solace in his hair. Her fingertips whispered over the soft black waves, riding the undulating thickness from his temple to his crown. She had seen courtesans make a man crazy simply by caressing the hair above his neck. So she threaded her fingers in between the silken waves and teased them out. "Page three."

Prescott closed his eyes, and a muscle in his jaw tensed. Mina's pleasure, as well as her confidence, grew with each degree of his increasing excitement. Her own desire rushed within her, but she quelled it. Even if she hadn't had an aim to accomplish, she was having too much fun watching the sadistic Lord Prescott surrender to her touch.

"My turn," he said, and brought his hand up the side of her arm. The feel of his fingers on her bare flesh brought an immediate jolt of desire.

"No. In this story, I do all the work."

His brow furrowed. "I don't think I like this story after all."

"You will," she promised. She took his wayward hand and brought it to her lips. It was a large thing, befitting a man of his size. "Page four." She took his small finger and kissed the tip of it. Then she did the same for his ring finger and middle finger. It was strange that his hands were so rough and callused, not at all smooth, as she expected a gentleman's to be. Then again, it didn't seem to matter too much, because her tender ministrations seemed to be having the desired effect: he shifted in his seat.

His index finger came next, receiving a soft kiss on the tip. He groaned at the sensation of warm wetness, so she deepened the kiss. This time, she let the tip of her tongue touch the end of his finger.

Prescott moaned. "Page five. Get to page five."

She smiled inwardly, awash in triumph. "No fair peeking ahead."

But she peeked . . . down at his trousers. The fold of fabric between his legs had grown taut. This was easier than she had thought. Lollie was right. Men were so easily seduced. She might not even have to sleep with him after all. Once she got her answer, she would undress him right here in the drawing room, then escape from the house and into the first hansom cab.

She placed her hand on his knee and splayed her fingers. Up her hand traveled and over the dense muscle of his thigh, which tensed at her touch. Her timid hand stopped at the tent of fabric between his legs, but curiosity, more than purpose, overcame her shyness. Softly, she caressed the rising mound, and was amazed at the sensation. Not just at the effect on her hand, but at the effect on her pride. She had aroused him.

His breathing quickened. "Free me."

"If I do, will you buy me a ruby?"

"Yes."

"If I kiss this digit here," she said, caressing the taut fabric, "will you buy me the best one, cut by the best jeweler?"

"Yes."

"Will you buy it at Halliday's?"

He groaned. "Can't. Halliday's closed down. But the very next best, wherever you like."

Now it was Mina's turn to breathe heavily. He knew her father was no longer in business! It had been only three months since the shop was shuttered and sold. A less frequent customer would not know this. But Lord Prescott did know it. He must know something more.

"Oh, no! How disappointing. What became of the owner?"

A thread of irritation entered his voice. "Can we talk about this later?"

"No," she replied petulantly, her fingers dancing upon the tip of his marble-hard erection. "I want to know now. What happened to Mr. Halliday?"

"He . . . was arrested."

Mina grew livid. He knew! "Why?"

He sighed wearily. "I . . . can't remember."

"Try."

He seized her wrist in his big callused hand. "I understand that you may not be terribly experienced at this, but the last thing a man in my present condition wants to talk about is another man. Do you think we could postpone the discussion until later?"

No, her mind screamed. Later would be too late. He would never talk about her father after he'd had his pleasure. The time to talk was now.

"Of course," she said pleasantly. "Whatever you ask. Shall we move on to page six?"

But Mina noticed a change in his demeanor. He seemed annoyed, impatient . . . angry even. Not at her, she was certain. But at something else. Whatever it was, it had distracted him.

"I can't believe I let myself get so far out of control," he said aloud to no one.

Mina redoubled her efforts. She pulled his collar down and placed a kiss on his earlobe. It felt soft and supple, and heavenly in her mouth. She felt his jaw tighten.

"I get the distinct impression I'm being toyed with. You are not trying to seduce me. You are trying to manipulate me."

Mina pulled back to look at his face. His ardor had vanished. "What on earth do you mean?"

"And what I want to know is . . . why?"

"Don't be ridiculous. I came here at your invitation."

"That's right. I invited *you,* not this . . . this . . ."

"Courtesan?"

"Precisely."

"Well, you paid for a courtesan, and you get what you pay for."

"Then perhaps I paid too much."

Mina's anger spiraled, but she didn't betray it. She had to steer him back to the Point of Surrender. She stretched up again and gave him a kiss full on the mouth. She turned her head slowly from side to side, just as she'd seen Lollie and the rest do. It was pleasant, and she found herself relishing the smell of his cologne. She even threw in a little moan for good measure.

He put his hands on her shoulders and pushed her down. He shook his head and smiled. "This is exactly what I mean. You look like a courtesan, but you kiss like a little girl."

That was it. He'd gone too far. Anger coiled within her, and she aimed it at the smirking mouth that insulted her. She raised her hand and slapped him on the face. Hard.

The eyes that had regarded her with amusement a moment ago now narrowed, and she glimpsed the depth of his anger.

"We've just reached the end of your book. Chapter one of mine begins now." He grabbed her forearm and pulled her in the direction of the door.

"Where are you taking me?" she cried.

"To the proverbial woodshed."

"I beg your pardon?"

"Not yet. But you will." He opened the door and stormed through, dragging her behind him. He strode past the stairs and down the corridor to another room. He flung open the door to a study and yanked her in ahead of him.

Mina shrieked as she nearly collided with a massive desk. She spun around to face him.

"Now, then," he began as he took off his jacket. "I am

going to ask you a few simple questions, and you are going to answer me. Honest answers will exponentially lessen the pain."

"Pain?" she gasped. "What pain?"

"*I* will ask the questions," his voice boomed. "Now, I am going to fetch my tawse from the drawing room. When I return, I expect you to be in position over the desk with your skirts raised to your waist and a sincere apology on your lips. Is that clear?"

Mina's heart was hammering so loudly she could barely hear him. She stared into his face, a mask of hard lines.

"I said, is that clear?"

Her instinctive physical response was to shake her head against the indignity of being spanked. But fear made her say what he wanted to hear. "Y-yes."

His lips thinned. "That's 'yes, *sir*'!"

Her throat tightened in outrage. "I call no man 'sir.'"

A satisfied smile spread across his face. "Then that shall be your first lesson." He turned around and walked out, slamming the door in his wake.

Oh, no! Oh, no! Oh, no! Mina felt as if she had just received her execution order. Now what was she going to do? She rushed to the door, and clutched the knob. But a sudden realization stopped her from opening the door. This man knew what had happened to her father. It was becoming clear that he was the man who had had him arrested. If she left now, she would never learn how to ruin him. At all costs, she had to stay.

The thought of being lashed by such a man turned her heart to water. But it would be far worse if she lost her golden opportunity to avenge her father. It was a double-edged sword, she noted ruefully. In order to hurt him, she would have to let him hurt her.

But maybe, if she was meek and docile, and did exactly as he asked, there would be no whipping. She looked around the room. It was littered with papers and ledgers. Books had been ripped from the shelves. The carpet was strewn with correspondence. It was as if the man had torn the room apart looking for something. The candles on the desk had burned low, but she could see newspapers scattered upon its expansive surface.

She glanced anxiously at the desk, and sighed pitiably. She knew this was not going to be pleasant. Humiliation burning within her, she placed her elbows on the desk, her nose inches above today's *Times*.

And read the headline.

PRESCOTT'S FUNERAL TOMORROW
LORD MAYOR'S AIDE TO BE GIVEN FULL HONORS

Lord Roderick Prescott is scheduled to be interred at three o'clock tomorrow following a ceremony that will be attended by many in Parliament, including the Lord Mayor, Alexander Bensonhurst.

There, above the article, was a line drawing of a man of about fifty with a large mustache and a bald pate. A man who looked nothing like the man she had tried to seduce only moments before.

Her mind reeled with questions that ricocheted unanswered from the paper. But there was one thing she knew for certain. The man whose footsteps she heard approaching had some explaining to do.

She stood in front of the desk, her arms crossed in front of her, one hand clutching the folded newspaper.

He rushed in, and was momentarily stunned to see her looking so defiant. She found she relished that particular look on his face.

Without his jacket, the man seemed even more threatening. The tight waistcoat outlined the hard sinews of his torso, and his shirtsleeves lent even greater size to his arms. The leather tawse in his hand would have made a lesser woman beg for mercy. But she was armed, too, with knowledge and a temper fit to explode.

"Before you administer punishment, please allow me to speak my regrets face-to-face."

"Your flagrant disobedience will cost you. Do not think that apologizing now will appease me."

"Perhaps not. I am sorry for disobeying your instructions. I know I am not allowed to ask questions, but there is one thing I must know before I subject myself to your chastisement."

He folded his hands over his chest, stretching to his full height. "Well?"

She lunged at him, smacking him with the newspaper. *"Who the hell are you?"*

Shocked by the assault, he raised his arms to fend off her blows.

She yelled at him, punctuating each syllable with a swat of the newspaper. "You—are not—Lord Prescott! You—are an—impostor!"

"Stop!" he cried out, sliding toward the corner.

"Explain yourself! You devil—you blackguard—you son of a bitch!"

To Mina's astonishment, the man started to laugh. Great bursts of laughter shook his shoulders as he tried to deflect her whacks. It was as if she were doing no more than tickling him. With an exasperated gasp, she hit him even harder.

"To think—I tried—to seduce you!"

The next few seconds were a blur. In one fluid motion, he seized her wrists in his hands and pushed her backward over the desk. With his leverage, he held her body down and ripped the shredded newspaper from her hand.

She opened her eyes to find herself lying prostrate on the hard wooden surface underneath a warm, masculine torso. Her hands were still manacled above her head in his fists, bringing her body into intimate contact with his. Her ragged breaths made her breasts rise and fall against his chest. Every inch of his body pressed against hers. She looked up into his smiling eyes, just inches from her own, bemusement playing on his features as he regarded her.

"By heavens," he said. "This is the real you."

"And who the devil are you?" she demanded, feeling more than ever at a disadvantage. As if her defeat were not humiliation enough, her body began to respond to the feel of his clothes against her exposed skin, to the intoxicating smell of his cologne, and to his eyes, which softened toward her.

"My name is Salter Lambrick. Chief Constable Salter Lambrick. I am investigating the murder of Lord Roderick Prescott. And until tonight, you were the prime suspect."

"Me?" Her breathing grew heavy once more. "Why?"

He straightened up off the desk, taking the warmth of his body with him, and helped her to a standing position.

"Because of this," he said, pulling a letter from the pocket of his waistcoat. The letter written to Lord Prescott in her very own hand.

"I didn't kill him."

"I know that now. Your belief that I was Lord Prescott was what convinced me. That and your utter obliviousness to the fact that you are standing not five feet from where he was found dead."

Aghast, Mina glanced to each side of her.

"Behind you."

She whirled around, instinctively backing away from the desk. The man's body stopped her retreat. She turned in his arms, and found herself captured in them. The sensation alarmed her.

"You're . . . you're a constable?"

"Yes."

Her mind reeled with the appalling threat of dead bodies, impostors, and the law. For once, she was grateful for his steadying strength.

"Come. I promised you dinner, and Mrs. Tolliver has prepared us something good."

Mina let the constable—the chief constable—lead her to the dining room, as myriad questions jostled each other in her mind, each demanding to be answered foremost. Once there, he seated her at the place to his right. A small, thin woman came in bearing a soup tureen that almost seemed to outweigh her.

The servant seemed to accept this man as her

employer, which confused Mina further. "I don't understand any of this. The butler . . . he announced me to you. He knows who you really are?"

The constable smiled. "They all do. They agreed to this masquerade until we could determine your innocence or guilt in the matter. I wanted the butler to have a look at you and tell me if you had ever been to this house before."

So much still didn't make sense. "So this is not your home?"

He shook his head benevolently. "No. This isn't my home, these are not my servants, these aren't even my clothes. And that was not my tawse."

Understanding dawned, and her body began to relax.

His wicked smile returned. "My tawse is much bigger."

She didn't find that especially amusing. "So this has all been one big lie? Your visit to the Pleasure Emporium, your purchase of my services, your . . ." She couldn't bring herself to say anything that would underscore what a fool she had been to try to seduce him. "It was all an attempt to entrap me?"

"In part. But there was something else about you, something I had to explore."

His condescending words incensed her. She felt an utter fool. She took a sip of wine to give her something to do. "Well, now that you've had your fun at my expense, I wish you all the best. Good evening." She rose to leave.

He reached up and encircled her forearm in an unyielding grip. "Not so fast. There's still a great deal more I wish to know."

"Well, Mr. Whatever-Your-Name-Is, I am not in a talking mood. Especially not with you. Now that I know there is nothing whatsoever tying me to you, I see no reason to continue our interview."

"I beg to differ." He pulled her back down roughly into her chair. "You can answer my questions here, over this lovely repast Mrs. Tolliver has taken pains to prepare, or you can answer them from behind prison bars. Either way, this interview will continue until *I* am satisfied."

You'll receive no satisfaction from me. Humiliation over the way she had fondled him stabbed at her again. She had acted like a two-penny whore. It made her sick to think what he must think about her. How he must have laughed inwardly at her ham-handed, amateurish attempts at lovemaking. She wanted to upend the soup tureen over his lying, deceiving head.

"What is your interest in Halliday's? The truth, now."

Mina pursed her lips. Though she was reluctant to provide him with an answer, it seemed only fitting that her unmasking follow his. "Emmett Halliday is my father. He was arrested earlier this year for fraud and theft. Crimes he *didn't* commit."

"Yes, I remember something of that case. He was accused of stealing jewels out of a necklace and replacing them with fakes."

"It wasn't a necklace. It was a tiara . . . more like an exotic oriental crown. And the replacements weren't fakes, they were semiprecious stones. He then turned over the tiara *and* the original gemstones to the client. Everything he was paid to do. There was nothing illegal in it."

"I seem to remember that the client, whoever he

was, pressed charges against him, claiming that he brought the tiara in for polishing and it was returned with the inferior stones. And that he didn't receive the real ones ever. He accused Halliday of jewel theft."

"All lies. And it was a closed-door trial. I never found out who preferred the charges against him. They claimed that my father's case involved national security and would not open the trial to the public. I was never even allowed to testify in his defense. He was convicted, sentenced, and consigned to some penal colony in Australia."

Salter leaned back in his chair. "Hmm. Yes, I am recalling the case more clearly now. The case involved a government official, and the judge thought it best to close the doors of the proceedings because of the political ramifications. These proceedings sometimes take years, but in your father's case, the trial was sped up and the sentence carried out quickly." He regarded her down-turned head. "And you thought Lord Prescott was his accuser?"

"My father had many wealthy clients, but only two of them were connected to the government. Only two men wielded that kind of political power. I intended to find out which, starting with Lord Prescott."

"Now I understand. Well, I'm afraid that avenue is closed to you. Lord Prescott was murdered."

Mina's nostrils flared. With Prescott murdered, she had revenge, but not justice. "How?"

"I'm sorry, but I'm not at liberty to discuss the particulars of this case until the murderer is discovered."

She crossed her arms in irritation. "I see. So I must tell you things but you will not tell me things."

He smiled that crooked smile of his, fully aware of how the imbalance of power rankled her. "That is the very definition of a constabulary interrogation, yes." He regarded her thoughtfully. "Mina . . . what kind of a name is Mina?"

She had no intention of telling him it was short for Wilhemina, a name she hated, lest he start calling her that. She narrowed her eyes at him, her tone mocking. "What kind of a name is Salter?"

He laughed, and for the moment, it made him less dictatorial and more human. "Touché. If you must know, my father was an ostler in the stables of a country squire named Lord Saltyre. Lord Saltyre was a very kind man, and he loved my family. When I was born, my father named me Salter in tribute to him."

Mina watched him take his soup. He ate with relish but not refinement, tearing off bits of bread and tossing them into his broth. She realized how much her fear had blinded her to the truth she'd sensed the very moment she laid eyes on him: this man was no gentleman.

"So you yourself are the son of a servant."

"Yes," he responded, before taking a gulp of wine. "Does that disappoint you?"

"It confirms my suspicions. Tell me, if you were raised in the country, what are you doing in London?"

He inhaled sharply, and paused for a moment, as if sorting through memories and leaching out their emotion before the retelling. "I had a brother. He died when I was eighteen. A couple years later I joined the cavalry of His Majesty's Army, and went to fight in the Irish Rebellion. I left the army just as soon as the war was over, and came to London. The constabulary was just being organized, and I threw in my hand. I found I had a much greater partiality for enforcing justice than for imposing foreign policy."

Mina could sense a wave of emotion behind his story, but he dammed it up rather skillfully. In comparison to his childhood, hers had been relatively uneventful. While she was growing up, other children had been cruel to her, so she shuttered herself up in her father's jewelry store, always engrossed in one book or another.

Mina watched Mrs. Tolliver bring out the second course, a savory-looking haddock in lemon-butter sauce.

"I have heard very distressing things about that war. I know it was not a decisive victory for our soldiers."

"There was much to endure. The atrocities committed . . ." His voice trailed off, a dark cloud passing over his features. "But I do not revisit the past. Tell me, what did you hope to gain by becoming Lord Prescott's mistress? Did you think he would fall so madly in love with you that he would reverse himself in court and have your father pulled out of prison?"

His sarcasm stung. "No, I am not so foolish as to think he would fall in love with me. But anyone who would perjure himself against an innocent man surely has skeletons in his closet. I made it my mission to find out as much as I could about Lord Prescott, so that I could uncover just whose skeletons they are."

"I see. So you set yourself on a vendetta."

Mina pursed her lips. "It is the only way."

"How did you know of Prescott's tendencies toward sadism?"

"My father told me. Apparently, when Prescott

came to the shop, he was crowing about his latest con-
quest. He shared the lurid details of his flagellant's an-
guish with my father. 'The lashes I inflict,' Prescott had
said, 'give me much more pleasure than the lashes she
bats.'"

"Surprising your father would relate the details of
such a sordid conversation with you."

"My father is very open and honest with me. We are
each other's company." She lowered her voice. "That
is, we were."

"Hmm. You mentioned there were two men you suspected of framing your father. Who is the other?"

"Frederick Stratton."

"Stratton. Lord Underwood . . ." He thought for a
moment. "There was a letter addressed to him on your
desk. You invited him to the bordello, didn't you?"

Mina nodded. "It was posted yesterday."

Salter sighed and shook his head. "You are going
about this the wrong way. Write him again and cancel."

"I will *not*."

"Miss Halliday, let the constabulary handle this."

Mina chuckled mirthlessly. "Your precious justice
system failed my father. But I do not intend to do the
same. If Lord Prescott is innocent of convicting my father, then nothing will come of my investigations."

"I am under orders to find the man who killed
Prescott. I won't have you meddling in this case."

"Do you mean to tell me that you would rather seek
justice for a dead man than for my father?"

"No, that's not what I'm saying. Justice belongs to
everyone. But this case is about finding a murderer."

"Oh, you are narrow-minded! My father is suffering

a sentence of hard labor in a foreign country for a crime he didn't commit, and you want to seek redress on behalf of a dead man?"

"I want to put a murderer behind bars. When my investigation is concluded, I promise I shall look into your father's case. If there is evidence to support his innocence, then I will personally see to it that he gets another trial."

"No."

"No?"

"Your offer is not good enough. The difference between us is that I do revisit the past. I think about my father and the injustice he suffers every single day. And I won't permit him to endure an undeserved punishment one second longer than he has to. I have leads of my own, and I intend to pursue them."

"Not when they intersect with my own, you don't. I caution you to desist from your investigations. You will only muck up the case and put yourself in harm's way."

"Am I free to go, Mr. Lambrick? This evening has been most trying, and quite frankly, I don't wish to waste another second arguing with you. I have other matters that are more pressing and of far greater importance."

He straightened in his chair. "In case I have been too circumspect with my meaning, my little Minnow, let me make myself perfectly clear. You are swimming around in a pool of sharks, and you're going to get eaten. You are to return to your books and your bar, and forget all about pursuing these two men. When I have successfully put Lord Prescott's murderer in prison, you may then pursue whatever course you choose, and

I will be happy to lend the full support of the entire constabulary to obtain justice for your father. But if you so much as put one foot within the boundaries of my investigation, I will lock you up until I have completed my mission. Now do we understand each other?"

Mina's eyes narrowed. "I understand you perfectly."

"Good."

"But you haven't yet begun to understand me." She got up from her chair and walked out.

Chapter Five

꧁

Lollie leaned against the door and let the shipping magnate place a goodbye kiss on each of her buoyant breasts.

She stroked his whiskered cheek. "Don't let it be another two whole months before I see you again. Otherwise, I may just forget all about you."

The man pressed his barrel-shaped belly against her, sliding his hand into her pantalettes. "Here's a little something to remember me by." He patted her bottom, and Lollie felt the crumple of the paper against her skin.

She smiled. "You are so good to me, Bartholomew. I'll save one of these bottles of Madeira you gave me until you come round again. I know a naughty little game that I'd just love to teach you."

The skin on his face crinkled as he smiled. "Until next month, then."

Lollie opened the door for him, and glanced out. She saw a carriage come to a halt in front of the Pleasure Emporium. The carriage door opened, and Mina stepped out. "Uh-oh."

"Sorry?"

She turned to Bartholomew. "I said, 'oh, no.' I do hate to see you go. Come back soon."

"Of course." He kissed her on the cheek. "Good evening."

Lollie didn't take her eyes off Mina, who threw a coin at the driver and stomped up to the house. Lollie followed quietly behind Mina as she tramped up the stairs.

Seconds after Mina slammed the door of her attic bedroom, Lollie opened it and came in. It was pointless to ask how it went, so Lollie just waited until Mina stripped off her gloves, tore off her hat, and flopped herself on the bed.

"I hate men!"

Lollie nodded, and sat next to her on the bed. "Congratulations. You're officially one of us, now."

Mina went on to describe the events of the evening to Lollie: how Lord Prescott turned out to be a constable, how the real Prescott turned out to be dead, how awry all her plans had gone.

Lollie put her hand on Mina's. "Did it hurt overmuch?"

Mina shook her head. "No. We didn't do it."

"Did he hit you?"

"No. Almost, but no."

A furrow appeared between Lollie's delicate eyebrows. "Then why are you so angry?"

Mina snorted. "Because . . ." The truth was too embarrassing to admit, even to Lollie.

"Because?"

Mina fished around for a substitute answer. "Because I wasted my whole evening, and this ridiculous getup."

"And?"

"And because I'm no closer to getting justice for my father than before."

"And?"

"And . . ." Mina's shoulders slumped. "And because I thought he really liked me." Angry, embarrassed tears welled up in her eyes. "But he didn't. He just wanted to question me. Oh, I'm such a stupid fool!"

Lollie rubbed her hand across Mina's back. "Poor duck. You let your emotions get in the way. We all make that mistake at the first. It's our tender hearts, is all. But ye've got to remember that they're quills, nuffink more. And this is just business. You're selling the idea of love, not the thing itself. It's easy to believe when they speak nice words that they really mean it. But they don't. And you must never fink less of yourself because of it."

"I just don't understand. You did everything possible to make me beautiful. I never looked as good as I did tonight. And it still wasn't enough."

Lollie dipped her head to look up into Mina's face. "You really liked him, din't you?"

Mina swiped her moist cheek and recovered as much of her poise as she could. "No, I didn't. And I don't. I wanted him to like me, that's all. So I could have the upper hand."

"Well, I've got a little somefink to cheer you up." Lollie held up an envelope. "It arrived by special messenger, and the carriage had a crest on the door."

Mina stared at the stiff cream-colored paper with the broken scarlet wax seal. "Who's it from?"

"Read it."

Mina unfolded the parchment.

My dear Miss Lollie,

I thank you for your kind invitation to visit. As a Royal Subject, you are entitled to an audience to discuss your petitions of His Royal Majesty's government. I will be happy to meet you at your residence tomorrow evening at six o'clock.

Very respectfully,
Frederick Stratton, Lord Underwood

Mina turned to Lollie. "He's coming!" She felt her heart lighten. "All right, Lollie. This time round, we're going to do things much, much differently. There'll be no mistakes on this one. Here's what's going to happen."

⌒"BLOW THE DAMNED THING already!" Salter cried impatiently.

Master Jack lifted his wizened face from his kneeling position in front of the strongbox. "Ye've got to have patience, governor. Safecracking is not a nervous man's game."

Salter paced about the room. "You've been at it for over four hours now. How long is this going to take?"

"It's like I told you, gov. This 'ere's a Bramah lock. It's unpickable, and has been for twenty-five years. No cracker in the world ever goes up against a Bramah. Not if 'e wants to get away with his skin from a box job before the alarm's raised. Fortunately—er, I mean, unfortunately—there aren't many of 'em out there. Too expensive, it seems. But what's worth doing is worth doing right, as me mum used to say."

Salter threw himself into the desk chair. "Thanks for the homily. How much longer do you need?"

Master Jack cocked his grizzled head. "Long as it takes, gov. Sometimes, she gives her secrets quickly. Sometimes, she don't."

"Well, see if you can't hurry her along."

"Sir," Master Jack assented before turning his rickety frame back toward the safe. He steadied himself on his knees, and patiently resumed his task of filing away at the wooden dowel from which he was fashioning a skeleton key.

Salter rubbed his forehead, an anxious gesture of a man who's going against his better judgment. Using a criminal to help solve this case was not a good idea.

Most people only knew London by day, a polished and sophisticated metropolis where polite and lucrative business was transacted. But at dusk, the city changed. It became like an upturned garden stone, teeming with nefarious creatures. As good and decent people slept, London's night dwellers moved about, compelled by a hunger to satisfy their own needs. It was here he lived, ate, worked, and breathed—circulating among the criminal element while trying to remain uncontaminated by it. Every lawbreaker he captured gave him a sense of consummate achievement, knowing he made the city a safer place for all the innocents. Each morning, as the heavy veil that had shrouded the city lifted and the dangers fled, his London once again became the place of cultural and historical renown, a place worthy of the monarch and the seat of government. Until dusk, that is.

"Just see that you don't use this service to the

constabulary for your own criminal purposes. If I so much as hear you've cracked another safe, Bramah or otherwise, you'll be in Newgate so quickly your head will spin."

Master Jack smiled weakly, revealing spaces where there should be teeth. "No such thing, gov. I'm an antique now. My days of running from the law are over. My knees ain't what they used to be, and the cold don't make it easier to move." He tried his wooden key in the cylindrical lock, took it back out, and sanded it some more. "This game is for younger men. Mind you, back when I was a lad, there wasn't a safe safe enough from Master Jack, and everybody knew it. But with every one of me mates dead and gone, my fame has grown that much fainter. There's not a lifter alive left from those days. My greatest achievements now live only in my own memory. That is, until this beauty here. You know, this comp'ny is offering a reward . . . two hundred guineas to whoever opens one of their locks. It hasn't been done. I must say this for the gentleman what owns this . . . this safe's as secure as they come. Whatever he's got in here, he don't want it disturbed."

"Don't get any ideas. You won't get famous for this. But you will fall into my good graces, and that's all the luck you can hope for."

There was a loud click, and Master Jack smiled. "She opened for me!"

Salter leaped to his feet. "Stand clear." Master Jack creaked to a standing position, and sat on a seventeenth-century sea chest, wincing as he moved his stiffened knees.

The hinges creaked as Salter turned the cast-iron

handle on the door of the safe. The contents were immaculately laid out, just as Prescott's study had been before Salter went hunting for clues. He reached in, pulled out a stack of papers, and riffled through them.

"Notes. These are all outstanding debts." His eyebrows lifted at the lordly sums on the notes. Salter knew that Prescott was an aggressive gambler, and that White's had records of gentlemanly wagers on which Prescott emerged the loser. It was conceivable that Prescott was killed by one of the men to whom he owed money, but it made no sense that nothing had been stolen, especially the untouched billfold inside Prescott's pocket.

Frowning, Salter looked through the rest of the contents of the safe: an ornate box containing dueling pistols, a small stack of banknotes, and a sack of gold sovereigns. Toward the back, he found a letter on crisp parchment. He unfolded it and read.

Prescott,

I tire of your repeated attempts to contact me. Let us bring a swift conclusion to our unfinished business. Tomorrow evening at six o'clock at my residence.

Stratton

His heart began to race, and blood thrummed in his ears. His thoughts flew to Mina. She had invited Stratton to the bordello to investigate him as well. Salter had ordered her to uninvite him, but he doubted she'd had the good sense to obey him. Her crude methods of detection would be transparent to any intelligent man. If she was discovered, there was no telling what the man might do to her. He had to get to Lord Underwood before Mina did.

Salter passed his hand inside the darkened safe to make certain he had everything. His thoroughness earned him one final reward. His fingers brushed a black velvet pouch undetected in the darkness. He drew it out and pulled open the drawstring. What he saw amazed him.

He pulled the largest of the jewels out of the pouch and held it up to the candelabra. It blazed with a deep blue fire.

"Jesus, Mary, and Joseph!" exclaimed Master Jack, leaning forward to get a better look through his tiny spectacles. "What a bonnie thing!"

Salter was dazzled by the tiny prisms that danced in the heart of the gem. There was no telling what something like this was worth. Mina might know. The opportunity to see her again lifted his mood, but he knew it was best to leave her out of the case altogether, for her own safety. He felt a twinge of regret at deliberately keeping away from her, but he quickly snuffed out the emotion, just as he did with everything else that distracted him from his work.

"I know someone what could sell that for you, gov," said Master Jack. "Give it to me and I'll look after it for you."

Salter gave him a withering stare. "The only thing I'm giving you is a ride back to Battersea. Now, get your things and let's go."

After leaving Master Jack at his dilapidated flat,

Salter went on to pay a visit to Lord Underwood. The butler informed him that Lord Underwood was not present, and was not expected back until the next day. Salter thought it best not to identify himself as a constable, so he did not press the question of Underwood's whereabouts. But he did sneak into the mews near Underwood's home to see if his carriage was there, just to make sure he wasn't really at home. There was no carriage there bearing his crest.

Salter heaved a profound sigh. He could easily deduce where Underwood might be. And he would be very cross if Mina got to him before he did. Very cross indeed.

Chapter Six

❧

One of the most popular attractions of the Pleasure Emporium was its large Roman bath.
Madame Fynch had decided to duplicate the spa at Bath
by installing a large marble tub in the teak-paneled cellar
of the building. The pool could easily seat six people,
and men would drink and socialize in the bath before being toweled off by the female of their choice and taken to
a room upstairs. The privilege of using the bath was ex-
pensive, as two servants had to tend to it exclusively just
to keep the waters hot. The Madame had installed the
bath independent of but near the kitchens, so that pots of
boiling water could be continuously brought out. There
was also another ingenious method of heating the water.
A heavy copper pail hung from a pulley over the center
of the bath, and a servant would scoop heated coals into
it. The pail would then be lowered into the water, and
clients cheered when the pail made the water sizzle.

Mina brought in a tray of port and set it down on a
small table. Lollie had already undressed Lord Underwood and had ushered him into the tub. He was a man
of about fifty, his hair thinning and graying. His chest
and his waist were the same width, and his skin had
taken on the flaccid texture that seemed to be common

among the wealthy, overindulgent gentlemen of Madame Fynch's clientele. Yet he was not an unattractive man, and Mina could see the shadow of a more handsome youth in his square jaw and piercing blue eyes.

Lollie cast Mina a meaningful glance. "Oh, Lord Underwood, I'm so grateful you could visit me tonight," she said, concealing her Cockney accent as best she could. "I was very much looking forward to your arrival."

"Not at all, my dear. And call me Frederick. No reason why we can't be good friends. And now that I see what a pretty thing you are, I've no reason to stay away."

"You're terribly sweet. You remind me of another gentleman who was here some time ago. His name was Halliday. Do you know him?"

Frederick leaned back against the wall of the tub, his eyes closed dreamily as he let the heated waters soothe him. "I don't think so."

Lollie knelt behind him on the deck and began to massage his temples. "Pity. He looked a great deal like you. Anyone would think you were brothers. He was a jeweler, I think."

Frederick moaned contentedly. "A jeweler, you say? Oh, yes, I do seem to remember a man of that name now. He had a small concern on Fulsom Street."

Mina, who had busied herself with folding towels, spun around to face Lollie. She gesticulated wildly to Lollie to press him for more details. Frederick's eyes were still closed lazily.

Lollie vigorously nodded her assent. "That's right. Don't you think you resemble him?"

A light frown touched his brow. "Not especially, no."

Lollie giggled. "I suppose not. You're much handsomer than what he is."

Mina cringed at the slip of Lollie's accent, but Frederick didn't seem to notice. Mina motioned to Lollie to keep going.

"Er, he hasn't been round in a while. Any idea what became of him?"

Frederick's expression relaxed. "As a matter of fact, I do. He—"

The teak door opened, and Mina cursed the interruption. She turned to look, and through the escaping steam emerged Salter.

There were so many emotions Mina felt, it was difficult to focus on just one. But had they been the only ones in the room, she would have leaped over the bath and strangled him.

"So this is where the festivities are held," said Salter jovially.

"Do come in," said Frederick politely. "I must say this is an amazing contraption. The water is infernally hot but remarkably soothing."

"Good. I could use a little relaxation after the day I've had." Salter bent low and extended his hand. "Miles Rainey. At your service."

They shook hands. "Frederick Stratton. Good to meet you. Won't you take your pleasure? The water is as warm as the company," he said, winking and jerking his head at Lollie.

"Indeed?" Salter replied, giving Lollie an appreciative look as he removed his coat. "Well, then, I heartily accept the invitation. Miss?"

Mina struggled with what to do next. She had been

so thrilled to have thought up a way to get Frederick re-laxed enough to talk without taking him to the Point of Surrender, and now Salter had come to ruin it.

"I say, miss?"

The repeated summons stirred her out of her black thoughts. Apparently, Salter meant her.

"Help me off with my clothes."

She glanced at Lollie, uncertain what to do. Lollie gestured at her to do as she was bid.

"You should have a woman do that," said Frederick. "Haven't you selected one yet?"

Salter glanced at Mina. "I'm rather partial to servant girls. Unfasten my waistcoat, girl."

Mina tethered her anger as she walked over to him. There was a teasing smile on his lips, and Mina itched to slap it off. It was one thing to pretend he didn't know her; it was quite another to humiliate her in the process.

He stood before her, the brocade silk waistcoat out-lining his broad chest and narrow waist. His arms hung lax at his sides, the loose sleeves adding volume to his already muscular arms. He was so tall . . . the top of her head didn't quite reach his shoulders. But she stared up at him squarely, silently communicating her irritation. Her fingers went to his first button and unfas-tened it. But the simple gesture of touching the warm fabric at his chest somehow diminished her anger. As her fingers smoothed over the silk, the buttons grew in-creasingly harder to undo.

"Now the neckcloth, if you please."

She looked into his face, and there was a huge smile on his lips. If Lord Underwood hadn't been there, she would have pushed him into the pool.

She untied the cravat and unwound it from his neck . . . no easy feat given his height. She yanked the loose cloth off him, hoping the friction burned him.

It must have, because he winced. He seized her wrist. "Gently, girl. Or my neck won't be the only thing smarting tonight."

She met the challenge in his hazel eyes.

"Now undo me here." He brought her hand down to the buttons of his trousers. She hesitated, realizing for the first time that she was about to make him completely naked. The idea raged inside her. She couldn't deny that she was intrigued at seeing him with no clothes on, but at the same time, she wished it wasn't now, when she could not afford such a stimulating distraction.

She knelt down to unfasten one of the two rows of buttons at his front. She couldn't help remembering the feel of his manhood standing tall and firm under the fabric, and there was a thrilling excitement at seeing what only her hands had known. Above her, he slipped his shirt out from inside his trousers and threw it over his head.

The sight of his naked torso made her fingers slip. His bare chest was like a mountain range with two large steppes lowering into a ridge of hills at his abdomen. So different from the men she had seen here. He was smooth, with only a small tuft of hair around each nipple. Below his navel was another line of hair, and it disappeared behind the fabric that was now trembling at her fingers.

Finally, she unhooked the last button. Modesty decreed she should let him take off his own pants. But curiosity and a certain erotic thrill made her lower the trousers from his hips.

There it was, the instrument of her undoing. His penis was thick and dark, and it stood out from a nest of hair between his legs. She had seen other men in brief snatches of nudity, but none of them wore it as confidently and proudly as he did. His thighs were smooth and hard, like a marble statue, and she delighted in stealing a brief caress as she slipped the trousers from him. Ashamed to stare much longer at his naked manhood directly in front of her face, she busied herself by slipping off his shoes and stockings.

Frederick had almost fallen asleep. "Rainey, try this girl. She is a sorceress with her hands."

Salter made a face as he slipped his foot in the steaming water. "Damn and blast!"

Frederick straightened. "First time in the bath?"

Salter nodded as he dropped down into the tub, immersing himself up to his neck. "Damn and blast!"

Frederick laughed. "Mine too. God help me if it isn't just what the doctor ordered."

"What are they trying to do, boil us alive?"

"It would appear so. Like Christian men in an Amazonian jungle."

"What's her name?" Salter asked.

"Haven't a clue. Polly, I think. What's your name, girl?"

"Lollie."

"That's it . . . Lollie. She wrote me the most scorching invitation with the devil's own hand."

"Did she now?" said Salter, looking Mina full in the face. Mina turned away, color filling her cheeks.

Lollie spoke up. "Frederick, you were about to tell me about our friend Halliday, remember?"

"Later, perhaps."

Lollie pouted prettily. "No, I want to know now."

"Come here, young woman," ordered Salter. "Can't you see the man is trying to take his ease? He doesn't want to be pestered about another man. Come give me a massage, too."

Mina was furious. She had half a mind to go and push his head under.

"What do you do for a living, Stratton?" he said, ignoring Mina's scowl.

"I'm Chief Secretary to the Treasury."

"Ah. A government man." Salter leaned back as Lollie began to massage the hood of muscle at his neck.

"Quite."

Salter cast the first line. "I've just heard about the Lord Mayor's aide. Pity about him, eh?"

"Yes. I've only just come from his funeral. Hundreds of people there. It was ghastly."

"Can't abide funerals myself. Don't like open caskets."

"Oh, well, his wasn't open. It was closed."

"Really? That's curious. I wonder why."

"Don't know for sure. I suppose the body wasn't a pretty sight."

"So he didn't die of natural causes?"

Frederick cast a surreptitious glance behind him, and leaned in conspiratorially. "That's what they would have us believe. But if you want to know what I think, I believe he was murdered."

"How do you know?"

"Well, to begin with, he was a coldhearted son of a bitch. There were lots of people who wanted him dead."

"Including you, it seems," Salter said pointedly.

The corners of Frederick's mouth dipped. "I had no love for him. Truth is, I'm glad he's gone. The man was a blackguard. And it's a foul thing when a man in his powerful position turns his mind to criminality. Do you know he once tried to blackmail me?"

"You don't say?"

"Wouldn't let him, though. I never could abide bullies. And wouldn't you know it . . . the minute I stood up to him, he backed down. He had gotten wind of one of my earlier business indiscretions, and he had threatened to make it public. I told him to go ahead. He didn't catch me cringing and pleading. The public would be forgiving of small peccadilloes. I let him take aim and fire, and when the bullet missed, he didn't reload. Never saw him again after that."

"Shocking. Do you think he was killed by someone he was trying to blackmail?"

"I have no doubt about it. The man was a scoundrel."

"What do you suppose happened to him?"

Frederick leaned in again. "I have it on good authority that he was killed in a duel."

Salter frowned. "A duel?"

Frederick nodded, entirely pleased with himself and his salacious bit of gossip. "I heard that he was shot in the face, and that's why his casket was closed."

Salter was crestfallen. "Who shot him?"

"No idea. Perhaps it was a man who had tired of

having Prescott parade his secrets in front of him. Good riddance to him, I say."

Lollie squeezed the muscles on Salter's shoulders. "I can't seem to work the stiffness out. You're wound tight as a drum."

Mina could see the disappointment in Salter's face. He was investigating Lord Underwood, and he had clearly reached a dead end.

"It's been a tiresome week." Salter closed his eyes and leaned his weary head onto Lollie's knees, surrendering himself to Lollie's ministrations.

As Salter groaned in pleasure, something jerked inside of Mina. It was a surprising emotion, something she hadn't felt in a long time—a disappointment elevated to an exquisite level of pain. Jealousy.

Lollie splayed her hands down Salter's muscled arms, her breasts coming into contact with the top of his head. Salter lifted his arms out of the water, and relaxed them across the deck. Her fingertips smoothed across the undulating curves.

Mina quelled her temper. Though Mina didn't like how much Lollie was enjoying rubbing Salter's spectacular body, it wasn't her fault that Salter was enjoying her company. In fact, Lollie was only here at Mina's request. So Mina aimed her full fury at Salter, and reacted on pure instinct. "Would you like me to bathe you, Lord Underwood?"

Salter's eyes sprang open.

"Certainly," responded Frederick emphatically.

Mina took a face towel and walked to the spot on the deck behind Frederick.

Salter spoke up. "Girl, go get me a cool drink."

"Not now, Rainey," protested Frederick. "I've shared my girl with you. Now you must share yours with me."

Mina knelt behind Frederick and dipped the towel into the hot water.

"Sorry, Stratton, but the heat of this place is getting to me. Can't I persuade you to take a glass of port with me?"

"Later, perhaps. I want to try your servant girl first. Scrub me nice and clean, girl." The leer on his face turned Mina's stomach, but she was determined to make Salter suffer as she had suffered.

Mina passed the wet towel over Frederick's shoulders. He shuddered at the warm sensation on his cool skin. She then smoothed it slowly over his chest, making Frederick inhale sharply.

Mina glanced at Salter's face. He wore a grave expression, his eyes trying to communicate a thousand things to her. Surreptitiously, Salter shook his head slowly, warning her to stop. Mina grinned mischievously. His anger told her that at least he wasn't indifferent to her. Besides, Frederick knew something about her father, so she decided it was time to press her inquiries.

"Damn, you're good too," exclaimed Underwood.

"You know, Lollie," began Mina, "you're right about Lord Underwood. He does resemble Mr. Halliday, the jeweler. You said you knew him, didn't you, Lord Underwood?"

Salter grew livid, and Mina delighted that she had ruined his happy feeling with Lollie.

"Yes, I purchased a set of earbobs from him for my

wife's birthday a few months ago. As a matter of fact, Prescott had recommended him to me. Curious thing, really. Prescott spoke very well about him one day, but not two weeks later, he turned on him. Next thing I know, Prescott's spouting curses upon the man. I don't know . . . seemed a fine enough fellow to me. Gave me a good price on my wife's earbobs. Actually, I should probably pay him a visit. Our wedding anniversary is coming up next month."

Now it was Mina's turn to be disappointed. Lord Underwood was not the man she had been looking for either.

"That's sufficient, girl. I'm clean enough. Now, it's time to get dirty." He rose from the tub naked, and Mina backed away from him. "Towel, girl!"

Mina sidled to the table and handed him a folded towel from the stack.

"Rainey," he began as he threw the oversized towel over his shoulders. "It was nice to have met you. Hope to see you again soon. Now I'm looking forward to a different sort of massage."

"You can't take her, Stratton," Salter said, indicating Mina. "I saw her first."

"Her?" responded Underwood. "Wouldn't dream of taking her. I paid to have a beautiful woman, not someone like this. Come along, Polly."

Mina felt as if her insides had been scooped out and were lying in a heap on the floor. She'd never felt so humiliated. She had been so pleased with herself that Salter had grown jealous over her; now it was apparent to everyone in the room, especially Salter, just how ridiculous she had been.

Lollie followed Frederick outside, chattering angrily at the man's back in a thick Cockney accent. Salter remained behind, silent.

Mina stood in the corner, refolding the towels, her back to the pool. She held her breath, waiting for Salter to emerge from the water and leave her alone. Finally, she heard him rise from the pool, water slapping the deck as it dripped from his body.

Just a few more seconds, she thought as a torrent of tears collected behind her closed eyelids. *He needs a towel, and then he'll leave.*

He walked up and stood behind her. Without turning around, she held out the cloth. All he had to do was take it.

But instead she felt his strong hands on her shoulders, and her tattered pride crumbled like a dry leaf. A sob escaped her lips, breaking through the dam of tears.

"Don't," he said. But she couldn't help it. She felt like an utter fool, and she wished the ground would swallow her up. The last person in the entire world she wanted solace from was the man behind her.

"Please just go away," she said, trying to keep her voice from sounding so pitiable.

"No."

She didn't have the strength or the will to argue with him. If he wanted to stay, then let him. She took the towel that she had refolded a dozen times, and pressed it to her face. And held it there.

He turned her around, and enveloped her in his arms. The compassionate gesture made her cry all the harder. He tightened the embrace.

She was grateful for his sensitivity, but it was more embarrassing to be pitied. The only thing she wanted to do was disappear. But the man held her fast and wouldn't let her go.

Finally, the worst of it was over. Though the tears still came, the sobbing had stopped. "Thank you, Salter. I'm fine now. Really. You can go. I'll be all right."

"Ah, but you see, there's my dilemma. I paid for a beautiful woman too. And I want you with me tonight."

"How could you mock me at a time like this?"

"I do find you beautiful. Of course, not now." A smirk appeared as he wiped a tear from her face. "When you've been crying like this, you look like a banshee."

She didn't feel like laughing, but her sorrow diminished at his playful jibe. "I'm sorry."

"For what?"

"For . . . I don't know. For showing my weakness, I suppose."

"That's nothing to be sorry about. We all have weaknesses. The only one who should be sorry is that insensitive ass. Would you like me to arrest him for you? I'll lock him up, and you can have a go at him with my truncheon."

A chuckle escaped Mina's lips. "Don't tempt me." Suddenly, she realized that Salter was completely wet and completely naked. She handed him a fresh towel. "Here, you'd better put this on."

Mina stole one last glance at his naked body before she turned around. What a beautiful man he was. She had been so distraught when he embraced her that she hadn't registered the feel of him. She knew she would berate herself later for not memorizing the way his body felt against hers. When she turned back around, Salter had tied the towel around his waist.

"I seem to have made you all wet," he said.

Mina's eyes bulged. "I beg your pardon?"

Salter pointed to her gown. She looked down and noticed her gray dress and pinafore were drenched from neck to hem by the warm water from his body.

"Oh. Yes, I see."

"Why don't you let me escort you to your room? You can change into something warm, and I can change back into my clothes."

She let him do just that. It seemed a long and very public walk from the cellar, across the parlor, and up the stairs to her attic room. But once inside the still womb of her tiny bedchamber, she felt safer and more insulated than ever, even if there was a half-naked man standing right in the center of it.

Salter put his clothes down on her desk and padded to her wardrobe. He opened the wooden doors and rummaged through her hanging garments until he found her dressing gown. "Here. Take your dress off and put this on before you catch your death of cold."

She felt silly feeling shy undressing in front of him, especially when his only clothing was a white towel barely covering his own nakedness, so she started to unhook the buttons at her bodice. It seemed to her an eternity the length of time it took to loosen her outer dress. All that time, she kept thinking how naked she would be with only her shift and corset left to preserve her modesty. It seemed ridiculous she should feel inhibited about underclothes in a place like this and at a time like now. And ridiculous was the last thing she wanted to feel.

She threw the wet dress on the floor and slipped on the dressing gown he held aloft for her. She slipped it on, and was instantly soothed by its thick warmth and softness. Although her outer dress had been her only decent clothing, she felt remarkably less self-conscious without it.

He poured her a glass of water from the carafe on her night table. "Please sit down."

It seemed odd that he was being so accommodating in a room that belonged to her, but she was enjoying his hospitality.

He placed the desk chair in front of her bed, and sat down upon it. Concern was scored on his forehead as he leaned forward, resting his elbows on his knees. "Are you warm enough now?"

She smiled sheepishly at him. "Yes, thank you."

The lines faded from his brow. There was an awkward silence, and her embarrassment returned. Not for herself, but for him. He had satisfied every obligation to be polite and gallant. She wanted to repay that by granting him an easy way to leave. "Thank you for being such a gentleman. You've been most kind, and I shall never forget it. But I should probably be getting back to work now. And I really shouldn't be keeping you any longer. Please . . . enjoy the rest of your evening."

He leaned back in the chair. "I want to, but you keep trying to get rid of me."

Color suffused her face. "I just thought you'd want jollier company."

"Jolly or not, I want to spend my evening with you."

She couldn't determine if he was telling the truth. "Well, I have my duties to attend to. Madame will miss my presence at the bar. I will get into a lot of trouble for being away from my station for too long."

"Well, then, I'll have a word with the Madame. I paid good money for you, Minnow, and I'll have no substitute."

They were kind words, but she couldn't read men well enough. A voice inside her insisted he was still just being chivalrous. "I think it only fair to warn you that you won't get the pleasure from me that you would from another girl. My advice to you, as a friend, is that you spend your evening in another bedchamber."

His lips thinned in irritation. He stood up, grabbed his coat, opened her bedroom door, and stepped outside.

A thousand emotions flashed across her mind, but none she wanted to claim. She had forced his hand, but he hadn't resisted. From the rubble of disappointment she was trapped under, the only beam of light was the knowledge that he would not stay unless he truly wanted to.

She heard the ponderous footsteps of Maggie, Cook's kitchen maid, on the hall floorboards. She must have come upstairs to change her apron, as she sometimes did when the need arose. Mina then heard Salter's deep voice. "Would you please do me the favor of bringing up a bottle of wine and two glasses? Perhaps some cheese and fruit too. And tell the Madame that Miss Mina will be otherwise engaged tonight."

She heard coins jingle, and Maggie gushed, "Thank

you, sir! Right away!" Her heavy footfalls faded down the hall.

Mina cupped her hand over her mouth to hide her smile. She had never felt so important—so wanted—and the joy it produced bubbled up from inside.

Salter came back in, tossed his coat back onto the desk, and walked around the bed. He lifted the covers and climbed in. She saw him shift under the covers, and then he slid out the damp towel and threw it on the floor.

Mina was thrilled he had chosen to stay with her, but this behavior exceeded the bounds of gallantry. "You're . . . in my bed."

"Yes, I am."

"Aren't you presuming a great deal?"

"Possibly. But the fact is, I'm cold."

Mina pursed her lips to keep from smiling. "And just where am I to be while you're warming yourself in my bed?

"There's plenty of room for you. Get in."

"I'd better not."

"It's going to be a long evening for you if you don't. I suggest you make yourself comfortable."

She leaned her back against the footboard. "How do you know your honor will be safe with me?"

Salter smiled. "I'll force you to keep your hands to yourself."

There was a knock at the door. Salter made a move to rise.

Remembering his nakedness, she stopped him. "Uh, I'll answer it. I wouldn't want you to catch your death of cold."

"As you wish," he said.

She went to the door and opened it. Maggie stood there with a tray.

"I brought 'im the tray 'e asked for. Ask 'im if it's all right."

Mina took the tray. "I'm sure it is. Thanks, Maggie."

Maggie pushed her florid face in through the door, and spotted Salter in bed. "I brought you some fresh rolls I just baked too, sir. They're still 'ot. Hope you like 'em."

Salter waved from the bed. "Thank you, Maggie."

Mina rolled her eyes. "Goodbye, now, Maggie."

"Ye've got a good one there, love," she said excitedly.

"Yes, well, that remains to be seen. Bye, Maggie."

Salter sat up in the bed, and took the tray from Mina. "What is that supposed to mean?"

"It means that I haven't made my mind up about you yet."

"Maggie had no problems on that score."

"Well, Maggie has more enthusiasm than discretion."

He began to open the bottle of wine. "Too bad the same can't be said about you."

Mina put her hands on her hips. "And what is that supposed to mean?"

"Men are not the enemy, Mina. I know some behave thoughtlessly, but you can't go through life imagining we are all out to get you."

"What are you talking about? I don't think that."

"Perhaps not deliberately, but your outward display says otherwise. You walk around in your own private world, and no one is ever allowed in. You keep yourself in a cocoon, as if you're afraid to show people who you really are."

"Don't be ridiculous," she said, though she was shaken by the truth in his words.

"See? There you go again. If you can't let people understand you, how can you hope to have them like you?"

The cork popped off the bottle, and he poured some into the glasses.

"And you are supposed to understand me? I hardly know you."

"That's just it. You don't know me because you're blinded by the darkness you surround yourself in. But I see clearly, and I can see the real you."

"How can you know me if I never gave you leave to?"

"Occasionally, I catch glimpses of you, when you think no one is looking. And that's the woman I want to get to know." He held out the glass to her.

"I don't know what to say to such a two-edged compliment."

"Have a sip of wine. Maybe she'll come out again, and we'll both get a chance to meet her."

She had no idea what the man was talking about. What a complete puzzlement men were. She spent half her time wanting to be with them, and the other half too baffled to want to. She shifted, leaning against the footboard.

He rested his naked back against the headboard and regarded her. "Why do women wear those?"

Her brows drew together. "What?"

He pointed with the glass. "Those. Corsets."

She looked down. Her dressing gown had slipped open, revealing the rounded tops over her cinched corset.

He shook his head. "I never did like those blasted things. They're so stiff and unyielding. Watching a woman's breasts trying to move inside that cage . . . it's like seeing a living thing trapped inside a statue."

Trapped. That was a good word for it. Sometimes she felt like that, a flesh-and-blood creature trapped inside rigid and unforgiving circumstances. As if she were living inside a cocoon.

"They look deucedly uncomfortable. Why do women wear them?"

She shrugged. "To look pretty." But as soon as she spoke the words, her countenance fell. Clearly, it hadn't worked for her. And being insulted by Lord Underwood made it all the more evident.

"Take it off," he said.

Her head snapped up. "What?"

"Take it off. You don't need it to look pretty. Besides, I much prefer a woman who can move freely, without trappings. Remove it."

Mina regarded him carefully, studying him for a hint of lewd intent. She could see that he was trying to make a point, and to be honest, she wanted to know what it was.

She pulled the bow at her bosom. As it loosened, she immediately began to feel some relief from the constricting stays. The looser it got, the more freedom she felt. As the garment unraveled, it seemed, so did her reserve.

She stood and shimmied the casing over her hips. She breathed easily, moved freely, and felt more comfortable. Her robe still protected her modesty, but now she felt more like a human being and less like a statue. When she sat back down on the bed, it was with the greatest relief.

"Better?"

"Quite."

He nodded appreciatively. "Yes, I prefer you thus, without all that paint and puffery from the other night. This is how you should have come to dinner."

Mina smiled, realizing she liked herself just the way he liked her.

Maybe it was his easy manner, or her growing comfort, or maybe even the wine. But there was something she had always wanted to know yet was too afraid to ask, and his extension of friendship offered the possibility. "If I ask you a question, Salter, would you swear to give me an honest answer?"

"Of course."

"You must swear to be truthful. Even if it means hurting my feelings."

He took a moment before answering. "I swear."

She quaked at the prospect of Salter's answer, but he was the closest thing to a friend she had in a man, and she felt she could trust him to finally answer the question that had plagued her her whole life.

"What do men see . . . when they look at me?"

His face was somber as he stared at her, considering his response. He was quiet a long time, and Mina began to wish she could retract the question.

"The honest answer is that I can't tell you what men see when they look at you."

She nodded, tucking the question back inside her heart.

"But I can tell you what I see."

With her silence, she gave him permission to continue.

"I see a woman afraid to be magnificent. A woman who sinks into the shadows, her eyes glued to the ground, trying to fade into the wallpaper. She's taken every offense and insult for gospel, but that's only because she's not had anyone to tell her otherwise. And the moment she steps out from the shadows and dares to believe the truth about herself, that's the day she will dazzle everyone with her brilliance. I'm sorry that I met her now, too late to undo some of the damage that's been done. But I'm glad that I'll be here from now on, to make sure it won't ever happen again."

Her lip trembled. She felt utterly naked in front of him, as if she had been stripped of every defense and deception. And yet there was no shame in that nakedness. What magic was this that let him see what other men could not? And what blessing was it that he wanted to?

"I don't know how to be unafraid."

He shook his head and sighed. His eyes traveled around the room, and landed on a spot on the wall.

"That painting. Where did you get it?"

She turned in the direction of his gaze. It was a small canvas of a wooden gate opening onto a path leading to a cottage in the background. Mina had become enamored of the ducks congregating around the open gate. "In the Cotswolds. My father bought it for me from an old man who was painting them in a field."

"What's it worth?"

She shrugged. "My father paid just a few pennies for it."

"That isn't what I asked you. I asked what it was worth."

Mina's brows drew together. "I don't know. He wasn't a famous artist. Just an old man who liked painting things."

"To you and to your father, the painting may be worth a few pennies. But consider: that painting represents a vision captured through the eyes of a man weighted with years and experience. It was painted at the height of his skill. And in the twilight of his life, considering how little remained to his days, he chose to invest his precious time in creating it. Not to mention what memory that particular cottage holds for him. Now, to that old man, what do you suppose the painting is worth? He may not have been famous, and you may not even know his name, but he created something of immeasurable value, something he prized very, very much. The fact that he sold it for so little does not diminish its value. Not to me."

Mina looked at the painting again. As she saw it through Salter's eyes, it became a masterpiece.

"You are a bit like that painting, Minnow. Remember how lovingly and carefully formed you are. Your thoughts, your talents, your memories, your mistakes . . . they all make the complete canvas of you. Even though others may mistake your worth, you must never value yourself any less."

Her eyes brimmed with tears, and two fell simultaneously down her cheeks. Maggie's words echoed: "You've got a good one there. Love."

"Come here," he said, motioning her to lie beside him. She did so.

She lay upon the bed, over the covers, facing him. *So this is what it feels like to lie beside a man,* she thought. How long she had fantasized about something like this. How often she had envisioned the sight of a man's arm over the edge of the sheets, his head on the pillow beside her, just like this. But her fantasies paled in comparison to the real thing. Because this time, she was not a brazen milkmaid, or a bored countess, or any of the other characters she had become in the sexual scenarios. This time, she was no one but herself—and his eyes were fixed fully upon her.

They lay awake talking for hours. He had given her something better than sex. He had shown her intimacy. She had no idea when slumber finally crept upon her, but she succumbed to it in the warmest contentment she had ever felt.

When she awoke, after the sun came up, he was gone. But there, on his pillow, was a note he had made on the blue paper from her writing desk.

Minnow,
   Thank you for letting me stay the night with you. I have never met anyone like you. You are a woman of many surprises, and I very much enjoyed your company. I will call again for you at noon today. There is something I'd like to show you.

*I didn't want to leave without saying goodbye,
but I also didn't want to wake you from your rest,
so I left a kiss upon your cheek.*

*Yours,
Salter*

Mina's hand flew to her cheek, as if to capture the fleeting kiss. Her eyes closed dreamily as she leaned back against her pillow. It felt as if her heart were floating three feet above the bed, and lightness was spreading throughout her entire body. Her first kiss from a man! She pressed the note—her very first love letter—to her chest. What a wonderful man! What a magical night! What an amazing feeling!

What if she couldn't keep him interested?

Chapter Seven

  "It will never work." The Right Honorable the Lord Mayor of London sat down with a black scowl and a large Scotch.

Sir Giles Mornay had the common sense to conceal his irritation. "My Lord Mayor, the efficacy of a government-funded police force has been proven. The constabulary has been operating in the London metropolis for some time now. As we predicted, the incidence of crime has diminished. The time is upon us to introduce such a force in the City of London."

Lord Bensonhurst folded a long leg over the other one. The Lord Mayor was a man of dignified bearing, with a singularly deep and commanding voice. Except for the full head of thick white hair and the deep grooves in the corners of his eyes, there was nothing about him that would betray the fact that he was well over sixty. "Sir Giles, you are an intelligent man, and a first-rate home secretary. I know that you have the security and safety of the public at heart. But I've made my opinions very clear on numerous occasions. I don't want a constabulary in the City."

Sir Giles glanced down. He wore thick, round spectacles, and the glow from the open window reflected crescents of light on his cheeks. "If I may say so, that sentiment is not based on a sound foundation. Here, in this square mile of important commercial and financial concerns, there is a great need for public protection. A certain amount of reluctance to change to new systems is natural, I suppose. But to keep the constabulary out of the City is an exercise in foolishness."

Lord Bensonhurst bristled, not expecting to be insulted here, inside his palatial residence, in the heart of the city he governed. "I beg to differ, Sir Giles. It isn't reluctance, or inertia, or even my own personal whim. The citizenry will not stand for it. To have an unwieldy, pseudomilitary organization in this city is an experiment in bad politics. Take it from me: most of my constituents will view the presence of your constables as a violation of their civil liberties."

Sir Giles's slow, measured words were his hallmark. Not a man given to histrionics, he instead preferred the temperate art of persuasion. "Have you ever stopped to consider that if a constabulary presence is felt in next-door Whitechapel, the criminal element would organically migrate into the City? Criminals will naturally go where the police are not allowed to."

Lord Bensonhurst sniffed. "The City is already well protected. Security is best left in the hands of those who have a vested interest in it. Each business hires its own protection. That is the way it ought to be. But to use public monies to fund a broad-based, unfocused enterprise is simply bad stewardship of resources."

"It isn't as if the City will collapse under the expense. Per capita, the City of London has the highest revenue of any London borough. And the area the police will cover is very small indeed. You wouldn't need too extensive a force."

"I just don't see the need in this constituency."

"No? Well, I am reluctant to remind you of your aide, the late Lord Roderick Prescott. Wasn't he murdered rather gruesomely here, in this City, which you say has no need of a constabulary?"

Lord Bensonhurst's ice-blue eyes grew flinty. "I think it in exceedingly poor taste that you should use the murder of a friend and colleague to make a point in an argument."

The crescents of light on Sir Giles's cheeks lengthened as he cast his face down. "My apologies. I meant no disrespect. But my wish is that this tragic incident never again be repeated. London needs an independent agency to safeguard the public welfare against crime."

Lord Bensonhurst sighed. "I see nothing wrong with this in theory. Personally, I've nothing against a publicly supported constabulary force. But to give one man rights over another, to dispense justice on the spot, is a formula for disaster. Men are corruptible beings, Sir Giles. Who is to stop your constable from abusing a common man's rights? You will need a police force for your police force."

Sir Giles raised his short grizzled brows. "There is some truth in that, Lord Bensonhurst. It does stand to reason that there may be a rotten apple in the barrel. But that is no reason to throw out the entire barrel. These men will be vetted by me. I will personally guarantee that the City police force will be men of upright moral character."

"Such as whom?"

"Well, Chief Constable Lambrick, for one. He's a fine officer, well experienced, and he's leading the charge in my program. He selected and trained an excellent force, and because of him and his men, crime and disorder have declined."

"Yes, I know this man. He is investigating Prescott's murder."

"And if I know my man, he will bring about a swift resolution to the case. Lambrick has brought hundreds of murderers to justice. He is patient, professional, impersonal—and above all, relentless."

Lord Bensonhurst tapped the arm of the chair with one long finger. "I'll tell you what I'll do. I'll accept your constabulary on trial. I will take on your Lambrick and his team while they work on finding the murderer of my aide. They shall be the City's first constabulary force, albeit a token one. I'll set aside monies from which to pay them, and they shall work for me. If your Lambrick is able to find the murderer and bring him to justice, then I'll consider signing the City on to your policing system. But if he doesn't . . ."

Sir Giles made no outward expression of his satisfaction. "He will not disappoint you. And I'll make certain that he fully understands the monumental importance of this case. To you and to the force at large."

"You have great expectations of this man."

"I must, to be able to feed my great hopes for the constabulary. The resolution of a murder such as this one is certain to drive home the point that a police force is just what this country needs."

Bensonhurst laughed. "So, you already envision policing the entire country, do you?"

Sir Giles raised his spectacled face. "As a matter of fact, I do. I hope one day to see uniformed constables patrolling the streets of England. And if, as I believe, you are pleased with the present constabulary, then I am sure you will have no qualms about offering your own support to bolster my petition to Parliament to effect just that."

"Then it's settled. Transfer Lambrick and his team over to my command. I'll let you know if a police force is worthy of your expectations."

BEFORE THE FIRST STROKE of noon from the hall clock, Salter's phaeton clattered to a stop in front of the Pleasure Emporium.

The ladies were having their breakfast in the dining room. Madame Fynch was not among them, as she customarily took breakfast in her study. But when the doorbell rang, Lollie jumped up to answer it.

"Good afternoon, Lollie," Salter said, removing his hat. "I'm here for Miss Mina."

Lollie invited him in. "Whom shall I say is calling . . . Lord Prescott, Mr. Rainey, Mr. Lambrick, or do you have a new name for us?"

He mirrored her sarcastic look. "Salter will do, thank you. Run along and get her for me. There's a good girl."

"All right," she said, a little withered, and went up the stairs.

As Salter waited in the parlor, Madeleine emerged from the dining room. The ladies traditionally didn't dress for breakfast, and Madeleine was still in her transparent violet peignoir.

"So, you are the Salter Lambrick we've heard so much about." Her generous lips pouted when she talked, revealing that sensual groove in the middle of her upper lip that intoxicated men.

Salter smiled down at her. "I didn't realize I was famous."

"In circles such as these, we discuss men quite a lot. Some men more than most."

"Then I'm flattered."

"But not embarrassed?"

He chuckled. "Mademoiselle, I haven't been embarrassed since I was fifteen years old."

"Interesting," she said, smiling. She sank onto the couch, allowing him a generous view of her cleavage. "Please sit down. Here," she said, patting the seat beside her.

"Very well. Thank you."

Her lips became a perfect O as she took his hand in hers. "What large hands you have. They are larger than any gentleman's I've ever known. You must be an athlete."

"Not exactly," he responded, flattered by the praise. "Although I do fancy myself a bit of a rider."

She leaned even closer to him, looking up at his face. "Really? Tell me, what sort of riding do you prefer?" she inquired, her black eyelashes fanning over her almond-shaped eyes.

⌒Upstairs in her room, Mina raced to complete the arrangement of her hair. She hopped around the bedroom frantically.

"Pins! Pins! I need more pins!"

Lollie watched lazily from a corner, munching on a piece of buttered toast. "Behind you."

Mina spun around to face her desk, and grabbed the jam jar containing her hairpins. She flew to the small mirror atop her dresser, folded the last tendrils into curls, and pinned them to her crown. She stepped back to assess the complete picture of herself. The pale blue dress was pretty but not especially becoming on her. Nevertheless, it was the only morning dress she had left and it matched her only reticule. It was her wilted brown hair that was the greatest source of her agitation, because she was unsure if the makeshift curls would hold. "How do I look?"

Lollie shoved the triangle of bread into her mouth and wiped her hand on the front of her chemise. " 'Ere. Let me fix that one."

"Lollie, no!" she cried, flitting away. "You'll get my hair all greasy!"

"Cor, you're in a right state! Anyone would think this was your weddin' night!"

"Don't be ridiculous," she said under her breath, a curious elation rising at the possibility. He had imprinted hope on her heart with a caress, and now it had grown into huge blossoms of joy. "I just want to look pretty, is all."

"You're really taken with him, aren't you?"

"No! No . . ." She wasn't sure how best to respond. "He's nice. I like him."

"Well, you've certainly changed your tune, 'aven't you?"

"Now I know him better," she said defensively. "He's a gentleman."

"With your nerves, Mina, the last thing you need is a gentleman. If you ask me, you could do with a good rogering."

"Ugh!" Exasperated, Mina grabbed her hat and reticule and trudged down the stairs.

Lollie shouted after her. "Mind he brings you back in a slightly more damaged condition!"

⁂DOWNSTAIRS, MADELEINE LAUGHED PRETTILY, flashing her beautiful white teeth. She had an easy, gay laugh, and men were drawn to her creamy charm. Her arm was already snaked around Salter's, and she let her breasts brush against his arm as she gave herself to the merriment.

Salter turned his head in her direction. "Tell me, mademoiselle, why is a delightful woman such as yourself working in a profession such as this?"

One fine brow arched into her forehead. "Ah, but you see, I shan't be here for long. My father's will has left me a considerable fortune, which I stand to inherit at twenty-five and upon marriage. I am but twenty-two now, and until then, I have to earn my living as others must. But I am using this time to my advantage, searching for the man who is a perfect fit for me." She sidled up to him even closer.

Mina stood on the last step, frozen by the sight of their closeness.

"A beautiful lady such as you does not need to search. I'm certain men must descend upon you in packs."

"True. But every pack is headed by a lead wolf, and only that man shall claim me."

"Well, that man is indeed a fortunate one."

Mina's heart chilled in affronted pride. "Good afternoon, Mr. Lambrick."

Salter rose from his seat. "Good afternoon, Mina. What a vision you are today."

Not, Mina noted, a vision "of loveliness." She adopted an air of frigid reserve as she approached the two of them. "Good afternoon, Countess. Thank you for entertaining my guest, and attempting to make him more comfortable. I'll ask the Madame if we should replace the settees in here with beds, in order to speed the process along."

Madeleine bolted from her seat. "Are you accusing me of stealing a customer?" To the Madame, it was perfectly acceptable to seduce any man who walked into the bordello, in order to foster the feeling that clients were not bound to any one woman. But to the girls, stealing a loyal customer could lead to a fight.

"In the first place, he's not my customer. And in the second place, you can have him."

Salter looked confused. "Er, have I missed something?"

Mina turned to him. "Yes. A wonderful opportunity. Good day to you." She turned to leave, but his hand on her elbow stopped her.

"I don't understand. Where are you going?"

"As far away from you as I can get."

His grip didn't loosen one bit. "Just a moment. You and I have an engagement."

"Believe me, Mr. Lambrick, you and I will *never* be

so engaged. And as for you, Countess, have a bath before you go fishing for more men. Your net is still full from last night's catch."

Madeleine's seductive face distorted into a mask of outraged ugliness. "Oh!"

Salter watched a humiliated Madeleine stamp up the stairs. He turned on Mina, a stern look on his face. "Was it necessary to be so rude?"

Mina folded her arms. "When I want a lesson in manners from you, Mr. Lambrick, I'll ask for it."

"When I think you need a lesson in manners, Miss Halliday, you'll get it. Whether you ask for it or not."

There was menace in his tone, but his high-handedness galled her. "I will not be lectured. By you or any man. Goodbye, Mr. Lambrick."

She made a move to leave, but he yanked her back like a tethered dog. "Let me go!"

"I don't take kindly to being dismissed in so cavalier a fashion. We have an appointment, and I expect you to keep it." He pulled her in the direction of the door.

"I don't wish to go out with you! You're kidnapping me!"

He turned on her. "You are wanted in connection with constabulary business. You will accompany me willingly for questioning, or I will arrest you in the name of the King. Either way, you're coming with me. Now, which is it going to be?"

Her resentment escalated to new levels. Here she had thought he was asking her on an outing, and all the while he was asking her to help him solve his precious case.

Although she had no choice but to go with him, she

was determined not to cooperate. Assuming her best ladylike hauteur, she jabbed her nose in the air and preceded him outside. He opened the door for her, and she ascended his carriage without accepting his proffered hand. He climbed aboard the phaeton next to her. He grabbed the reins, made a clicking sound, and the phaeton lurched forward.

Mina looked in any direction but his. She hoped her frostiness drove home the point that she would never speak to him of her own accord again. Still, from the corner of her eye, she noticed how his dark gray coat stretched over his broad shoulders, and how the sunshine lit the crests of his black wavy hair. The breeze carried the scent of his soap.

"You were quite vicious with Madeleine," he remarked.

Silence.

"Are you so sure she deserved such ill treatment?"

Silence again. But an answer burned within her.

"I thought she was very gracious."

She simply had to set him straight. "Gracious? She's not gracious. She's insatiable. She's only after the best man, and usually that means whoever another woman has set her sights upon. She likes to feel victory over other women, and men are her trophies."

He smiled, deepening the grooves in his cheeks. "I see. So you've set your sights upon me, is that it?"

Her face colored as she struggled to explain her meaning. "No, I—"

"Wait . . . were you jealous over me?"

"Don't be ridiculous," she said, turning away. "I hardly even know you. But the point is, she *thinks* I like you, and that was tantamount to tossing down the gaunt-let. She had to claim you for herself to prove she is the better woman. And as far as I'm concerned, she can have you. Not because she's better, but because if you want her, you deserve her."

He smiled broadly. "You *are* jealous."

She itched to slap the smug look off his face. "To be jealous, I'd have to want you. And I don't. Right now, I wish I'd never even met you."

"If you are thinking I'm attracted to Madeleine, once again, you're monumentally mistaken about me. I pity her."

"You pity her?"

"She thinks she is searching for the right man in a place such as that. Men who frequent those establishments are not to be desired."

"For once, Mr. Lambrick, I'm entirely inclined to agree with you."

He gave her a withering look. "You know what I mean. She claims she is looking for a wolf, and believe me, she's going to find him. Speaking as a man, I can tell you that we have a positive talent for sniffing out the weak ones. Some women are like wounded gazelles, and Madeleine is one of them. She's positively screaming to be hunted and devoured. And not in the way she hopes. Because by the time he's through feasting on her, there'll be nothing left of her to recognize."

She had never given Madeleine so much thought. But Salter seemed to read Madeleine as clearly as if her whole life were printed on her face. She was amazed by his skill at sizing people up. "Madeleine is a grown woman who has a great deal of experience of the world. Why should you pity her?"

"I pity all of you. You more than the rest."

"Me? Why should you pity me?"

He didn't respond, but his eyes spoke his answer, and she understood it all too clearly. He was reading her too, and his truthfulness left her bruised. She wanted to be regarded with desire, not pity. And especially not by him.

"Stop this carriage."

"Why?"

"Because I've grown weary of this conversation. Let me off."

"Settle down. We're almost there."

"I have no further need of your company, Mr. Lambrick."

"But I have need of yours."

"That is not my concern. I'm not going anywhere with you." She bent forward, grabbed the reins from his hands, and gave them a firm yank. The surprised horse stopped suddenly.

Before Salter could react, she leaped off the phaeton and marched up the street. Here, in broad daylight, with so many people around, he wouldn't dare seize her by the hand again in so brutish a fashion.

She was almost at the corner when she felt a tug at her elbow. He spun her around to face him. She was about to verbally tear into him, public be damned. But before she could mouth the first insulting word, he bent down, grabbed her legs, and folded her over his shoulder like a sack of meal.

"What are you doing? Let me go!"

The man made no sound, but instead strode purposefully up the street. "Put me down!" she cried, humiliation burning at her ignoble position. As they passed the phaeton, she came to the frightening realization that he planned to carry her the rest of the way.

"Salter, no! Stop! Stop, I tell you!" Forcefully, she pummeled his back, hoping the pain would make him stop. But her upturned bottom received a very sharp smack, and she cried out as it absorbed the sizzling impression of his large hand. She provoked him no further. "Stop, please. I'll walk from here. Wherever you wish."

He turned onto the front steps of a house, though she couldn't see whose. Salter was very tall, and she was already high off the ground, but bouncing up the stairs over his shoulder was a fresh adventure in fear. "Please put me down!"

Her protests were a waste of breath. Not until he stood in the foyer, closed the door, locked it, and pocketed the key did he bend over and let her slip off his shoulder.

Her pride stung, not to mention her behind, but she tried to recover her earlier frosty composure as best she could. "That was the most humiliating thing I've ever been subjected to."

His jaw squared in challenge. "The day is still young. Give me time."

Her chest caved as she considered the prospect.

"Now," he began, smoothing out his hair, "if you would be so kind as to join me in the study, there is something I wish to show you."

For the first time, she looked around. She was back

at Lord Prescott's town house. She glanced up at him uncertainly. Straightening her skirt, she turned in the direction of the study while he asked the butler to look after his horse down the street.

The study was nothing like she remembered. The books were back on their shelves, the desk was clean and orderly, and newspapers were nowhere to be found. She could finally see the pattern of the carpet.

"Lord Prescott kept a strongbox here behind this oak panel," he said, tugging on a door at the foot of a column, which opened to reveal a safe. "I thought surely its contents would tell me why he was killed. But they raised more questions than answers." From his pocket, he pulled a wooden dowel with notches at the end, and inserted it into the hole on the safe's escutcheon. He yanked on a handle and the safe opened.

Mina watched as Salter drew out a black velvet pouch and pulled on the drawstring. "Among the other items in his safe, Lord Prescott had this." He pulled out something and placed it into her hand.

It was a very large sapphire the color of a stormy ocean. The stone was heavy in her hand, and light reflected off its mirrored surface. She held the stone up to the light of the window, and peered into its depth.

"I remember you!" she exclaimed under her breath, memories streaming from the stone as she held it aloft. She turned to Salter in amazed disbelief. "Where did this come from? Before it wound up in Lord Prescott's safe?"

He sat on the edge of the desk. "That's what I was hoping you could tell me."

Mesmerized, she cradled it in her palm like a baby

bird. "Well, there's one thing I do know. My father held this stone in his very own hand."

He crossed his arms. "Explain."

Her brow furrowed, not knowing where to begin. A thousand details ran through her mind, and she raced to put them in a coherent order. "This stone came from the tiara I told you about. My father showed it to me. It was an exquisite creation . . . Indian or Burmese, perhaps. Gold filigree openwork, with lots of jewels in it. This stone was in its center."

"Are you certain of that?"

"I'd stake my life on it. Rare gems are like snowflakes—no two are alike. And this one is very rare indeed. Even to the naked eye, you can see the inclusion that gives it its uniqueness. It bears a tiny star inside. See?"

She watched as his hazel eyes penetrated the stone. "I see it. There's a sort of blemish inside it."

"That blemish, as you call it, is the very thing that gives it its worth. If we had a loupe, you could see how that scar actually multiplies the sapphire's refraction."

He held it up to the light. The sapphire burst into blue fire, twinkling like a star.

"There were other stones in the tiara," she continued. "A dozen rubies . . . and a host of diamonds."

He stared at her, comprehension materializing on his face. He upturned the black velvet pouch on the desk. Out fluttered a shower of jewels—a dozen rubies and a host of diamonds.

A muscle in his jaw tightened. "These must have been the jewels your father was arrested for stealing."

She fingered the stones, marveling at them as if they

were little drops of sunshine. A ragged breath filled her lungs, and it felt as if it were the first breath she had taken in months. "Lord Prescott . . . it *was* he who accused my father." She had to sit down. "But why? What would Prescott stand to gain from having my father arrested?"

Salter shrugged. "Silence. It's possible he was trying to cover up the switch in jewels."

"Why?

"Perhaps he wanted to keep what he'd done a secret. Perhaps the tiara wasn't his to alter. Perhaps he wanted to sell the jewels to pay off his debts. Perhaps all three."

Mina waved the ideas away in disgust. "Well, that doesn't concern me. I don't really care why he did it. The point is, here is evidence that my father is not guilty of stealing the jewels from that tiara."

Salter's thoughtful scowl faded. "If these were the gems your father was accused of stealing, then we can petition the courts to set your father free."

Mina clasped her hands and pressed them to her forehead. "Thank God." She sighed once more. "Can we go now?"

"Where?"

"To the magistrate."

His serious expression returned. "I'm afraid not."

Mina's face crumbled. "Why not?"

"Because I still don't know who killed Prescott. And if he was killed for these, then I can't let on that I have them. Not yet."

"Do you mean to tell me you would let my father stay in prison while you search for another criminal?"

"I have to, Minnow. It's my job."

She bolted out of the chair. "To hell with your job! My father is rotting away in some vermin-infested prison on the other side of the world. Here in my hand is the key to unlocking his chains. And you want me to give that up for your suppositions?"

"Mina, please calm yourself. I want justice for your father as much as you do. But there is a killer out there, and I want him caught, if for no other reason than to prevent him from killing again."

"What if my father dies in prison? You're not as anxious to prevent that."

"Of course I am. But I have to investigate this matter, and your input is invaluable. Please cooperate with me on this."

His plea moved her. But no matter how she turned it over in her head, his purposes were not as important, nor as urgent, as hers. "You are a very talented constable. I have every confidence that you will find this man you seek. Without the aid of these," she said as she scooped the stones back into the pouch.

"Minnow," he began, "I'm not letting you leave with those stones."

She thought quickly. "I know that," she said, setting down the pouch and picking up a large, heavy book from the desk entitled *The History of Astronomy*. "That's why, against my best wishes, I have to do this." She swung the heavy volume at his head. Hard.

The force of the blow sent him sprawling across the desk, dazed. She snatched the pouch and took off toward the kitchen in the rear of the house.

Once in the courtyard, she found her way though the

side alley to the street and ran down the thoroughfare in the direction of the river. She had to get to Bow Street, to a magistrate's chambers, before he figured out where she was going. But in her rush, she forgot her reticule at the house, leaving her with no money for a hansom cab. She had to make it there all on her own.

Chapter Eight

❧ *Idiot. Fool. Ass.* He called himself every name he could think of as he took off after her. The woman had caught him completely off guard. Damn him for losing focus on his job. And damn her for being so distracting.

He had underestimated her. But it was not a mistake he would make twice. The knot at the hairline above his left eye throbbed mercilessly, and the bouncing ride on horseback only made the pain worse.

Salter reined in his horse at the end of the adjacent street. She could not have headed back toward the Pleasure Emporium, or he would have seen her. He shook his head in frustration, and was rewarded with a new level of pain. He ground his teeth, and turned his horse in the direction of the river. She was probably headed directly to Bow Street.

From Prescott's town house, she would have to travel about a half-mile to the Thames, and then another two miles along the river. He lifted his collar against his neck, and blew a dense puff of air onto his clasped hands. The sky threatened rain, and a chill impregnated the air. Urging the horse into a brisk canter, he zigzagged through the labyrinth of London's lanes and alleys, hoping to spot her.

Finally, he reached Thames Street, the long thoroughfare snaking alongside the river. He looked to the left; the angering sky had begun to drive the few remaining pedestrians from the street. The river lay ahead of him, and then he looked to the right.

Squinting, he saw the figure of a woman looking over her shoulder as she walked along the street. He blinked, unable to even make out the color of the woman's dress. But when he nudged his horse in the woman's direction, she broke into a run.

Mina.

Every nerve and sense blazed to life. His entire body heated instantly, like that of a panther who had scented a gazelle. He galloped toward her, quickly narrowing the distance between them. He would catch up to her in no time.

But Mina must have panicked at his rapid approach. She darted across the street in front of an oncoming stagecoach. His heart skipped a beat. "Mina!"

If the driver hadn't reined in his horses violently, he would have run her over. Mina scurried safely past and toward the embankment.

Thank God. He heaved a profound sigh, and then dreamed up ways of killing her for almost getting killed.

He saw Mina duck into a warren of empty wooden crates and discarded shipping boxes stacked high at the foot of the bridge. *Clever rabbit,* he thought, realizing she would now be inaccessible to him on horseback. He jumped off his mount and followed her through the piles of debris.

The massive brick footer cast a dark shadow over

the area, concealing her location even more. He listened for her footfalls, but the soft ground on the shoulder of the river muffled any sound.

Just as he was squeezing between two large wooden crates, a wooden plank flew right into his gut.

He doubled over, grimacing in pain. The next thing he felt were her clasped fists being brought down hard on his exposed neck.

He fell in a heap on the damp grass. Damn if she didn't fight like a man. But pure adrenaline gave him the presence of mind to reach out and latch on to her ankle before she could run away. She fell face-forward in front of him.

Now he had her. He stood, and hauled her to a standing position. Angry and steeled with resolve, he threw her across both his shoulders like a felled deer.

"All right, Minnow. It's time you cooled down." He marched down a derelict jetty underneath the bridge, his booted feet pounding against the unsteady boards. When he reached the end of the jetty, he threw her unceremoniously from his shoulders, her body sailing through the air before landing with a loud splash in the murky water.

She sputtered uncontrollably in the freezing water, flailing her arms. "I can't swim!"

He folded his arms across his chest. "Preposterous. All Minnows can swim!"

She sank into the water, her feet kicking behind her. "Salter!"

His scowl returned. "You're in about four feet of water. Stand up!"

Her hands landed on a wooden brace about five feet from the jetty. She clawed at the pole to raise herself out of the water. When she straightened up against it, she realized he was right; she could touch the riverbed with her feet.

Her dumbfounded expression drew a laugh out of him. Outraged, she spat a mouthful of wet curses at him.

He knelt on the edge of the jetty, cocking a surprised eyebrow. "A foul mouth like that will fill with foul water. I advise you to shut it."

A sullen look came over her features, which were plastered with wet hair.

"Now then, my little hellcat, as I seem to have your undivided attention, please be so kind as to hand over the jewels."

"I don't have them. Because of you, I accidentally dropped them in the water. If you want them, you'll have to come looking for them yourself."

"I don't think that will be necessary." He drew his pistol from the holster underneath his jacket, and leveled it at her. "And neither do you. Give me the jewels."

She blanched as she pushed the wet hair from her face. "I told you I don't have them!"

He pulled the trigger. The bullet screamed through the water to the left of her. Though it didn't touch her, its high-speed velocity superheated the water, scalding her on her left hip.

"Liar, liar, pants on fire."

Outraged, frightened, and incredulous, she didn't know which emotion to register. "What are you trying to do, kill me?"

"You started it, Minnow." Nonchalantly, he began to reload his gun.

"Dammit, I'm telling you the truth!" she shouted back.

"You have a very creative way of determining what truth is. Now, I'm going to ask you again. I do not want lies, equivocations, or refusals. Please hand over the jewels." He trained the gun on her once again.

She stared into the barrel. "I . . . I . . . hid the pouch in a tree. Help me out of here and I'll go get them for you."

His mouth pursing in grim determination, he pulled the trigger again. This time, the bullet penetrated the water on the other side, igniting the water and burning her right hip. She rubbed her side where the bullet had singed her. He began to reload, but she did not want to see where the next bullet was headed.

"All right, all right!" she cried, reaching between her breasts and pulling out the wet pouch. "Here are your jewels!" She held the pouch aloft as far as she could stretch her hand.

He took the pouch from her and shoved it into his coat pocket. Then he holstered his weapon.

"Now help me out of here!"

He took her wrist and drew her toward the jetty. Then, bending low, he slipped his hand between her breasts, gripped the lacing of her corset, and hauled her out of the blackened water.

Her shriek of affronted modesty was as loud as the gunshot.

"How about that?" he said, dropping her on her feet

onto the pier. "Those blasted corsets *are* good for something."

Both hands flew to her bosom. "How dare you!"

He gripped her under the arm and dragged her back to the street to his patiently waiting horse. He reached inside his saddlebag and pulled out a pair of shackles.

She struggled violently against his viselike grip, but moved him not one inch. "What are you doing?" she asked foolishly as he clasped them around her wrists in front. "Take these off me at once!"

"You tried to kill me twice today. I have no intention of giving you a third opportunity." He tied a rope to the chain between her cuffs, and jumped upon his horse. "Come along."

The horse sprang forward, pulling her with it. "You expect me to walk?"

He looked down at her. "Prisoners don't ride with constables."

"Is that what I am? A prisoner? And just what am I being charged with?"

"Assault on a police constable, interfering with an ongoing investigation, and swimming in a prohibited area."

"Swimming in a—" She would have told him exactly what she thought of him, but her insults would have fallen on his horse's ass. But her anger soon gave way to discomfort. She was sopping wet, shivering from the cold, she'd lost a shoe, and something slimy kept brushing against her leg.

She drew stares from passersby. She must have looked a bedraggled fright, and there was a fetid smell that clung to her wet clothes. She was actually looking forward to getting to the jail. At least there she would be out of the frigid air. But more importantly, she could appeal to another constable—a sympathetic one—and finally get her father's case reopened.

Salter's horse turned off Thames Street, and she realized with alarm he wasn't headed toward the Bow Street station. "Where are you taking me?"

He gave no answer. But a few blocks later, he stopped in the middle of a street lined with brick buildings. He alighted from his horse and led it to a mews between two tall buildings. He stabled the animal, removed its saddle and bridle, threw a woolen blanket over it, and shoveled fresh hay and oats into the trough. He gave its neck a gentle pat, and then picked up Mina's tether and walked ahead of her toward the front door.

Although the space was dimly lit, she was grateful to be out of the biting cold. A door on the ground floor opened, and the foyer was flooded with light from the flat.

An elderly woman clutching a shawl around her shoulders emerged from the room. She was thin with a slight stoop, giving Mina the odd impression she was made of twigs. "Good evening, Mr. Lambrick."

"Good evening, Mrs. Tilbury. Whatever you've got for us tonight smells heavenly. Steak and kidney?"

"Beef and potato."

"Mmm. Nothing I like more than one of your delicious pies for supper."

The woman's milk-rimmed eyes trailed up and down Mina's form. "I didn't know you were bringing company, Mr. Lambrick."

"This isn't company, Mrs. Tilbury. That is, not any-more. She is a prisoner, and I would be very much obliged if you would bring up with my supper a sand-wich for her."

The old woman glanced suspiciously at Mina. "All I have is bread and cheese."

"That will do. Won't it, Minnow? Say thank you and come along." Mina almost tripped on the stairs as he dragged her by her lead.

He took her to a flat on the next floor. The sitting room was clean but sparsely furnished, with only a few odd ornaments to indicate that anyone lived there at all.

"This way," he said, pulling her toward the bedroom.

She resisted. "I'm not going in there with you."

He chuckled, holding a hand to his heart. "With the way you smell, Minnow, I assure you your virtue will remain sacred with me."

Her mouth flew open with offended pride.

He brought her into the bedroom, a much larger but equally Spartan room without much décor other than a few curious articles atop the fireplace. There was a wardrobe at one end, a bed in the center, a tub and washstand in the far corner, and a table and uphol-stered reading chair next to the fireplace.

He tied her lead to the metal grating on the hearth, and lit the wood. "You can warm yourself here."

The length of rope didn't allow her much freedom of movement. She had to bend low just to be able to move her hands. "May I at least have the chair?"

"And have you stink up a perfectly good chair?"

She ground her teeth and knelt at the fireplace as it crackled to life. "Far be it from me to continue to offend your nose as a result of my poor choice in swimming locales. Let me have a bath then."

"Sorry, Minnow. I'm not asking that poor old woman to haul water upstairs at this hour. You can sleep on the floor tonight."

"On the floor?"

He ignored her protest as he slipped off his coat. Over his white shirt, she could now see the holster, a leather strap that went around his chest to support the pouch under his left arm where his pistol rested. From his coat, he removed the wet satchel containing the jewels, and poured out its precious contents into the empty basin on the washstand.

So close, she thought, and yet impossibly far.

There was a knock on the door. "In here, Mrs. Tilbury," he called out.

The old woman came in bearing a large tray. He took it from her and set it down on the tea table by the fireplace.

"Mr. Lambrick!" she exclaimed as the light from the fire illuminated his face. "You've been hurt!" Even with her arm outstretched, the small woman couldn't reach all the way up to his brow.

"It's nothing to be concerned about."

"That's a frightful lump. A compress of vinegar and water will bring down the swelling."

"No need. It'll be all right in the morning."

She pursed her lips. "However did you get it?"

A loud breath escaped him. "I turned my back on a delinquent."

The old woman gasped and turned upon Mina. "Did you do that to him?"

Mina grinned sarcastically at Salter. "I merely wanted to prove to him that one didn't need a book on astronomy in order to see stars."

Salter narrowed his eyes at her, mirroring her expression.

Mrs. Tilbury wagged her finger at Mina. "Well, shame on you, you naughty girl! Serves you right to go to jail. Imagine striking a man as noble and good as Mr. Lambrick. You ought to be sorry."

"I *am* sorry. Sorry I didn't hit him harder."

"Oh! The youth of today, Mr. Lambrick! Where is this world headed?"

"It's a crooked world, Mrs. Tilbury. It falls to us to straighten it out."

As Salter showed the old woman to the door, Mina looked wistfully at the tray. On one plate was a whole meat pie steaming from the cuts on the pastry shell. Its warm aroma filled the room. On the other plate were two thick slices of pale bread and a square of yellow cheese. Dejected, she bounced back onto her haunches. Even the horse got fresh oats and hay.

Salter came back to the room, and sat in the armchair on the other side of the hearth.

"How long do you intend to keep me here?"

"As long as it takes."

"For what?"

"To solve my case. Without any interference from you." He took the plate of beef pie and placed it on the floor in front of her.

Immediately, a jolt of guilt flashed through her. "This is your dinner."

"I know. I'm giving it to you."

She couldn't understand why he was being so nice to her after all the ways she had hurt him. Maybe he was giving her the better meal to make her feel guilty. Well, she wasn't about to let him manipulate her.

"I don't want your food," she said haughtily, holding it aloft to him with both tied hands. "I'll have the other."

Firelight twinkled in his eyes as he stared at her from the chair. Moments passed, and she got that uncomfortable feeling again, as if he were seeing far more than she'd care to show.

"You don't much care for people, do you?" he asked.

She set the plate down, the weight of it suddenly too heavy for her. How could he sap all her strength with a few insightful words? "Don't be ridiculous."

"You seem to give a kindness and an insult the very same value. Like men. All have the same value to you. And it isn't a very favorable one."

She had to turn away. The shrewdness of his words stung. All men tried to hurt her, in one way or another. Even a compliment often concealed a barb.

She picked up the plate again, without looking back at him. "Thank you for the meal," she said, but her appetite had significantly diminished.

They ate their supper in silence. She was happy he didn't engage her in conversation, because she wanted to avoid his scrutiny. What an enigma he was. Though she tried, it was impossible to calculate just how he planned to wound her. She knew the disappointment would come eventually, so she challenged him at every step to provoke the eventual attack. She just didn't want to be caught by surprise, as she was with Lord Underwood, because it invariably left her defenseless and bloodied. Was it possible that maybe—just maybe—Salter wasn't out to hurt her at all?

The food was still warm in her belly when she lay down on her side on the hearth rug. The fire had driven away the chill, and the hot coffee was actually making her sleepy. "What is that?" she said, staring at the delicate porcelain figurine of a dancing female courtier. One tiny hand had broken off.

His eyes followed her gaze to the mantel. "The doll?"

She nodded, stifling a yawn.

"That is a memento of my wife."

She sat upright. "Your wife?"

He loosened his cravat. "We were married when I was twenty. She was but eighteen. We were in love. I was in love," he corrected.

There was a long silence. "What happened?" she prompted.

"I went off to war. The Irish had revolted, and we were sent to quell the rebellion. Awful, bloody thing it was. Our mission was to control the insurgence, but it seemed that our government was more bent on punishing and destroying than merely restoring order. The brutality of it all . . . was unimaginable. I wanted desperately to come home. I missed my wife and the peace of my life in England. I was away for almost two years. Our separation was difficult for her too. We were married only eight months before I was called for duty."

"What happened to her?"

"She found solitude too difficult to bear alone."

Illumination dawned. "I see." She waited until he spoke more on it, but nothing was forthcoming. "Did you divorce her?"

"No. I moved out of our home. A month after I returned, she died giving birth to another man's child."

It was hard to imagine such betrayal. "That must have been very difficult."

He nodded stiffly. "First I lost her heart, then I lost her fidelity. Then I lost her."

She glanced back at the figurine. "If she caused you so much pain, why do you keep that?"

He stared directly at her. "To remind me of our better times. In the end, she made mistakes that cost us her happiness and mine. But that doesn't diminish her value to me."

She imagined herself in his place. "I don't think I could be as forgiving as you."

"Forgiveness has a way of turning into forbearance. I no longer expect women to be pure. Or faithful."

"You mustn't let such cynicism take root on the basis of one woman."

"No. It's on the basis of all women." His words were pregnant with meaning, but he didn't seem to want to confess any more.

"I suppose, then, that all women have the same value to you," she said, throwing his words back at him. "And it isn't a very favorable one."

His head jerked backward as he regarded her. He was quiet a long time. "Here, take this," he said, pulling the blanket from his bed and handing it to her. "It's getting late, and I've a lot of work to do tomorrow."

She took the blanket from him, and watched as he removed his shoes and lay on the bed fully clothed. He extinguished the candle by his bedside, and laid his head on his forearm. He heaved an audible sigh, and then was quiet.

Now that she was ostensibly alone and unwatched, she removed her dress and corset, leaving only her chemise. She tossed the foul-smelling garments in the corner, and folded herself in the delicious warmth of the blanket.

It did not take long for Salter's steady breathing to lull her to sleep.

꿍THE MOMENT MINA AWOKE, she was aware of two things: the cramped discomfort of having slept on a hardwood floor, and the noxious odor of the Thames emanating from her still-damp chemise.

She groaned into consciousness, and sat up. Her hair spiked stiffly in several directions, and her arm was asleep from having used it as a pillow. Her greatest and only wish in the whole world was a nice, hot, comforting bath.

Though the curtains were closed, the sunlight glowed through them. Mina looked at Salter's bed. He was gone.

She looked around the room, as if it were large enough to lose a man in. An intense and peculiar loneliness pervaded her heart. She tightened the blanket around her. She wanted someone there with her. And not just anyone. She wanted Salter. His absence left an enormous vacuum in the room and in her sense of peace, and she needed him to fill it back up again. It had quickly become her greatest and only wish.

As if in answer to prayer, Salter opened the bedroom door. "Ah, you're awake."

She couldn't help but smile at seeing him again. It refreshed and restored something inside her.

Salter was carrying a cistern. He upended it into the tub, and Mina noticed steam rising from the bath.

"Is that really for me?"

Salter chuckled at her excitement. "With the way you smell, it will benefit both of us."

She couldn't get mad. In the span of a moment, he had made both her wishes come true.

Mrs. Tilbury walked in, a sour expression wrinkling her face even more. In the crook of her arm was a towel and a cake of soap. "I've brought you this. At Mr. Lambrick's request," she hastened to add.

"Thank you. Thank you both."

The old woman's face softened a bit. "I trust you won't be wanting those clothes anymore." She jerked her head at the mound of wet clothes in the corner.

"Oh, no. They're past all hope of cleansing."

"Very well, then. I'll take them to the dustbin. Dear me, I don't know if I have anything that will fit you."

"At this point, Mrs. Tilbury, I'd wear those curtains just as long as I could have a bath."

Salter lifted her shackled wrists, and pulled the key from his pocket. "If I take these off, will you promise to behave yourself?"

Mina watched Mrs. Tilbury as she poured something pink into the tub. She nodded.

Salter jerked on her chain. "If you show yourself to be troublesome, I will bind you hand and foot to the end of my bed. Is that understood?"

She looked up at him earnestly. "Yes, I promise."

When he took the heavy metal shackles off, she began to feel more like herself again. Mrs. Tilbury left the towel on the washstand and a washrag over the edge of the tub, and left the room to find something for her to wear.

"Mind you wash behind the ears. I'll check you over afterward." He smiled, and locked the door.

Mina bounced over to the tub. A heavenly rose-scented steam wafted from the water. She threw off the soiled chemise, and climbed naked into the tub. She winced at the heat, but unable to wait a moment longer, she immersed herself in the water.

Delicious. She soaped the washrag thoroughly and scrubbed herself all over. Her abrasive cleansing left her skin pink and tender, but refreshingly clean. Her hair received two washings.

When she emerged from the tub and dried herself off, she fairly squeaked. She wrapped herself in the towel, glorying in the freedom from being dirty. Mrs. Tilbury, however, hadn't yet come back with clothes, and she was starting to get a little chilly. After spending the night the way she had, she did not want a damp towel against her skin. She looked at the giant wardrobe on the far wall and took an uncertain step toward it.

She opened the doors and looked inside. His clothes were neat and pressed, but nothing like the coats he wore when he impersonated Lord Prescott. These were a common man's clothes, polished but modest. She ran her hands over the fabrics. Even in these clothes, he could look dashing. He didn't need a parliamentarian's coat to look like a nobleman.

Mina pulled out one of his shirts and held it aloft by its shoulders. Yes, Salter was a large man indeed. She held the linen to her nose. This was *his* scent. Clean masculine spice, and the smell of sunshine. She smiled and put it on.

She fairly swam in the voluminous fabric. The hem came down to her knees. But it was warm and concealing, and blissfully clean. She went to the washstand and found his comb. She raked it through her hair, wincing as it battled with the tangles.

She heard a soft knock at the door. "May I come in?"

"Yes."

She heard the key turn in the lock. The door opened. For a moment, he stood in mute surprise as he studied her in his clothes. Embarrassed, she clasped her hands in front of her.

"I'm sorry. I didn't have anything else to wear."

He blinked, and shook his head. "Of course. No, it's all right. You . . . you're perfectly welcome to anything I—"

She was puzzled by his reaction. She thought she looked a monstrous fright out of a dress and in a man's clothes. But to judge by his expression, anyone would think he was fascinated.

She sat upon his unmade bed. "Thank you for the bathwater. I can't tell you what a pleasure that was for me."

"Happy to give you such pleasure . . . that is, I'm happy you were pleased." He heaved a profound sigh. "Do you mind if I wash now?"

Mina was smiling on the inside. Was it possible she made him nervous? "By all means."

He took one last look at her, and then turned his attention to the washstand. Impatiently, he tipped the ewer into the basin, removed his shirt, and began to splash water on his face.

The sight of him performing this simple action was mesmerizing. The sunlight from the window glowed on his laborer's body. His Sisyphean shoulders bulged with muscle. His back was a triangle of bone and sinew narrowing into a tight waist. The smooth, bronze skin promised heavenly pleasures if licked. He had a body like a sculptor's model—or perhaps he himself was the work of art. Whatever else could be said about him, he was a proper man. The sight of him there and the smell of him here made her senses go wild, and she ached to reconcile the two.

But there, on his side, just under the ribs on his right, was a giant bruise. She had done that when she swung the plank of wood at him. It was an unsightly thing, marring the beauty of his spectacular body. It saddened her to think she had inflicted it upon him, infecting him with ugliness. She became aware of an irrepressible desire to smooth it away, to reverse the damage and remove the hurt. She stood up.

She walked over to where he was shaving and stood behind him. Her fingers touched the bruise lightly. Salter turned around.

Her eyes flew to the blue-black ring on his forehead above his left eye. She had done that too. It was the evidence of her wickedness, how she had hurt him. She regarded his handsome face as he stared down at her in puzzlement. Her fingertips brushed the wound. "I'm sorry."

The corners of his mouth lifted, and he nodded. And then something happened that she never thought would. He opened his arms and enfolded her in them.

She had often fantasized about the lurid sensation, the eroticism of this act. A man's clinch was supposed to be a clumsy, groping prelude to sex. But this was different than she imagined. This was a tender embrace of shared affection. Never did she expect the breath of life it gave her, as if their heartbeats were somehow intensified by their proximity to each other. Closing her eyes, she absorbed the feeling, memorizing it, knowing it wouldn't last.

It was over sooner than she wanted. He gently pushed her away. She didn't want to look at him, lest he see in her eyes how much the simple embrace had meant to her. But she felt his fingertips under her chin, making her look into his face. He lowered his head, and she closed her eyes.

The kiss came softly, gently, a velvety feathering of his lips. Nothing at all like the exaggerated kisses exchanged at the Pleasure Emporium. This was shockingly genuine, warmly surprising. She was wearing no beautiful dress, no courtesan's cosmetics. She spoke no erotic words. She was nothing but simple Mina. And yet his kiss came anyway.

Gradually, the kiss deepened and intensified. His lips became more insistent, as if he were trying to communicate something to her. She wanted to understand him, but her reasoning mind was dulled by a fog of pleasure. He pressed himself against her, with only a thin fabric between their naked skin, and the feeling made her swoon. His lips smoothed over hers, bringing forth a tendril of erotic pleasure from between her legs, a breathless desire to be filled and fulfilled.

Her fingers splayed across his back, the hard muscle tightening at her touch. His skin was warm and golden, and she found herself aching to know every inch of his body. Her hands skimmed down the crest of his buttocks, and he moaned.

"Mina," he breathed, and the sound of it resonated inside her. His mouth drew a steamy trail to the base of her jaw, and her head fell back in surrender. His hand cradled her head, threading his fingers in her wet tendrils. Her hands climbed up his chest, like a vine seeking warm sunlight, and entwined around his neck. As his mouth licked a trail down her throat, she whimpered in distress.

His manhood began to swell, and she immediately went still. A crimson flush heated her face. She had never been held against a man's aroused body, and the sensations dizzied her. Soft lips against her skin, but a firm pressure against her tummy. Modesty protested, but her own desire drowned out the voice. Even if she wanted to form an objection on her lips, her mouth was smothered underneath his. His hips rocked gently against her.

"Mr. Lambrick," called Mrs. Tilbury shrilly from the sitting room. "May I come in? I've brought some clothes for your prisoner."

Mina shut her eyes and let out a sigh of frustration.

Disappointment darkened his expression. "Leave them on the chair, please," he called out in a gravelly voice.

"You've also got a visitor, Mr. Lambrick."

He heaved a sigh. "Be right out." He brought his voice down to a thick rumble. "It doesn't end here, Minnow. We have more to discuss on this subject."

She nodded, perhaps too eagerly. The anticipation of more left her quite breathless.

He wiped the remaining shaving soap from his face and drew out a fresh shirt from the wardrobe. She watched him shamelessly as he dressed. It was such a pity that his stunning torso had to be covered by so much fabric. How her hands hungered to continue their exploration of his body. She was finding it difficult to come down from the intoxication of his kiss.

He slipped on his waistcoat, gun holster, and coat before opening the door. "Come, Mina," he said, holding out his hand.

She slipped her hand in his, and they went out to the sitting room together.

When Mrs. Tilbury saw Mina, she gasped in horror. "Good heavens! Whatever are you wearing?"

Mina looked down at the long shirt that fell open scandalously between her breasts. "There was nothing else in there. And much as I tried to convince him, Mr. Lambrick wouldn't allow me to walk around nude."

Salter shot her a scowl. "Stop trying to shock Mrs. Tilbury."

"There's no modesty left in today's young girls, Mr. Lambrick." Mrs. Tilbury's hands were clasped under her bosom, a heap of fabric clenched between them. "I've brought you this, girl. Put it on." She held out a dress that looked as if it were very fashionable about twenty years earlier. "It belonged to my daughter."

"Thank you. It's lovely."

Mrs. Tilbury's hard look of disapproval softened at Mina's courtesy. "There's a gentleman downstairs to see you, Mr. Lambrick."

"Send him up, if you please."

Mina watched Mrs. Tilbury disappear through the door. Her thoughts turned to Salter. What she wouldn't give to feel one more kiss, one more moment sheathed in his tight embrace.

She felt a hand on her stomach, and she was pulled backward against the wall of his body. His breath was a hot gust against her cheek. "I wish we could continue where we left off."

The words barely made it out. "As do I."

"But we have company."

"Send him away." The words sounded pitiable even to her own ears.

He placed a soft kiss on her cheek. "No. Now go get dressed."

He had wanted, so he reached out and took. She grew jealous of that boldness. She turned in his arms, and slipped her hand under his coat to stroke his muscular back. He inhaled deeply, and his back grew even bigger. He bent down and pressed another searing kiss on her eager mouth. Mina almost smiled into it. She wanted, and she reached out and took. It was a glorious feeling. Her free hand cupped his face, his sideburns damp where he had shaved. *More,* her body cried out, though she didn't have enough hands to grasp all she wanted.

A smile moved across his lips as he gripped her arms firmly and pushed her away. "Mina, if you can't keep your hands to yourself, I shall put the shackles back on you. Go inside the bedroom and put those clothes on. If I have to dress you, I shall do it in front of my guest."

Reluctantly, she pulled away. "Very well," she pouted, the electric currents in her body shooting off into nowhere. "But I shall never be in the mood for you again."

"We'll see about that," he said confidently as he tied his cravat.

"I mean it," she said, disappointment leaking from her. "You can put something on your mantel to remember me by. A quill pen. Or better yet, a book on astronomy."

"How about if I just set you atop the mantel and bring you down every time I want to play with you?"

She walked into the bedroom, smiling secretly. She would not be entirely opposed to that.

SALTER HAD JUST COMPLETED the knot on his cravat when he heard the sharp rap of a man's walking stick on his door.

He opened it. "Lord Bensonhurst! I did not expect you."

"Have I come at an inopportune time?"

"Not at all. Please come in." He stood to one side as the Lord Mayor strode past him. Salter waited for an aide or a clerk to follow him, but there was no one with him. It was unusual for a man like Lord Bensonhurst, so consumed by governmental affairs, to be unaccompanied by an entourage.

Despite his dignified age, Lord Bensonhurst retained the vigor of a much younger man. He was slender but tall, and his frame gave him a quiet strength.

The white whiskers down the sides of his face balanced the shock of white hair at his crown. His movements were elegant as he doffed his hat and gloves.

"I'm sorry to drop in on you unannounced, but I had grown worried about the case." Lord Bensonhurst had a large voice—loud enough for Parliament, yet diplomatic enough for the Prime Minister. "I tried visiting you at the station, but your men told me you would not report in today."

"Yes, sir. Upon your request, I've been working on this case exclusively. I left my subaltern, Constable Dalton, in charge of managing my department."

"And what have you turned up?" he said, gracefully folding his body onto the settee.

"A good deal," Salter answered, sitting opposite him in a chair. "Although I've not identified *who* killed Lord Prescott, I think I may have discovered *why*."

Lord Bensonhurst raised two thick white eyebrows. "Indeed?"

"Yes. In Prescott's safe were a number of articles that painted a vivid picture of the reasons he may have been murdered. It may interest you to know that your senior aide was very deeply in debt."

"I'm not surprised," sniffed Lord Bensonhurst. "The man was an incorrigible gambler. Not to speak ill of the dead, but a good deal of his money was made at the tables. He had the devil's own luck at cards. Much good it did him in the end. The devil plays favorites, it seems, and every man's luck runs out eventually." Lord Bensonhurst drew a gold box from his pocket and pinched some snuff into his nose. "So you think he was killed by a man to whom he owed money?"

"I haven't ruled that theory out, sir, but another one poses greater likelihood." Salter reached toward the inside pocket of his own coat, and pulled out a pouch. "I think he might have been killed for these."

Salter turned the pouch upside down on the table and the jewels trickled out.

"Extraordinary!" exclaimed Lord Bensonhurst. He picked up the large blue gem. "Where on earth did he get these?"

Salter's gaze locked on the older man. "That's what I was hoping you could tell me."

Lord Bensonhurst's blue eyes stared quizzically back at Salter.

"From the vowels in his safe, we can safely surmise that he did not have enough money to repay his debts. But alongside them was a sizable fortune in gemstones, enough to pay all his debts a hundred times over. How did he come by them?"

"Why do you think I would know the answer to that?"

"As your aide, sir, Prescott would have come in contact with the same foreign dignitaries, ambassadors, and potentates as you. Is it possible he might have stolen these gemstones from one of them?"

The crease between Lord Bensonhurst's eyebrows deepened. "Possible, but not likely. Are you claiming Prescott lifted their purses like some ruddy pickpocket?"

"No, sir, I—"

"I mean, the man had some scruples."

"Yes, sir. I'm merely trying to determine how he would have them in his possession."

"If they had gone missing from one of this country's

guests, don't you think I would have heard about it? If something had been stolen, as host to all visiting dignitaries, I would hear of it, wouldn't I?"

Lord Bensonhurst's eyes turned icy, and Salter thought it a fearsome thing. "Yes, sir. That's true."

"Why are constables always looking for filth where none exists? Prescott may not have had nefarious motives. He might have been asked to keep them for someone. I mean, he didn't sell them, did he?"

"Well, sir, he might not have had the chance."

Lord Bensonhurst's scowl blackened. "I can say definitively, Chief Constable, that Roderick Prescott did not steal these gems from any government representative to London. Anyway, how do you know these gems had anything to do with foreign dignitaries? How do you know they didn't come from some rich widow or other?"

"The provenance of these stones leads me to believe that they came from someone you may have been in contact with."

"Provenance? What provenance?"

"I have it on good authority that these gemstones were taken from a tiara brought by a foreign potentate."

"What authority?"

Salter stood up. "Her." Lord Bensonhurst turned in the direction of Salter's gaze.

Mina smoothed out the front of her dress and walked into the drawing room. She was dressed in a royal-blue spencer made of shiny material that made her feel extremely conspicuous. The long-sleeved confection was beautiful but outlandishly outmoded. The peplum on the rear of the jacket hung over the miles of wide skirt that Mina suspected was supposed to be lifted by a crinoline. Thank goodness Mrs. Tilbury hadn't offered her one.

"Lord Bensonhurst, may I present Miss Mina Halliday. Mina, this is Alexander Bensonhurst, Lord Mayor of London."

"I'm very pleased to meet you," she said, curtsying.

"Likewise, Miss Halliday. Do sit down."

With characteristically precise timing, Mrs. Tilbury brought up a tray of tea and breakfast cakes. Mina offered to pour, and the old woman made a quiet exit.

"The Chief Constable here tells me you offered some expertise on the provenance of these jewels. Perhaps you'd be good enough to educate me."

"Certainly," she said, offering Lord Bensonhurst a steaming cup. "My father is a jeweler. He had a growing concern on Fulsom Street. These jewels came to his shop three months ago mounted in a beautiful tiara, the likes of which I had never seen before. It was exotic—Indian or Burmese—more like a crown than a simple tiara."

Salter accepted the cup she offered. "I seem to remember that last winter, we had a visitor to this country from Asia, though I can't recall exactly from where. I believe they came to pay respects to the King and Queen. It would make sense to suppose that this exotic tiara was brought by this visitor, either worn by one of his wives or brought as a gift of homage to our Queen. Perhaps you can recall better than I."

"And you believe it somehow landed in Prescott's possession?"

"Yes, sir. Either by legal or illicit means."

Lord Bensonhurst sighed deeply. "My agenda is quite full, as I'm certain you can appreciate. But if what you say is true, then I feel honor-bound to look into this matter myself. Let me take the jewels with me."

Salter shook his head. "I'm afraid that won't be possible, sir. The jewels are evidence in an ongoing investigation. If the murderer was after these gemstones to begin with, then it is imperative that I hold on to them to provoke the criminal into revealing himself."

"I see your point. But is it safe to leave so much valuable evidence here in your flat?"

Salter gathered the fistful of gemstones back into the pouch. "Not to worry, sir. They'll always remain within arm's reach."

"Well, I shall trust your judgment and experience of these matters. Tell me, Miss Halliday, how can you be so certain that this tiara was where the jewels came from? Although lovely, these could have come from a piece worn by any woman at any ball in London."

"Not these. These I remember very clearly. This sapphire is special. My father pointed out its exceptional quality to me not long before he was arrested."

The older man blinked. "Arrested?"

Mina flushed. "Er, yes. My father was commissioned to remove the stones from that tiara, and replace them with similar, inferior-quality stones. Shortly after he finished the job, he was taken away, charged with thievery and fraud. But he is innocent. He did precisely what he was asked to do, and turned the tiara and the real gemstones over to the client. The fact that they were now found in Lord Prescott's safe tells me that it was Lord Prescott who hired my father, Lord Prescott who had him arrested, and Lord Prescott who kept the real jewels."

Lord Bensonhurst nodded slowly, absorbing her words. "This is a very sad tale, Miss Halliday. I can certainly understand what you must have gone through. Tell me, now that your father is imprisoned, what has become of you?"

Mina's face reddened. "Well, it's a bit embarrassing, I'm afraid. I was forced to enter employment."

"Employment? You had no family to support you?"

"I'm afraid not."

"At what, may I ask, are you employed?"

Mina glanced at Salter. "Er, well, I sought work as a writer."

"A writer? You mean, like a journalist?"

"No, not exactly."

Salter ended her hemming. "She is employed as a writer at a house of ill repute, sir."

Illumination dawned on his features. "Oh. I see."

"I know how this must make me look, Lord Bensonhurst. But I am a decent girl who's had to make certain compromises to keep from starving. I have nothing whatever to regret, except the absence of my father from my life. I know that he is imprisoned unjustly. And these jewels in Prescott's safe prove that he was not the one who stole them. As London's Chief Magistrate, you must have it in your power to see that my father gets a second trial to prove his innocence. I beseech you . . . will you arrange it?"

Lord Bensonhurst nodded. "You have my word that I will look into the matter. If your father is indeed innocent, then the truth will come out. Do not fear, Miss

Halliday. Lambrick and I will get to the bottom of this together."

Mina smiled. "Thank you," she said, so grateful that she even wanted to accord him a title she never used on any man. "Thank you, sir."

"Miss Halliday, I have no wish to trouble you further while this matter remains unresolved." Lord Bensonhurst came to his feet. "Lambrick, walk me out. Miss Halliday, good day to you. I hope we are able to reunite you and your father very quickly."

Mina almost giggled. "Thank you very much!"

Lord Bensonhurst and Salter stepped out into the hall, and began their descent down the staircase. On the landing, Lord Bensonhurst whirled upon Salter.

"What in God's heaven has gotten into you, man?"

Salter froze mid-step. "Sir?"

"I came here to get hard facts about who killed my senior aide, and I am drawn into a web of intrigue surrounding a stolen Oriental tiara and an innocent persecuted man, like some drivel plucked from the pages of a ladies' fiction magazine!"

"Sir—"

"Were you even listening to that claptrap? As a man, I can certainly respect your prurient interest in offering that woman a sympathetic ear, but are you telling me that you are basing the course of your investigation on the fantastical stories drawn from a prostitute with a convict father?"

"Sir, I know how this may sound to you, but—"

"Now listen very closely, Lambrick. I don't want this scandal to haunt me any longer. An assault on the King's government is an assault on the King. I want this murderer brought to justice. And let me remind you that your own career is on the line as well. If the constabulary cannot find a man who killed a senior member of government, how can they be relied upon to protect society at large? For both our sakes, I want you to do your job. At this point, I wouldn't care if you pinned the blame on a vagrant, just as long as we can have an end to it. No more stories, no more intrigues, and no more attempts to besmirch a man whom I personally hired. Is that understood?"

Salter ground his teeth. "Yes, sir."

"You have forty-eight hours to find the man. If you can't do it, I'll find someone who can."

Salter watched the man pound down the remaining stairs and slam the front door.

Chapter Nine

Business was notoriously slow on Mondays, so the ladies at the Pleasure Emporium customarily took the day to go on an outing. It became their day for going to market, seeing a show, or walking in the park. This day, they had decided to attend a Gypsy fair that had been erected just outside London. They rose early so that by noon they'd be on their way.

The Gypsy fair was Lollie's idea, and she was the most excited to go. She had heard about a woman there who could tell her future just by looking at the palm of her hand, and she was eager to have it done. Serafina and Madeleine volunteered to stay behind to tend to any customers.

Two coaches were hailed and sat waiting outside as the girls finished putting on their gloves and hats. There was a knock at the door, and Lollie wrenched it open to calm the impatient driver.

"Keep your codpiece on, we'll be right th—!" The rest of Lollie's rebuke evaporated as she opened to door to a particularly handsome man. "Oh. Hello."

"Mornin', love," he said as he took off his hat. "I'm 'ere to see Madame Fynch. She round?"

Lollie's gaze feathered over his face and body. He

was a tall fellow, with tousled blond hair and a musical voice. A swarthy complexion contrasted with a shimmer of golden stubble and the most striking cerulean eyes she had ever seen. His suit was inexpensive but clean, and it was completely filled by what her practiced eye could tell was a very muscular physique. He was so unlike her customary clientele that he immediately caused a stir in her.

"Naow," she answered in her comfortable Cockney, which she did whenever she heard a fellow commoner speak. "She's out on errands today. Anything I can do for ya?"

"Dunno. My name's Constable Alcott. I'm under orders from Chief Constable Lambrick to collect Miss Mina Halliday's clothes."

"What for? You doing 'er washin'?"

The man smiled, revealing a row of perfect white teeth that triggered a smile from her. "Nah. She's being detained while an investigation is carried out. It may take several days, so she's going to need some clothes."

Lollie cocked her head appraisingly. "Oh. Well, you'd better come in, then."

The man walked past her, and Lollie inhaled a fragrance of lime-scented toilet water that immediately kindled her senses. She took a quick glance in the mirror to check her hair, and followed him into the salon.

The rest of the girls fluttered out to the foyer. "Lollie, where are you?" cried Evie.

"Wait here," Lollie told the man. She glided back to the foyer, hoping to ignite his interest with a swivel of her hips.

She closed the door to the salon. "You go on without me. I think I may have a quill."

Evie pinned her hands to her hips. "But it's our day off. Let the Countess take him."

She wasn't about to go haring off when such an unusually handsome prospect presented himself, and she certainly wouldn't relinquish him to Madeleine. "Naow. I'll take him. He seems interestin'."

Charlotte rolled her eyes. "For heaven's sake, Lollie, this outing was all your idea. I thought you wanted to know your fortune."

She shrugged. "Seems my fortune found me. Go on. I'll catch up to you later."

Amid their protestations, Lollie ushered the nine ladies out the door. Now she had time alone with the gorgeous man. If he paid her, so much the better, she thought as she pinched her cheeks to heighten her color. If he didn't . . . well, she'd do this one for free.

"So, what's this, then?" Lollie asked, breezing back into the room. "You arrested my friend?"

"Not exactly. She's . . . how can I put it? Under constabulary protection."

"Protection? Who from? She in danger?"

A dimple darkened his cheek. "I wouldn't worry about 'er, miss. She'll be safe as houses under the Chief Constable's supervision."

The cleft in his chin was equally mesmerizing. "Will you be watching over her as well?"

"I'll be protectin' 'em both. That's my job. To protect the public."

"Does that include me?" she asked, a wink in her voice.

He smiled self-consciously. "'Course it does." He focused those piercing blue eyes on her. "Unless, of course, you do something 'gainst the law."

Now it was her turn to blush. It was not something she did often. "Me? Never."

"In a place like this, someone may get the wrong idea about you."

She sidled up to him on the settee. "Well, if they do, then I'll just have to set them straight, won't I?"

She peered into his face. Cor, what a dasher he was. He had the prettiest eyes. Thick brown lashes, the kind you only see on young children; thick eyebrows feathering all the way back to his temples; thick blond hair all rumpled from his hat. She wondered if everything on his body was as thick.

Her gaze swept over his shoulders. They stretched the fabric of his gray coat. He fairly radiated strength. A head-to-toe male. All she could think about was being facedown on a pillow.

Instinctively, she leaned in.

Her closeness seemed to unsettle him. "I'm sorry, what did you say yer name was?"

She flashed a grin, and let her tongue dance over her name. "Lollie."

"Hmm. Miss Lollie, I've come for Miss Mina's clothes, so if it's not too much trouble, perhaps you could get them for me."

A bashful man. How refreshing. "In time. I thought we could become better acquainted first. You already know my name, so what can I call you?"

"Charles." He shrugged. "Chase."

"Chase," she repeated, her full lips kissing the word.

"I like the sound of that better. See? Already we're becoming good friends."

"You, uh, all alone 'ere?"

"Just about."

He fiddled with the brim of his hat, which hung between his knees. "Well, you don't have to be. Fancy a drink down at the Bit and Bridle? I's planning to meet me mates there to toss back a few tans. You're welcome to join us if you like."

He was asking her on an outing. This was precious. "Sounds a lark, but . . ." The Madame would kill her if she went out with a quill without telling her. "I think we could have far more fun if we stayed right 'ere."

He nodded, then laughed awkwardly. "You're awfully pretty, Miss Lollie, but I'm . . . well, I'm on duty. I'm not really supposed to be stopping. I've got an idea. Can I call for you tomorrow? There's a show at the Tinwhistle that's good for a few laughs. I've already seen it twice. We could go to the pub for a bite beforehand."

It sounded wonderful, but the Madame would never approve of her being taken out by this man. Even if he wasn't a man of the law, he was a commoner. It was bad for business for the girls to be seen with men who weren't of a certain social standing. The perfect opportunity was right here. And right now.

"We don't have to go out for a bite, darlin'. You and me got lots to savor just between us." Her breast pressed against his arm as she brushed a long lock of her hair against his face.

The sensation made him close his eyes. She smiled in triumph.

"Miss Lollie . . ." There was a tremor in his voice. He couldn't even bring himself to look at her. Lollie smiled. He was one of *those*. Some men were like volcanoes; temptation would build up within them, each word and caress edging them closer to eruption until they exploded. She would need to coax him along.

"You're a man accustomed to taking orders. Tell me, would you take orders from someone like me?"

His brows drew together.

"For instance, if I were to order you to kiss me here," she said, holding out her wrist, "would you do it?"

His expression became inscrutable.

"Or here?" she said, pointing to her lips. "Or even here?" she continued, her finger traveling to the division between her rounded breasts. "Would you do that too?"

A muscle tightened in his jaw. "Miss Lollie, I think you might have arrived at the wrong conclusion. I'm not . . . yer type."

Seductively, she leaned back against the settee. "Why don't you let me decide that?"

His eyes raked over her languid form like a caress on her skin. She offered him the most tantalizing view, encouraging his eyes to take their fill.

His gaze returned to her face. "And you're not mine."

At first, she didn't understand him. It didn't make sense—he was supposed to lean over her, put his hand on her thigh, and mutter something lewd and guttural in her ear. He was supposed to force a kiss on her lips while pawing at her breast. It was what all men did.

Except this one.

"Oh," she said, straightening up. There was very little Lollie did not know about sex. She had seen and done it all, and if she hadn't seen it or done it, she most definitely knew about it. There were as many sexual predilections as there were people in the world, and she was open-minded enough to take this one, whatever his pleasure might be. "Well, I can become your type. I'll change into a coat and breeches, hide my hair in a hat, and strap on a godemiche. If you've a little imagination, you won't be disappointed. I promise you."

She wasn't ready for this kind of explosion. His face contorted into an appalled expression, and he bolted out of the seat.

"I'm not a poofter! You think just because I don't jump you and thump you that I'm a bloody fairy?"

She straightened, her heart hammering her chest. Silence seemed the wisest reply.

"Well, I'm not! Yer not my type 'cause I don't particularly care for forward women. And certainly not for any sort of man! Blimey!"

"Sorry," she said in a casual tone, attempting to belittle her transgression.

His mouth pressed into a thin line, and he put his hands on his narrow hips. "Please do me the favor of packing Miss Mina's things right now. Or show me where they are, and I'll do it meself. Your choice."

"All right. I'll be right back." She stood up stiffly and crept away under his fiery gaze.

As she filled Mina's valise with a few days' worth of clothes, Lollie puzzled over Chase's response to her invitation. She could read a man as well as if he had every lewd urge stamped on his face. All quills were alike. All men were after her for one thing. How could she have misread him so? He said he didn't like for-ward women. That was a new one. Whether here at the bordello or on a Covent Garden street corner, if she didn't flaunt it, she didn't sell it.

She shook her head in self-reproach. He didn't come here as a quill, she realized. This breed of man was someone she was altogether unfamiliar with. He was a commoner, yet didn't behave commonly. He was not a gentleman, but acted as if he was, and a chival-rous one at that. He didn't ask her for anything, and yet she threw her body at him as if he were a hungry lion. For the first time, a man was being nice to her *without* an ulterior motive.

He had treated her like a lady, and she had acted like a whore.

She knelt on the floor to retrieve Mina's shoes from under the bed. *Chase.* It was a good name for him, be-cause clearly he liked to do the chasing. On the job . . . and in the bed.

She trudged down the stairs with the bundle. He was sitting on the edge of the settee, his elbows propped on his knees, and he was staring into the distance. The moment he heard her approach, he stood up.

He accepted the stuffed valise from her, but re-mained where he was. "Look, er, I'm sorry for torching up like I did. I didn't mean to upset you."

She hung her head. "Naow. I'm the one who should be sorry. For being so vain. I figured any man who didn't like me must lean, you know, himwards. And I shouldn't've come on to you like I did. I found you 'tractive, is all."

He grinned wanly. "Thanks. Yer not s'bad yerself."

An awkward silence stretched between them. She could easily have filled it, but the only thing she knew to do would surely displease him all over again.

He leaned in close. "Look, I hope you don't mind me sayin' so, but some blokes don't need to be on top of a woman to feel like a real man. Some of us think that happens when we make a woman feel like a real lady. D'ye understand what I mean?"

Lollie nodded. She understood . . . she had just ruined her one chance with a prince.

As she watched him walk out the door, a dark cloud settled around her heart. It was like nothing she had ever experienced before, and it dissolved her confidence as surely as if it had been drenched in acid.

Rejection.

Now she knew how Mina felt.

MINA FELT AS IF she were walking on bubbles.

Her father would soon be receiving a new trial. The Chief Magistrate of London, Lord Bensonhurst, had promised her he would see to it himself. It was only a matter of time before her father was acquitted and would finally be returned to her embrace.

Although this made her deliriously happy, there was another, more immediate and more visceral cause for her elation. It was the new awareness that she was a woman of beauty, a woman who was desirable. The man sitting next to her on the phaeton had kissed that awareness into her.

As their carriage wended up St. James Street, she inhaled the crisp air. She had never felt so alive, so feminine, as she did at that moment. Women walked arm-in-arm with their husbands down the street, and she knew how they felt. *I am one of you now,* she wanted to shout.

But there were other voices shouting too, voices that she was trying her best to ignore. They were reminding her in none-too-gentle ways that she was deluding herself yet again. *You're not the beauty you think you've become, and you never will be. Aren't the decades of neglect proof of that? If he declares you pretty, it's only because he wants something from you. He is like all the others . . . a sleeping cobra. It's only a matter of time before he, too, will strike.*

As the phaeton slowed to a halt, Salter turned to her. "Now remember your promise to me. You can come with me on this investigation so long as you help and not hinder. Otherwise, it's back to the shackles until I've solved this case. Is that understood?"

"For the hundredth time, yes," she said testily, as if she were answering the voices instead of Salter.

Salter ignored the sharp remark and tossed the reins to the groomsman outside the front door of White's. Privately, he frowned upon such clubs, which excluded men of inferior rank and birth. Only the political and social elite were allowed through their doors, which irritated Salter to no end. When men associated only with "their own kind," they developed a skewed perspective of who they were. Salter preferred to socialize with people of all kinds. Not only did it ground him in reality, but the stories common people told were infinitely more interesting.

A bespectacled man stood behind a podium in the

foyer, his long sideburns bristling up from his cheeks. He peered at them over his round frames as soon as they stepped over the threshold. "Deliveries through the back," he tossed at them before returning his attention to what appeared to be his member's book.

Salter chuckled sarcastically. He supposed that in his gray trousers and black tailcoat, he probably couldn't pass for a member. His appearance was most certainly not up to Beau Brummel's exacting standards. Quite frankly, he didn't care.

Nor did he care for being dismissed so casually. He strode up to the majordomo. "That information will be useful to the deliveryman. I require a bit more than that."

For the first time, the man focused his full attention on him.

"My name is Chief Constable Salter Lambrick. I'd like to ask you a few questions about the late Lord Roderick Prescott."

The man put his quill down. "Yes, sir? How can I help you?"

"You can start by giving me your name."

"My name is Oakes, sir. Whitcomb Oakes. I'm the chief steward."

"Well, Oakes, perhaps you'd be good enough to show me the betting book, where I may see the entries for Lord Prescott."

"I'm sorry, sir. That is private information. Only White's members may contribute or refer to the book. Club policy."

If there was one thing that irritated Salter, it was dusty

little men who hid behind arbitrary rules. "Oakes, I am investigating the questionable death of Lord Prescott. You have two choices: either you can let me see the book, or I can confiscate it while the investigation is carried out. Which would you prefer?"

The man lowered his voice. "But sir, the book is confidential. I can't allow outsiders to see it."

"You can trust me, Oakes. I won't let on. Besides, I'm only interested in Lord Prescott's bets, and I doubt he'd lodge any complaints against you for showing them to me."

Visibly, the man weighed his options. "Very well, sir. Come this way."

He went through a set of double doors and preceded Salter into a large room.

So this is how the other half live, Salter thought. A bay window stood imposingly at one end of the room, allowing an unimpeded view of St. James Street. Sunlight from the window filled the vast gaming salon, gleaming off the clusters of brown leather chairs. Card tables dotted the room, their green baize felt looking like small patches of well-mowed lawns. The wallpaper was a deep forest green, in sharp contrast to the fashionable pastel colors the ladies selected to decorate their parlors. The room smelled of tobacco and liquor, exuding masculinity from every corner.

Salter followed Oakes to one of the massive fireplaces. From the mantel, Oakes pulled down a large leather-bound volume. He opened it, removing a leather strap sewn to a fox's tail that was used as a place marker, and thumbed backward a few pages.

"Historically, Lord Prescott wagered a great deal, but he always had the wherewithal to pay his debts. Lately, however, some members had begun to complain that he was not settling his wagers in a timely fashion. It is a serious accusation—cause for dismissal—and Lord Prescott was close to losing his membership at White's. As you'll see from these pages, over the last couple of months, a number of Lord Prescott's wagers remained outst—" Oakes looked up, and his gaze riveted to a spot just behind Salter.

Salter's brows drew together as he followed the direction of Oakes's gaze. All he saw was Mina.

Oakes's eyes grew round as saucers. "That's a woman."

Salter grinned cheekily. "That's right."

"But, sir, this is White's. No women are allowed on the premises."

Salter took the book from Oakes's numbed fingers. "We won't be long."

"B-but this is impossible. Intolerable. You can't have a woman here."

"I'll try to remember that if the romantic mood strikes me. May I trouble you to excuse us?"

Mina walked gingerly under the man's shocked expression. He could not have appeared more appalled if she were smeared head to toe in mud.

"Sir, this violates a tradition that has endured more than three-quarters of a century! No woman—not even a sovereign—has ever set foot inside these rooms. I must ask her to wait outside."

Salter was astonished. The man was more flustered over the presence of a woman in the club than of a constable probing into a murder. "She is invaluable to my investigation. She stays."

Choking on unvoiced objections, Oakes stormed off.

"I'm not supposed to be here," she whispered.

"Neither one of us is. Pompous prig. His brain has been addled by this stultifying atmosphere."

Mina giggled. "When a man lashes out that vehemently, it usually means he's got something to hide."

The pages of White's betting book contained wagers over just about anything. Not only were there entries for boxing matches and cricket games, men had also bet on which debutante would be deflowered first and on what day an older member would die.

Salter also noted that when a debt had been satisfied, a mark was placed at the end of the entry. "According to the ledger, Prescott failed to make good on some of his wagers. Let me see . . . as near as I can make it, he owed about three thousand guineas."

"Three thousand! To whom?"

He flipped some pages. "A number of men. Avonlea, Bramstoke, Garrett . . . perhaps eight or ten in all."

"Do you think one of these men got tired of waiting for his money and accosted Prescott?"

His lips thinned. None of the evidence pointed to robbery. "I doubt it. If they killed him, they would never collect. A man's wagers die with him."

"I don't understand it," Mina said, flopping down upon a leather chair. "If Prescott was close to being disgraced for failure to pay his wagers, why didn't he sell the jewels?"

"Maybe he didn't have enough time."

"My father was arrested three months ago. Prescott had the jewels for that long. You don't think that's enough time?"

"Perhaps it was too risky. Maybe he didn't want to be discovered with these particular jewels."

Mina shook her head. "The headpiece in its entirety would be risky to sell. But cut up into pieces like that, it wouldn't be. With the exception of the large sapphire, I doubt selling the individual stones would raise any untoward attention."

Salter slammed the book shut. He was focusing too much on what he saw, and not enough on what he didn't see. What was he missing? His mind leaped through a host of possible scenarios, like a chess player planning his next move.

Mina bit her thumbnail. "Unless he was waiting for something better to come along."

By degrees, Mina's words infiltrated his thoughts. *Something better.* That was it. He was holding out for a better offer. "I think you have it, Minnow."

"Have what? What do I have?"

"The answer. A gambler balances risk against rewards. Prescott was waiting for a greater return from somewhere else."

"But he could have easily sold those stones to a dozen jewelers here in London, and gotten a very fair price."

"True. But maybe a fair price was not the return he was after." At Mina's puzzled expression, he explained. "If he was going to risk discovery by selling the jewels, he would wait until the payoff was likely to be best."

"I still don't understand why he would have been killed. Other than by me, of course."

Salter smirked. "Well, you bring up a good point. There are four principal motives for which a man is killed: revenge, jealousy, fear, or greed. We can safely rule out greed, because robbery was not the motive. Jealousy was also not likely, as Prescott was a confirmed bachelor, and his choice of female ran to the kind he paid for. That leaves revenge or fear."

Mina shrugged. "Lord Prescott was a powerful man. Lots of people might have feared him. And the man was no angel, so he may have been killed for revenge too."

Salter rubbed an open palm against the lower half of his face, a gesture that put him into deep thought. Fear or revenge . . . either prospect produced dozens of suspects, hundreds even. It would take months to narrow down the possibilities.

His hand passed over a spot on the right side of his jaw. There was a jagged column of rough hair below his sideburn. He had missed that spot while shaving this morning. A surge of irritation and impatience flooded through him. He was missing something from this case as well, and Salter was certain it should be as plain as that spot on his face. Yet like that spot, he could *feel* it, but he couldn't *see* it.

He would need a mirror . . . of sorts. Someone in whose reflection he could see more clearly what he had been missing.

"Let's go home, now, Minnow. I need to pay someone a visit."

"Who?"

"I failed to consider one more motive. Not fear *or* revenge, but perhaps fear *and* revenge. Whoever turned Rutting Roddie into Rotting Roddie was definitely trying to bury something, and I don't mean his corpse."

Chapter Ten

The rain pelted the large window in the dining room of the Pleasure Emporium, blurring Lollie's view of the street lamp across the road. The spattering drops on the glass fractured the glow into a thousand pieces.

She propped her long face weakly against her fist. She was grateful for the inclement weather. Rainy evenings usually meant very quiet nights. Tonight, she wanted solitude.

She sighed. That wasn't exactly true either. There was one man whose company she wanted.

Chase.

She couldn't stop thinking about him. She'd give anything if she could start over . . . meet him for the first time. She had made such a fool of herself. But humiliation was only part of the reason for her morose state of mind. She had proven to herself how superficial she was. In had walked a beautiful man, and that was all she could see. She couldn't see past the surface to notice what a special person there was inside. Truth be told, she had forgotten that such men existed. She just assumed that good and decent men were found only among elderly country parsons. But she hadn't even given Chase the chance to show her who he was.

She had treated Chase just like men had always treated her. And he had reacted with just as much indignation as she should have done so many years ago, before she learned to accept such ill treatment as flattery.

And now that she had shown herself to be a sex-mad harlot, this particular gentleman would never walk through that door again.

Suddenly, she heard a rap on the front door. The ether of hope lifted her heart, and she closed her eyes to listen for a Cockney accent. Serafina opened the door, and a man blustered in from the rainy street. "Horrible night, what?"

Oh, no. Not him.

"Where the devil is Lollie?"

She heard Serafina's gentle voice welcome him softly, escorting him to the salon. Then the dining room door—the only barrier between Lollie and *them*—opened. "Lollie, Mr. Woodruff ees calling for you," said Serafina.

Lollie rolled her eyes. "I don't want to see 'im tonight. Please take 'im for me?"

"I'm expecting someone." Serafina came forward a few steps. "What ees wrong?"

"Nothing. I just don't feel like it." Lollie heard her own voice crack, and turned away before any more emotion betrayed her.

"Wait here. I'll see if Madeleine can take heem."

The rustle of Serafina's strawberry-colored gown faded beyond the door, leaving Lollie in silence. She realized how badly she needed someone to talk to. Her thoughts were torturing her, and the last thing she wanted was to be alone with them. Her head fell forward into her hand, her uncoiffed hair making a curtain of isolation around her. When Serafina laid her hand on her shoulder, she nearly jumped.

"The Countess has heem now," she said.

"Thanks, love. Tonight is just . . ." There was no way to finish the thought.

There was no need. The large black doe eyes blinked back in understanding as Serafina sat down on the seat. "What ees hees name?"

Lollie poured out the whole ugly story. How lovely she found Chase, how wantonly she had offered herself, how he had rejected her advances. "But the thing that really twists my garter is that I just didn't know how to talk to him. I didn't know what to say, what to do, that wasn't just what I'd always done to seduce a quill. I just couldn't, I don't know, be me. Just me."

Serafina's eyes fell. "When I was eighteen, I was married to a man. He was a very wealthy man from Alameda, with many vineyards. It was a good match for my family. He was a good man, a decent man. But I did not love heem. I had been enchanted with stories of pirates and thieves, men who were—how you say?—rokes."

"Rogues," Lollie corrected.

"Yes. And my husband was no rogue. He was dull. Kind and generous, yes . . . but so dull. He treated me like a lady, and even though I was little more than a child, all hees associates respected me as if I spoke for heem. And the servants would never cross me for fear of hees anger. Everyone mirrored hees treatment of me." Serafina's ladylike posture crumbled. "But though I loved heem, I still desired the forbidden. When he was on top of me, I would dream of my handsome pirate. It became so that my husband could never compare with my dream lover, even in the daylight hours when he tended to my every need. For our second anniversary, he purchased a beautiful diamond necklace for me. My parents, they held a ball to celebrate. And it was at that ball that I met my handsome pirate lover."

Lollie's mouth fell open. "Never!"

She nodded, light shimmering on her glossy black curls. "He was an Englishman. Very charming. Very handsome. Eyes of a color blue like . . . like the sky on a warm summer day. He was an associate of my husband's, a man who owned many ships, who had come to buy sherry for export to England. And he was everything to me that I had dreamed of. He advanced upon me shamelessly. He caressed me and whispered to me—all within sight of my husband. I was more afraid of my husband seeing heem than he himself was. It was so dangerous, so forbidden. And I fell in love on the spot.

"I should have seen what was to happen. But I didn't want to. I was so in love with the excitement. Before long, he had hees cargo purchased and was ready to sail for England. And when he asked me to come with heem, I did not think too long on it. I collected my jewels, some money, and went with heem. I never wanted to hurt my husband in this way. He was certain to endure shame and suffering because of my infidelity and escape. But I pushed all thought of heem out of my head, something that my lover helped me to do."

"What happened?"

"The moment I set foot upon English soil, the man

who had become my pirate lover vanished. Instead, he became just a man. As we were pulling into port, he thanked me for sharing hees bed during the voyage, but explained that he had to go home to hees wife and children. He was a—how you say—a rague."

Lollie smiled. "A rake."

"Yes, a rake. In truth, I deserved that treatment. Was I not a rake with my own husband? But in my fantasy, my handsome lover would never have done that to me. I learned that fantasies are just happy dreams we enjoy for a while. They are not meant to be lived."

Lollie absorbed Serafina's words. "Chase is no rake. He's the opposite, in fact."

"Yes. That ees why I say my story. Every day, I wish I had not left my husband's side. I did not realize how good he was to me. Now I know. Now I see that bad men do not bring happiness. And every night I spend with these bad men, I know I deserve this treatment. I traded away my life of dull goodness for a life of disappointing excitement. If this Chase ees a good man, who sees you as not for just sex and treats you as what you're worth, then this ees a man you should never let go."

Her chest caved. "But what if I already ruined my one chance?"

Her soft hand rested on Lollie's and squeezed. "Make for yourself another."

MAKE FOR YOURSELF ANOTHER. It was the soft flame of hope that fueled Lollie's tremulous happiness. The words kept time with the sound of the horse's hoofbeats during the carriage ride.

Other than the police station, the Bit & Bridle Pub

was the only place she knew to look for him. She knew the place well; she used to work the street three blocks down, and many a quill had taken her there for a quick pint on their way to the dark alley behind the flower shop, where they would take her up against the wall. It had seemed a lifetime since those rough days on the street. If it weren't for Madame Fynch, who had offered her work from the relative safety of the bordello, she shuddered to think where she might be now.

The Bit & Bridle smelled exactly the same. Fatty mutton sizzled on a spit in the kitchen; pungent ale flowed from aromatic wooden barrels behind the bar; wood shavings and threshing covered the floor around the bar. It was early, and the dining room was not yet full. She easily found a table in plain view of the bar and door.

"Lollie, is that you?" came a rotund voice behind her. "I thought you'd turned up yer toes."

" 'Allo, Ralphy. Cor, you've put on weight!"

The man chuckled. "Yeah, about eleven stone of 'er. I got married."

"What'd you do, swallow 'er?"

His jowls jiggled in protest. "Now don't you give me any of your lip. Say, what you doing 'ere? You on the streets again?"

"Naow. I'm 'ere to meet me friend."

"Oh, I see. Is that what they're calling 'em these days?"

"Blimey, Ralphy . . . it's nuffink like that. He's just a bloke I know."

"All right, all right. Will you be having anything to eat?"

"Sure. 'Ow 'bout one of them bowls o' stew you were always on about?"

"Mutton stew. That's me specialty. Coming right up."

Lollie adjusted the pleats at her chest. She had been careful to dress as modestly as she could, and she knew this dress would do nicely. It was a virginal white confection with tiny green leaves around the hems and bodice. Feminine yet unpretentious, the dress covered her best assets and left only her face to do the talking for her.

The door to the pub opened and there stood Chase Alcott, more beautiful than she remembered. His navy swallowtail coat was faded in places and the white cravat was loosely tied, but he may as well have been wearing a crisp military dress uniform. He carelessly wiped the drizzle from his hair, making the blond locks spike up in places. While making some comment about the weather to the woman behind the bar, he smiled broadly, and it set off a gorgeous dimple on his masculine cheek. Lollie forgot to breathe.

The breathlessness changed from nervous anticipation to outright anxiety. What did she think she was doing? Appearing at his favorite pub in the hopes of running into him? She was being precisely what he said he didn't like, forward. But how could she give him a chance to pursue her if he never saw her again? And what if she failed to attract him? Her hips and breasts were surefire magnets for a man's attention, but without using them, she doubted she could do it. Was her personality going to be enough?

A blind panic seized her. She grabbed her reticule and bolted from the chair, aiming for the kitchens to duck out the back door. But before she could get more than two paces from the table, she nearly collided with Ralph.

He fought to stabilize the bowl he had balanced on a tray. "I brought it out as fast as I could, love. You didn't 'ave to check up on me."

She returned to the table, embarrassment coloring her face. What was wrong with her? She was an experienced woman, skilled in the art of seduction. Here she was acting like a lovesick schoolmiss, awkwardly avoiding a boy while trying to get him to notice her.

Apparently, it worked. If he hadn't noticed her before, he noticed her now.

He started to walk over to her table, and Lollie completely lost all train of thought. What was she going to say?

"Well, fancy that. Miss Lollie! Whatever you doin' 'ere?"

She sat back down stiffly. "I come 'ere all the time. Don't I, Ralphy?"

He set the plate down. "No."

Lollie could have killed him. She'd try to trip him when he left.

Ralph looked Chase up and down. "Dear me, Lollie. Don't tell me this pig's snout is your friend."

Chase crossed his arms. "Evenin', Ralphy. Try not to waste all your charm on me. Save some for Mrs. Birkett."

Ralph straightened as best he could, and looked down his fleshy nose at Chase. "At least 'er tab is all paid up."

"Friday, Ralphy," he said with an exasperated sigh. "I get paid on Friday."

Harrumphing, Ralph wedged the tray under an armpit and stomped off.

Chase shook his head. "He does that to me every month. Like clockwork. Right around the day I collect me wages. May I sit down?"

Lollie nodded, watching his trim body alight on the chair.

"Don't let me keep you from your meal."

Lollie glanced down at her stew. She'd forgotten she'd ordered it. "Care to join me?"

"Love to." He flagged down the pub's only serving girl and asked for a plate of mutton chops.

Now that they had exchanged pleasantries, there was nothing but the weather and the price of sugar to talk about, and she wasn't about to do either. She tore off a piece of bread and put it in her mouth.

"Have you come to give me a tongue-lashing for the way I behaved yesterday?"

A tongue-*lashing* was not precisely what she had in mind. "Naow. I was, uh, worried, 'cause I, uh, I'd forgotten to give you something of Mina's."

He shrugged. "What?"

Yes, what? echoed her frenzied mind. She drew open her reticule and fished around in it. Coins, a handkerchief, a forgotten bag of humbugs ... ah! "This." She placed the object in his large palm.

"A thimble?"

At his incredulous look, Lollie thrust her chin out defensively. "Yes. It's Mina's lucky thimble. She never leaves home without it. She's probably frantic right now, wondering where it is. And since you didn't tell me where that brute was holding her, I couldn't take it to her meself."

"I see," he said, pocketing it with a smile. "Well, I wouldn't want a lady to be without 'er lucky thimble. I'll take it to 'er in the morning."

Once again, she felt crushed by the weight of her own folly. She would never be able to pull this off. Without using her body, she just didn't know how to talk to a man. "Right. Well. That's a load off my mind."

He stared at her, bemusement playing on his face.

"Right. Well." She couldn't take any more of this. She felt utterly transparent. "I'll be off, then."

She stood to go, but his hand on hers stopped her. "Don't."

Her chest rose and fell behind the organdy pleats. *Don't what? Don't make a fool of myself? Don't crave you?*

"Stay. Please. I want you to."

She looked into his penetrating blue eyes. There was no more bemusement, no more secret understanding. Just a sincere request, and the barest hint of fear she'd say no. It was enough for her. She sat down.

He wrung his hands. "I'm glad you came all this way to find me. I can see what a caring person you must be, bringing Miss Mina's lucky thimble and all."

"Thank you." She knew the real reason she had come, and so did he. She couldn't look at him.

"I bless my own luck you're here, because I don't think we got off to a very good start. And that's been bothering me."

The diminishing candle of hope sputtered back to life. "It has?"

He nodded. "I didn't mean to be so sharp with you. I know you was just doing your job."

Lollie puzzled at his meaning. "What d'ye mean?"

"I wasn't angry so much with you as I was with your profession. I didn't like being taken for a mark."

"Oh, no. I wasn't trying to fleece you—"

"No, no, I deserved it. You don't know this, but you actually gave me a taste of me own medicine."

"I don't understand."

Chase sighed heavily. "Before I became a constable . . . I led the life."

She cocked her head. "What sort of a life?"

"You know, a street life. A less-than-honorable one. I used to be a thief. Best lifter in London . . . or so I fancied meself. I could take a gentleman's purse without 'im feelin' a thing. And I was a cracker at doing the ladies. A quick slice of this," he said, touching the ribbon that served as the handle to her reticule, "and she wouldn't know what 'appened till she got 'ome."

Lollie tried to imagine him sidling up to an unsuspecting woman and stealing the reticule from her gloved hand. It didn't fit.

"'Course I was a little younger in those days. Skinny runt with no brains and even less sense. Some days, I'd be able to take home enough to support me family for a week. Minus a bit for meself. I'd do me duty as man of the house, and then the rest of the time I just larked about with me mates."

An alarm went off inside her. "So, you're married?"

He chuckled, and she caught a glimpse of his straight white teeth. "Nah. Me father died when I was a scrapper, so I had to do for me mum and four sisters.

Mum hated the fact that I turned out to be such a scamp. She was always on me about getting a proper job. But the life was just too much fun. Until, of course, I got caught."

They talked through dinner, over dessert, and beyond coffee. Almost two hours had passed and the conversation still had not wound down. Lollie was enthralled by his discussions of everything from criminal schemes to self-defense, from use of weaponry to questioning a suspect. Lollie recognized in Chase's life the inexorable drive to survive, something she could identify with in her own. But a chasm appeared in that Chase was not as given to compromise as she herself had always been. There was no tale of valor in her past, no honorable accomplishments to share. The less he knew about her vocation and how she got here, the better. So whenever he became curious about her, she deflected his questions and instead drew out more of his exciting stories.

"Lollie, Lollie," he remarked, the candlelight twinkling in his eyes. "Is that your real name?"

"Naow. I gave meself that name. I don't much like me real name."

"Which is?"

She jabbed her nose in the air with mock offense. "I don't know you well enough to tell you."

"Go on," he insisted, his dimple reappearing.

"I don't want to say. You'll laugh at me."

"I won't. Come on, then. What's your real name?"

She squared her shoulders. "All right, then. Me real name is Blanche."

He snorted, and a loud guffaw reverberated through the pub.

"You rotten bastard!" she chided, stifling a smile. "You said you weren't going to laugh!" She reached over and cuffed him on the shoulder. But the sound of his merriment soon sent her into peals of giggles.

The pub had thinned to a handful of mostly drunk laborers. Chase suggested they take a walk, and she agreed. She wound her wrap around her shoulders, collected her reticule, and waited by the door while he put the cost of their meals on his tab.

Just then, a man at the table by the door reached over to where she was standing and shoved his hand between her bottom cheeks, making her yip in surprise. "Oy, darlin'," he said, his voice gravelly with liquor. "When you're done wit' 'im, 'ow 'bout lettin' me 'ave a go?"

Lollie looked with dismay at the large sooty smear on her brilliant white dress. *Ruined,* she thought. *It's all ruined.*

Chase flew past her and seized the man by his grimy lapels. He yanked the man out of his chair and slammed him against the wall.

"Lay a hand on her again and you'll lose it at the elbow!"

The man's slowed reactions finally registered shock and fear, and he nodded as earnestly as he could. Chase let him go, and the drunken man crumpled to the floor. He spun round to check on Lollie, but she was nowhere to be found.

She was halfway down the street when he caught up to her.

"Lollie! Wait!"

She didn't stop running until his hand on her arm halted her. Tears streaked her face. "Let me go!"

"No," he said, tightening his grip. "Why are you running? 'Cause of that saucer?"

She closed her eyes tightly, releasing another swell of tears. "You really want to know? You want to know where Lollie was before today? Right here, on this corner. And there. And behind that wall there. This," she said, twisting her stained dress around to show him, "is who I am. And that saucer, I did him once inside a stable for three shillings."

Chase's face cascaded from concern to distress to disgust, making Lollie's chest cave in with despair. But at least it was all out in the open. No more polite pretenses. And now that she had vomited out the whole ugly truth, she wanted to escape the horrible stench of her own sordid past. She bolted past him.

"Stop!"

She had never heard him shout with all his voice. The sound reverberated in the still night. She came to a halt underneath a street lamp.

"Just stop." He advanced upon her slowly, his face materializing by degrees in the yellow glow. "Courtesan, streetwalker . . . three guineas or three shillings . . . it don't matter which. Either way, it saddens me."

She didn't expect that. Fresh tears spilled from her reddened eyes.

But this," he said, pointing to the stain on her skirt, "is not *who* you are. It's what you *do*. So stop. Just stop."

He didn't know what he was asking. "How can I?

It's all I know. All I've ever known. Can't do nuffink else."

"'Course you can." His eyebrows tented in the middle, and his hand stroked her face softly. "Do what it is you were put here to do."

His touch electrified her. It was, at once, more pure and more intimate than she ever thought possible. It banished the sadness, leaving only wonder. "And what is that?"

He smiled gently, and that charming dimple reappeared. "You're going to have to find that out for yourself."

A chill descended upon her suddenly, and she began to tremble.

"You're shaking," he said, removing his coat and settling it on her shoulders. "My flat's just round the corner. You can warm yerself there, if you like."

Unbidden thoughts flashed through Lollie's mind, most of them indiscreet. They began when he slipped his warm, limewater-scented coat onto her back. Erotic visions of making love to him flowered uncontrollably in her mind. Her practiced eye instantaneously spotted a half-dozen places they could do it, completely unseen by the public, before they even got to his flat. But something prevented her from opening herself up to that possibility. Although she knew the pleasure would be heavenly, something warned her that the beautiful closeness that had sprung up between them would be irreparably sullied if they drowned it out with sex.

"Just take me home, Chase. My home."

He nodded, and hailed a hansom cab.

They didn't speak during the brief ride from Stepney, but inside her, a symphony played. He had his arm round her shoulders, but it felt as if he held it round her heart. How could she have known so many men—yet never have felt this?

He reached down and took her hand in his, and Lollie's whole body felt caressed by that tender gesture. What magic did he hold that he could make a woman like her feel like an inexperienced maiden? Whatever it was, she wanted more. Much more.

The carriage slowed in front of the Pleasure Emporium, and Lollie considered changing her mind. She could go back to his flat, and let human nature take its course. Or better yet, invite him in, maybe even taking him to the Eden Room, the enclosed conservatory in the rear of the house, and lose herself to him amid the plants and vines. But it wasn't enough. Not nearly enough.

He helped her alight from the carriage, and she returned his coat. "May I call for you tomorrow?"

She smiled, feeling alive with delight. She lifted her face to him, and let her kiss speak the yes that was inside her heart. It was forward and brazen, but there was too much emotion to convey in such a brief, tepid word.

"I . . . I just want to say that," Lollie managed, "that I enjoyed being with you."

"Me too," he answered, smiling down at her.

"That thimble . . . d'ye think I can have it back?"

His brows drew together as he reached into his pocket. "I thought it was Mina's lucky thimble."

A blush colored her cheeks. "It's my lucky thimble now."

He reached down, lifted her hand, and placed the

wooden object on the edge of her fourth finger. Almost like a ring, but not quite.

"Until tomorrow, then?"

She nodded, and began counting down the seconds.

Chapter Eleven

 "No!" she shouted above the clatter of the horse's hooves. "I don't want to!"

"Mina, I've already explained—"

"Why can't I go with you? I want to talk to Lord Bensonhurst too."

Salter looked over at her as she pouted on the other side of the phaeton's bench. "No. Now, you've helped me tremendously on this case. You have the makings of a fine constable in you. But you must let me handle this interview by myself."

"Why?"

"It's complicated."

"Then use really small words so I'll understand you."

He straightened to his full authoritative stature. "Because I said so. Is that plain enough for you?"

She leaned back against the seat of the carriage and crossed her arms, prickled by his confident air of superiority.

"You can count yourself lucky that Mrs. Tilbury is out of town. Otherwise, it'd be back to the shackles with you. I'll faithfully recount the substance of our conversation, word for word. But you must wait for me at the Pleasure Emporium."

"I won't."

"Mina . . ." There was warning in his voice.

"Not until you tell me why I can't go with you."

He shook his head, and slowed the carriage onto the shoulder of the street. "You can't come with me because Lord Bensonhurst doesn't believe you."

"That's not true. He's going to get my father a new trial. He promised me."

His brow tightened with concern. Carefully, he picked through Lord Bensonhurst's diatribe to remove all of the statements that would hurt Mina's feelings. "He wasn't being honest with you. He was merely being polite. He has no intention of getting your father out of prison."

The air was stolen out of her. She had been floating high on the hope that Lord Bensonhurst would seek exoneration for her father. Now that hope crumbled like an ancient tower, and she found herself among the ruins with no clue how to dig herself out.

"Lord Bensonhurst doesn't believe anything you told him." Salter rested his hand gently on hers. "But I do. I know you're telling me the truth. And I'm going to do all I can to make sure your father gets his case reviewed."

The world had gone dark for Mina, but Salter's words sparked a glimmer of optimism.

"Wait for me at the bordello. I'll be back straightaway. I promise."

She was conscious of the pressure of his warm gloved hand on hers. It was difficult to refuse him anything when he touched her. She nodded weakly.

"Mina, look at me."

She did so.

"You're not alone anymore."

Mina absorbed his words one by one. Was it possible to let someone into her solitary life? Was it possible he wanted to be there?

His expression grew pensive, as if he himself were contemplating the weight of his meaning. He leaned down and pressed his lips against hers. It was brief, perfunctory, and communicated to Mina his avowed friendship. A hint of a grateful smile lifted the corners of her mouth.

But Salter didn't move. The pensive look came over him again, and his eyes drank in Mina's face. His expression was inscrutable, but she could tell a million thoughts were racing through his mind. Finally, he settled upon one, and his head lowered once more.

He kissed her again, but this time it was far different. As his lips caressed hers, she became aware of a host of hidden emotions and buried desires, his and hers. It was as if his heart were trying to speak something directly to hers. And her heart heard him loud and clear.

I love you.

Elation filled her, and she didn't know how she was going to contain it. Even if she let her heart burst into a million blissful pieces, she just knew that each one of those pieces would shout as much back to him: *I love you too.*

There was a smile on his face when he broke the kiss, one unlike any she had seen on him before. He fairly glowed with love. *For her,* she reminded herself.

He urged the horse forward. They reached the door entirely too soon, and she didn't want to part from him.

He helped her down from the carriage. As they stood at the door together, he enfolded her in his arms and gave her one last kiss.

"Hurry back," she said breathlessly.

He nodded curtly, leaped upon the conveyance, and raced off.

Though Mina stood by herself, she knew she was no longer alone. She bounced through the bordello door.

The place was quiet as she wended her way through the salon. Only the ticking of the mantel clock split the silence. It was just past ten o'clock in the morning, and none of the ladies had awoken yet. She started up the rear stairs to her bedroom when she heard a noise in the dining room.

She left her valise on the step. When she opened the door to the dining room, she saw Lollie with a cup of tea, giggling softly.

Mina looked around the room, but saw no one else.

"Welcome back," Lollie said. "I thought he'd never return you."

"What are you doing up so early?"

A smile spread across her face. "I haven't been to bed." She took a sip. "With anyone," she added.

Mina sat down. "You've got a peculiar look on your face. What are you so full of cream about?"

Lollie blushed, something Mina had never seen her do before. "I've found 'im, Mina."

"Who?"

"Me prince."

Mina smirked. "Your prince? Who?"

Lollie smiled dreamily. "Charles Cavill Alcott."

She frowned, repeating each name. Suddenly, illumination dawned on her. "You mean that young constable who brought me my clothes?"

Lollie nodded. Animatedly, she told Mina all that had happened since Chase stepped through the front door. She described in perfect detail the look of his face, everything from the varying color of his eyes to how his dimples showed when he was in a playful mood. Unabashedly, she told of how she'd thrown herself at him and how he rejected her sexual invitation. How he seemed to want more from her—not just her breasts, but the beating heart behind them.

"He's changed me, Mina. I don't know how, but he's changed me. I don't even know who I am anymore."

Mina smiled at Lollie's unearthly change in demeanor. It was staggering what the love of a good man could do to a woman.

Mina poured herself a cup of tea, and told Lollie all that had happened since Salter whisked her away. It had been an adventure, but the crowning glory had been the kiss they shared outside just then. She confessed to Lollie that living at the bordello had made her feel like a thistle in a field of tulips. Yet of all the gorgeously colored cups with their slender beautiful stems, it was *her* that Salter stopped to pick.

Lollie giggled. "Wonderful thing to have a man in your life, eh?"

"The *right* man," Mina corrected. "Salter's got this amazing ability to see what other people can't. And I desperately want to know what else he sees in me. When I see myself through his eyes, I like what I see. It's like he can somehow make me better than I am. Like he's—"

"Changed you," Lollie finished.

Mina smiled broadly. "Irreversibly."

The door creaked, startling them both.

Madame Fynch. And she did not look happy.

"So! Changed, are we?"

Mina's heart nearly stopped beating. She felt as if she had been caught with her hand in the Madame's treasury. In an instant, she mentally replayed her lengthy conversation with Lollie, wondering how much Madame Fynch had overheard.

"You're a foolish girl, Mina. You've fallen into the same trap that has ensnared women since the dawn of mankind. You've confused being desired with having worth, and you've given a man power over your own self-esteem. I suppose for a plain girl such as yourself, a man's attentions may feel like the best thing that could ever happen to you. But men the world over know that their favors are merely a tool to get what they want out of a woman without having to force her. Your precious constable is no different. Even now I can read you well enough to know that he hasn't bedded you. What does that tell you? He knows that it's what you most desire, and he will dangle it in front of you like a piece of scrap meat in front of a starving dog.

"As for you," Madame Fynch continued, the anger in her eyes slicing through Lollie. "I'm most disappointed in you. I believed you to be smarter than that. Of all the girls in my employ, you are the only one who grew up in the profession, the one with the most experience of men. I assumed that you had learned by now that men are all the same. Prince Charming exists only in fairy tales, and you more than anyone should know that. I suppose you think you're in love. You're not. He just scrubbed a few of the calluses off your heart, and it's left you tender. But even if you are in love, he better *not* have changed you. I don't employ nuns. Give him your heart, if you must, but the rest belongs to me."

Madame Fynch folded her arms. "There will be no more leave for either of you. For disappearing without permission, you are both restricted to the premises until I tell you otherwise. I *will* restore order to my house. Lollie, you will return to your duties *tonight*. I lose money when customers must wait around for the next girl to become available because you're not here. And you, I want ten new letters on my escritoire by this afternoon—unsealed. I want you to prove to me that they're up to your usual standards. And in case you're wondering, your 'princes' may *not* come to call. Lambrick has used up all the credit in his account when he absconded with you these many days, and I don't even want to meet his protégé. The last thing I want around here are constables nosing into my affairs. Is that clear?"

Madame Fynch flamed out of the dining room, leaving them to languish in the oppressive reprimand.

Mina had gravitated from shock to shame, and was now roiling in resentment. "Of all the insufferable, obnoxious, mean-spirited—" Her invective was halted by Lollie's desolate expression. "Loll, don't tell me you feel offended by that horrible woman."

Lollie shook her head slowly. "She can say what she likes about me."

"Then what's wrong?"

"Tonight, Mina. What am I going to do about to-night?"

𝒢MANSION HOUSE WAS AS beautiful as it was impos-ing. To visitors from other governments, its Palladian architecture and artwork conveyed wealth and refine-ment, enabling the Lord Mayor to represent the City of London in elegant style. But for those heads of state less friendly to the country, its size and majesty were designed to impress upon them the assurance that En-gland was unarguably the most powerful country in the world, and that it would behoove them not to forget it.

Salter removed his hat and handed it to the steward. He knew something of Mansion House, because the residence was the only one with its own court of law. Though he had never been to the upper floors before, he sometimes escorted prisoners to one of the ten hold-ing cells for men, or occasionally the one for women, affectionately termed the "birdcage." As he was taken through to the Lord Mayor's offices upstairs, he caught glimpses of the sprawling interior. Clearly, what he had been told of the house had been a gross understate-ment. The kitchen ranges were large enough to roast an entire ox. Fluted columns of the Corinthian order tow-ered fifty feet high along the vast Egyptian Hall, where the Lord Mayor held banquets for four hundred guests at a time. The immense Greek sculptures along the walls looked to be thousands of years old.

The Lord Mayor's private office was just as ostenta-tious. The desk that dominated the room gleamed in cherry mahogany notes. Tomes hundreds of years old lined the shelves two stories high. Against one wall was a large cabinet that displayed all the Lord Mayor's insignia—the Seal, the Purse, the Mace, and the Sword. Draped inside was the famous collar of SS, a chain of S-shaped links that Salter had seen worn by the likes of Sir Thomas More in paintings.

The Lord Mayor rose from his chair, and extended his hand. "Lambrick! What a surprise. I must have conjured you because I've been thinking of you all day."

Salter took him by the hand. "Favorably, I hope, sir."

"That depends on the news you bring." Lord Bensonhurst waved Salter to a chair. "How speeds your progress on the case? Has your suspicion alighted on anyone yet?"

"Not as yet, sir. But I feel close to an answer." Ignoring Lord Bensonhurst's look of irritation, Salter reached into his coat pocket. "Allow me to show you something."

He unfolded a page of newsprint, which he had obtained from the archives at the newspaper office shortly before arriving at Mansion House. "This is an article published in the *Times,* dated November 27, 1812. It describes the visit to this country made by emissaries from the King of Siam. It was one of your first official state events."

"I remember it. What about it?"

"King Rama's emissaries had come on a journey of peace, in the hopes of strengthening Siam's relations with England. The King sent tokens of his country's esteem for Their Majesties—a dozen Dutch dressage stallions for King George, and a priceless tiara for Queen Charlotte. 'The tiara,' it says, 'is of incomparable beauty and value, having twelve rubies, one hundred diamonds, and a large sapphire. The gems were chosen to symbol-ize the colors of Britain's Union Jack. The most singular piece is the single sapphire. The gem is about the same size as a robin's egg, and a light shining into its smooth surface is refracted into six rays, hence the name, the Star of Bangkok, and was taken from the royal diadem of the King's great-grandmother.' Sir, I have that very gemstone in my possession."

"Not that drivel about the missing tiara again!"

"Sir, hear me out—"

"No," he retorted, his eyes flashing blue fire. "I warned you about listening to that whore's story, didn't I?"

"She's not a whore, sir," Salter responded sternly. "And her story rings true."

"I don't care! This is a murder investigation, and you're out chasing fantasies about Siamese crowns!"

Salter raised his voice. "It's my belief that whoever murdered Roderick Prescott did so to keep him quiet about the theft of this tiara, a theft which Prescott per-petrated. And this person—"

"You're a stupid man, Lambrick. If you must know, that tiara is safe in the Tower of London along with Her Majesty's other jewels. I myself took it there."

"Sir, Mina's father made a duplicate of this item. We should check the Tower to make sure the authentic tiara is actually there—"

"Enough! I won't have my aide's character called into question on something as ridiculous as this. My God, man, can you not see how she has duped you? She will say anything to get her father freed, and she is using you to get me to do it."

Salter shook his head. "She would never do that, sir. I know her well enough to believe that."

"Well, I'm not as gullible as you are, Lambrick." Lord Bensonhurst stood. "Nor as sympathetic. To her or to you. You've failed utterly in your assignment."

"Sir, I haven't failed. I just haven't succeeded yet."

"I have no confidence that you will. And I can no longer stomach your incompetence or your insubordination. I am relieving you of your command. Indeed, of your commission. I don't want cock-stupid men on my force. I'll get someone else to do your job. One who doesn't consort with liars and goddamned prostitutes!"

Salter bolted out of his chair, valiantly warring with the powerful urge to drive his fist into Bensonhurst's mouth for slandering Mina again. Why couldn't he make Bensonhurst understand? Dread of scandal aside, Bensonhurst shouldn't be thwarting his investigation. And to be discharged in the bargain—it was the height of injustice.

Then something Mina said popped into his head. *When a man lashes out that vehemently, it usually means he's got something to hide.* Suddenly, Bensonhurst's reaction spoke loud and clear. Though he was shrouded in fury, Bensonhurst was practically bleeding with panic. It was a smell Salter knew well—fear emanating from a cornered murderer.

Lord Bensonhurst rose from his chair, signaling the end of their conversation. "There will be no more investigation. I'm concluding it now as an unsolved murder. You've bungled it from the start, and now the murderer has gotten away. Consider yourself lucky I don't have you arrested for abetting a criminal act."

"Yes, sir," he responded, feelings of revulsion and indignation swarming in his head.

Lord Bensonhurst held out his open palm. "Hand over the jewels you found in Lord Prescott's strongbox. They belong to Prescott's estate, and I intend to make sure their value goes to the next of kin."

Salter looked at Bensonhurst's outstretched hand. Well manicured and clean, but stained with invisible blood.

"I don't have them with me," he lied.

"I'll send a servant with you to retrieve them."

"That won't be necessary. I'll bring them by myself," he said, flinging the words over his shoulder as he stormed out.

A scowl darkened his brow. Salter had his man, but this was no common street killer, no thug for hire. This was the Lord Mayor of London, a man second in rank only to the sovereign himself. How did one bring such a man to justice?

Chapter Twelve

It was hard seeing Lollie so morose. Mina had always been drawn to the combination of Lollie's high spirits and low-class wit, and the fact that Lollie had lost her sparkle infected Mina's own mood.

Lollie sulked about the room, prolonging the task of getting dressed for the evening. Her gorgeous lilac velvet gown with the deep décolletage was tossed carelessly onto her bed, and her stockings had fallen to the floor, forgotten.

"Loll? What's wrong?" Mina asked.

"I'm not feeling well, Mina. I can't go downstairs tonight. I don't want to be with those blokes. I can't bend back my lips, hoping it'll look like a smile. Listening to their problems and all their complaints about their wives, and then spreading meself open for them. I just can't."

"Did Chase ask you to quit the business?"

"Not exactly," she replied, wiping her nose. "If he had, I probably would have told him to go stuff himself. He likes me, Mina. *Me*. He didn't tell me to quit, but he wants me to. Not for his benefit, but for mine. Thing is," Lollie said, hazarding a look at Mina, "I want to too. Don't look at me like that. I know ye think I've gone daft. Maybe I have." She picked up the wooden thimble from the nightstand and fingered it gently. "A time was when all I wanted was a stiff man and a stiff drink. Now I've met Chase, it seems that ain't enough no more."

Mina sat on the bed and looked up at Lollie. "This is a big decision. What would you do?"

She chuckled feebly. "I asked Chase that same question. Know what he told me? He told me whatever I was put here to do."

She walked over the clothes on the floor and sat on the chair. She brought her knees up to her chin in a protective gesture, and wrapped her arms around them. "So I got to thinkin', what was I meant to do? Didn't seem I was fit for much. So I thought, maybe I should ask God, you know? I don't think I've prayed—properly—since I was thirteen. So I told Him 'bout Chase and 'ow much I liked him. And Mina, I swear I could hear each word of His answer in my heart. He said," she began, then choked on her emotion, and all she could do was whisper. "He said, *'I'm glad. I saved him just for you.'*"

Mina watched as Lollie wiped her wet cheeks on her dress, and waited until she was ready to continue. Soon she took a deep shuddering breath, and shook her head. "That's why I can't go downstairs. Not tonight. Not ever."

No girl had ever quit while Mina had been working there, though it certainly happened that several were discharged. A girl would get pregnant, or would contract some ugly disease, and she would have to go. Or someone would defy Madame Fynch, and she'd be sacked on the spot. But no one had ever willingly left.

The money was too good, and the girls put up with a lot in exchange for the security of having a place to stay, and the privilege of getting to bed only gentlemen of a certain class.

A rising panic filled Mina's heart. "Lollie, Madame Fynch won't let you stay if you don't work. Where would you go?"

"I dunno. There's an old client of mine what owns a building, but even if he 'ad any vacancies, he knows what I do and he'd want to be paid in trade. I've got a cousin in Yorkshire, but I don't want to leave Chase behind in London."

"What about him? Would Chase let you stay with him?"

"No doubt. But I've a strong feeling that would be a big mistake. I've made a cock-up of my life so far. I don't want to ruin what's left."

Mina reflected. It was not going to be easy for Lollie, and she wondered if Lollie had any idea what she was up against. For girls like Lollie, with precious little education and no breeding, there weren't many options available to them. All the women Mina ever knew were either married or prostitutes. Either way, their bodies were no longer theirs. There was a third option—to go into service, as Mina had—but she suspected that Lollie lacked the humility to follow that profession. Besides, with her beauty, she wouldn't last long as anyone's maid before a gentleman of the house would corner her in a scullery or stable and change her back into what she was trying so desperately to escape right now.

"Talk to Madame Fynch, Lollie. Tell her you'd be willing to stay on as a maid. Or you can tend bar, and

I'll go write letters all night long. She'd like that, I know she would. It's nowhere near as lucrative as what you're used to, but it'll let you remain in safety among your friends."

"D'ye think she'd agree to that?"

Her look was so desperate that Mina wanted to let her hope. "The only thing you can do is try."

IT WAS A FURIOUSLY busy night. Parliament was in a special evening session and when it adjourned, a good number of men from the winning party came to the Pleasure Emporium for a celebration. There weren't enough ladies to go around, so Madame Fynch held an impromptu party in the courtyard to keep them all entertained at once. She brought out a shadowbox, a theatrical piece she had picked up on her travels. The front of the box was covered by a large screen of parchment, and it was illuminated from behind by candles. Tessa and Margot went behind the curtain and, selecting some of the shadow puppets, put on a most ingenious but decidedly naughty performance. Disguising their voices, they created a wickedly funny scene in which a man comes home to find his wife in bed with the chimney sweep. The man runs after the sweep to beat him up, but a cloud of soot prevents the man from finding him, and instead he assaults a visiting vicar. Growing amorous for his wife, the husband puppet—which had an enormous, fully articulated phallus—mistakenly goes after the chimney sweep. The scene had the audience in stitches, and soon many of them wanted to try their hand at a roguish improvisation.

As Mina was busy pouring drinks for the raucous gathering, her own heart was heavy with worry. While everyone laughed around her, it seemed that only she was aware of the imminent catastrophe about to befall her friend. Lollie had come down to the courtyard for only a moment to call the Madame's attention, and then they both disappeared into the house. They were gone a long time, and each second that passed multiplied Mina's anxiety. Still, she comforted herself with the glimmer of hope that Lollie could stay. After all, Madame Fynch was a savvy businesswoman, and sacking Lollie would not be in the house's best interest. This sort of thing must happen a lot among courtesans. Falling in love with a client would be temporarily bad for business, but according to Madame Fynch, love didn't last. If this was true, it would be only a matter of time before Chase realized the error of his ways and Lollie would return to her duties much wiser and less apt to stray again.

Just as two Members of Parliament, to the cheers of the entire audience, were creating a puppet scene in high falsetto voices of the world's fastest wedding consummation, Madame Fynch returned to the courtyard alone. She picked up her portfolio and began to write in it.

Mina waited for Lollie to emerge from the conservatory door, but nothing happened. Finally, she could no longer stand the suspense and started back into the house.

"Where are you going?" Madame Fynch demanded without even taking her eyes off the paper.

"I was going to fetch another keg of ale from the cellar."

Madame Fynch's eyes flashed in ire. "No you weren't. You were going to satisfy your curiosity as to what's become of Lollie. Well, let me put your mind at ease so you can concentrate on your duties. She's been terminated."

"What?"

"You heard me. I've sent her packing. I'll not have layabouts working for me."

"But Madame, perhaps this love phase will peter out. She might return to her senses, sooner than you'd imagine. If you terminate her now, you'll have lost out on all her potential income."

The Madame's face never changed expression. "She was good. Easily one of the best, despite her commonness. Maybe even because of it, who knows? But she's no good to me anymore. She can be replaced. There are hundreds more like her. I can easily find another Lollie." The hardness on her face intensified. "And another Mina. Get back to work."

The evening seemed interminable. Those who didn't collapse in drunken heaps in the salons staggered to a bedroom with a girl, where she dispatched him in haste as there were others waiting.

When the Madame wasn't looking, Mina crept upstairs to check on Lollie. She was nowhere to be found. Her clothes were gone, her things were gone. Mina checked her own room, hoping to find a note, but there wasn't one.

Mina was bereft. She came back downstairs to the salon, worry etched on her face. She plodded over to the bar, and collected more glasses to take to the courtyard.

Suddenly, the front door opened and in walked a figure she knew well.

Salter.

Panic rolled over her like a giant wave. Madame Fynch mustn't see him. After the dressing-down she had received that morning, there would be hell to pay if the woman saw her talking to Salter.

She flew toward him. He opened his arms, thinking she was going to embrace him, but she just pushed him against the door. He stared down at her in puzzlement.

"Salter, leave!" she insisted.

"I just got here. Are you trying to get rid of me already? I haven't had a chance to offend you yet."

"Now, please! I don't want you here." She tugged on him but he didn't budge. A man his size moved only when he wanted to.

"Why not?"

There was no way to explain it all before Madame Fynch walked into the room. How could she tell him that her immediate future hung precariously over an enormous abyss, and that if she was fired, she'd fall into it? She didn't have any significant savings to be able to put a roof over her head, nor did she have any prospect of another situation. Unlike Lollie, Mina had no cousin in Yorkshire or sympathetic client who might take her in. Without a job, she'd be destitute and homeless.

She thought quickly. "Please come outside with me so I can kiss you properly."

He smiled. "That's more like it." He held the door open for her, and Mina darted out.

It was a lovely evening, but Mina only felt the chill.

It had seemed a hundred years since she had seen Salter last, though it had only been that morning. Now that she was free of the oppression and sadness of the bordello, she found that the sight of him gladdened her heart immensely.

"Where have you been all day?"

His wide lips pursed. "Well, if you must know, I took a stroll through Hyde Park, shared tea with a friend, and played lawn tennis in the afternoon. Where do you think? I went to see Lord Bensonhurst."

"Why did it take you so long?"

The smirk returned. "Did you miss me?"

"Don't be ridiculous."

He took her hands in his. "From you, that means yes."

Her small hands were completely engulfed in his larger ones, and the sensation gave her a delightful thrill. At that moment, she wished her entire being could merge with his.

Her voice became wistful. "I wish I'd have gone with you."

"Why? What's happened?"

"First tell me what Lord Bensonhurst said. Did he give you any idea who the murderer might be?"

"I'll say he did. I know exactly who the murderer is. Bensonhurst himself."

"What?"

"It was him. I'm sure of it. Murder is like fire. You don't play around with it without your fingers getting burned."

"How can you be certain it was him?"

"It all fits. The tiara was sent from King Rama the

Second of Siam, as one of several gifts to curry favor from our own sovereigns. Because of King George's illness, the King and Queen were both indisposed and couldn't receive Rama's entourage. I suspect that instead, he presented the tiara to Bensonhurst, who of course should have conveyed it to Queen Charlotte. Instead of doing that, however, he gave it to his aide, Prescott, and instructed him to take it first to your father's jewelry shop to have the pricey jewels cleverly switched for lesser ones. The Queen would probably never set eyes on the tiara, anyway, but even if she did, she'd never suspect that its gems were not the ones originally set into it. Prescott, who was so heavily in debt, did as his employer asked but saw a more lucrative opportunity for himself. He held on to the gems, and did something Bensonhurst hadn't counted on. He blackmailed his employer to keep silent about the switch. My hunch is that Bensonhurst paid Prescott off—hence the money I found in the safe—but when he came to collect the jewels, Prescott didn't keep up his end of the bargain. He had no intention of giving back the jewels, not while Bensonhurst was willing to buy his silence. Bensonhurst was so furious, he picked up the first thing he saw—Prescott's leather whip—and strangled him with it."

Mina's mouth had hung open the entire time Salter was talking. "Did you arrest Lord Bensonhurst?"

Salter sighed heavily. "I'd love to, but I can't. Problem is, I can't prove any of it. And even if I could, Bensonhurst sacked me."

"Oh, that rotten bastard! What can we do now?"

"We? *We* will do nothing. *I* will be finding a way to

bring him to justice. Which, admittedly, won't be easy. Short of the King, Bensonhurst is the most powerful man in London. He has the ear of the monarch, and he knows every diplomat and leader in the world. You don't just walk up to a man like that and arrest him without having enough evidence to prove your case."

"But you have the jewels."

"That isn't enough, Minnow. I have to prove that Bensonhurst ordered the jewels switched, killed Prescott, and tried to cover it up—and I have to do it without casting our country into international embarrassment. If it is discovered in the world arena that a man as highly ranked as Bensonhurst could perpetrate such a pedestrian crime, it would be a humiliation for the Crown. The King has been through enough with his illness."

Mina could see his deeply felt loyalties, and it endeared him to her tenfold. "So what will you do now?"

"Tomorrow morning I'm going to see if I can get a look at that tiara in the Tower. If the gems in that headpiece match the gems I have in my possession, I'll go see one of the magistrates . . . assuming, of course, Bensonhurst hasn't already informed them I'm no longer a constable. If so, I'll talk to my man, Chase Alcott. He'll follow through on the case for me."

The mention of Chase drove a stab of fear through her. Because of Chase, Lollie had been sacked. Mina, too, had been warned about talking to Salter. She had to return to her duties before Madame Fynch came looking for her.

"I have to get back! Come for me tomorrow. Or better

yet," she said, mentally fabricating a story for the Madame that she would need to go purchase more ink and a stack of blue writing paper. "I'll meet you at noon at your flat. We can talk then." She made a move for the door, but his hand tightened on hers.

"Just a minute. What about my kiss?"

"Here? Salter, people will see."

"I'm hoping that they do."

"Very well. A quick one." She stood in front of him and raised her face to his.

The smirk returned, deepening the furrow on his cheek. The challenge lit up his eyes.

He leaned down and placed a soft yet unbroken kiss on her lips. At first, the long kiss seemed awkward, but she didn't move. Soon the alchemy of his mouth against hers, his hands on hers, and his heart against hers created an intoxicating sensation that she wished would last forever. Slowly, the magic worked its way through her anxiety and slipped her to a place where there were no tiaras, no bordellos, no bad men. His hands slid up the back of her arms and wound around her back, enfolding her in the safe cocoon of his embrace. She opened her mouth to his, and his tongue swirled beneath hers, licking the untouched pinkness underneath. It made her swoon with longing.

Her soft moan made him tighten his embrace. She rested against one of his great arms as the other came round the front and lifted her breast. *More,* her frenzied mind cried, as his warm hand caressed her left breast until her nipple rose in response. Her whole body was on fire for him. But to her greater delight, his body seemed to be on fire for her as well.

"Salter?"

"Hmm?"

"Would it be terribly wrong of me if I fell in love with you?"

He smiled then, but it quickly faded. A troubled look came over his face. It was not the expression she expected. Had she gone too far? But he kissed her again, long and slow, and it fanned the flames that had begun to lave between her legs. She knew she wanted him, but she didn't know how to ask. Why didn't he make the next move? It was dark, it was quiet, it was time. Why didn't he rescue her from this torment?

Suddenly, he broke the kiss. "It's time I go," he said, pressing his forehead against hers.

Why? "Not yet, please. I know a place where we can go . . . to talk."

"I can't, Minnow. Not right now. Tomorrow. I'll see you tomorrow."

As he retreated down the street, she inhaled sharply. She could kill him for leaving her smoldering like a forgotten fire. She could feel each erotic sensation intensifying, even in his absence, like embers illuminating the dark. His scent still clung to her, and she gloried in the lingering impression it left.

But something had gone wrong. She cursed her own ignorance. If only she knew what to say, how to act, to get him to want to make love to her. It was all so new to her, and she was so close. She wanted Salter—only Salter—but she didn't know how to get him. What was the magic word to entice him to say he loved her?

She frowned in puzzlement, and started up the steps to the door. Suddenly, she caught a glimpse of something that obliterated any remaining joy. There, in the bordello window above her, was the Madame's face, looking down on her in anger.

Mina felt as if she had been dunked in icy water. The chill went down to her bones. Her knees shook as she took the steps up to the front door.

Madame Fynch was waiting for her in the empty parlor. "How dare you disobey my explicit instructions!"

"I didn't," she said, knowing she bloody well had. "He came to the door."

"I told you I didn't want him calling for you. Period."

"I tried to send him away, Madame. Honest."

"Yes, I can see how hard you tried."

Mina had the decency to look down.

"I am not accustomed to being contravened, especially not by servants. As you are unable to submit to the rules of my house—"

The Madame must not finish that sentence. As soon as it was spoken, Mina knew her word would become law. "Madame, please, I wasn't trying to—"

"—you will leave immediately."

"Madame, no!"

"Don't say I didn't warn you. When that lawman got stuck to the bottom of your shoe, I gave you the chance to scrape him off. But you didn't. So out with the lot of you."

"I didn't let him in. I saw him outside."

"I don't care. I didn't want you to see him at all."

Mina bristled at the unfairness. "You can't dictate who I see."

"As long as you work for me, I can. But no longer.

Now, you are free to see whomever you like. For all the good it may do you. Go pack your things now, or we'll throw everything you own into the fire."

"Please, Madame, he is not investigating you or your business. It isn't you he wants. It's me."

A razor-blade smile cut across her face. "Is that what he told you? You stupid girl. You are more naïve than I thought. A constable is interested in only one thing, my pet. He doesn't care about justice. He cares about power. Once a man wields authority, there is nothing more he craves. Even sex no longer arouses him as much as acquiring more dominance. Your constable is on the road to political success. Today Chief Constable, tomorrow Magistrate, and from thence into the House of Commons. Your precious hero is only after power, and he will offer you whatever you desire to achieve his aim. And you," she said, sneering, "are so very cheap. He bought your heart with a simple kiss."

TEARS BLURRED HER VISION as Mina packed her belongings in her father's valise. There was a knock on her door before Margot opened it. She leaned her tall, thin frame against the doorjamb, her mahogany tresses tousled by her last client. "You ready?"

Mina pursed her lips. Madame Fynch hadn't had the common courtesy to escort her out herself. She had sent her informer to watch Mina leave.

Mina didn't bother to answer. The sophisticated Margot wore a cynicism that Mina found hard to like. Although Margot could declare a connection to the aristocracy, she was nonetheless jealous of the commonly born Lollie. Though Margot herself was lovely, her willowy form was nothing at all like Lollie's voluptuous one, and she had lost several clients to Lollie's full breasts and rounded hips. It had set Margot irretrievably against Lollie—and therefore against Mina.

Mina wiped the wetness from her face. With renewed dignity, she picked up her valise and strode stiffly to the door. "You can tell Madame Fynch for me that I . . ." Mina struggled for the right stinging words to leave behind. "That nothing had better happen to Lollie out there, or she'll have to answer to me."

Margot chuckled at Mina's threat, but silently walked Mina out to the front door. Margot had the final word when she slammed the door shut behind Mina, and it sounded like a cannon blast in the night.

Mina stood on the front steps for some time, wondering where to go. A chill wind blasted her from the side, nearly taking her mobcap. Shivering, she lifted the collar of her spencer and took her first step out into the unknown.

Her options were limited. She had enough money to let a room for a week or two, but how would she find one at this hour of the night? She could find shelter from the cold at a pub, some of which she knew would be open all night, but she'd have to keep buying drinks to be able to stay inside. Plus, she had no wish to be accosted by drunken men. She just wanted a quiet place to sleep. If only she knew where Lollie had gone, she could join up with her. They could keep each other company.

There was one other option, but she didn't want to

explore it. Salter. If only she could be sure that he really loved her. But it didn't add up . . . what would someone like him see in someone like her? He could never understand how precarious her sentiments were. She could withstand it if a man humiliated her. But not Salter. Anyone but him.

She leaned into the gathering wind. It was pushing her in the opposite direction—toward Salter's flat, she couldn't help noticing. Where was she headed anyway? Why couldn't she shore up with Salter, just for one night? It was the only way she'd be certain of his affections. The more she climbed against the bluster, the stronger the wind seemed to become. Although she was in no mood to test him tonight, Salter's home was the only sensible place to go.

She made her way to Salter's street. Mrs. Tilbury, who lived on the ground floor, would be the first to awaken to her knocking. Mina would make the necessary apologies. But when she walked up the steps to the front door, Mina realized there'd be no need. The door was ajar.

"Hello?"

There was no answer. She stepped into the foyer, and called up the flight of steps. "Salter? Can I come in?"

A thunderous sound came from the upper floor, like an army marching through the house, and Mina instinctively hid in the dark recess under the stairs. Four large men, kerchiefs concealing their faces, came running down the stairs. They disappeared out of the front door, leaving Mina breathless with astonishment.

Her frantic thoughts flew to Mrs. Tilbury. If those

ruffians had broken into her place, they wouldn't need to lay a finger on her to harm her. The frail old woman's heart could scarcely take the fright. She tried Mrs. Tilbury's door, but it was locked. Puzzled, she crept up the stairs toward Salter's flat.

His door was wide open. She walked inside, and blood drained from her face. The entire flat was vandalized. The settee was overturned and knifed through, the tables were upended, and every object was thrown to the floor. Even the rug was flipped upside down. The only light came from the pale moonbeams streaming in through the window and from an overturned candle on the floor whose flame had set fire to the carpet. Mina quickly stamped it out with her foot.

"Salter?"

There was no answer. She looked around the room but didn't see him. She crept to the bedroom, and found it also in disorder. It was as if a giant had shaken the entire building and set it back on its foundation upside down.

"Salter?"

Again no answer, and Mina was never happier to know he wasn't around. Those men were looking for something, and she knew precisely what it was. But she had no way of knowing whether the ruffians had found the gems or not. She walked back into the parlor, sidestepping the toppled chairs, and planted her foot on the overturned carpet.

But instead of flattening against the floor, the carpet stayed put, as if there were something underneath it. Mina was so surprised, she tripped over the wooden kitchen chair and landed squarely on her rump. From this angle, she saw it . . . a still hand sticking out from beneath the rug.

Her own hand flew to her mouth to prevent herself from screaming. But when the initial horror passed, she grasped the rug and flung it away.

Her beloved wasn't moving.

Chapter Thirteen

She knelt by his side. "Salter!" she cried. No movement.

His body lay facedown, and Mina couldn't tell if he was breathing. "Salter!" she screamed again. Still nothing.

With a strength she didn't know she possessed, she heaved on his heavy, motionless torso. His body flipped over, and he made an unconscious grunt.

Awash in relief, she checked him for injuries. The dim light from the window cast a pale glow on his body, but it was enough to see that the four men had beaten him mercilessly. There was a gash across his eyebrow that was oozing dark blood, a small cut above his nose, a large discoloration on his cheek, and his bottom lip had begun to swell. But there were no knife or gunshot wounds.

His eyebrows drew together as he drifted into consciousness. "Minnnn . . ."

"I'm here, love. I'm right here."

He struggled to speak. "Go . . ."

"The men are gone. We're both safe now."

Just as she spoke those words, she heard a sound at the door and froze. A violent protective instinct snaked up from her belly. She seized a brass candlestick, and her arms filled with coiled strength. She'd never thought herself capable of killing, until now.

The door creaked open, and Mina braced herself behind the upended settee. A small female figure stood in silhouette in the doorway.

Mina relaxed, both her fear and strength draining away. "Mrs. Tilbury!"

"Who is it?" the old woman cried, her nervous voice cracking as she strained her eyes in the dark.

"It is I, Mina. Mr. Lambrick is hurt badly. We're here behind the settee."

Mrs. Tilbury picked the candle off the carpet and reached for tinder in the pocket of her apron. "Oh, my dear. It was awful! Those men crept in through the front door. They went directly up the stairs and pushed their way into Mr. Lambrick's room. I heard them yelling and they began to fight. Oh!"

Mrs. Tilbury lifted her hand to her mouth as, lit candle in hand, she finally got a look at Salter.

"Oh, my goodness! The poor thing! What've they done to him?"

"He needs help, Mrs. Tilbury. Fetch a surgeon."

"O-of course. Mr. Havelock, he's two doors down." Mrs. Tilbury flew out of the room, more spry than Mina had given her credit for.

Quickly, Mina placed a pillow under Salter's head. She cursed herself for taking so long to get here. If she hadn't let pride and doubt confuse her steps, she would have come to Salter's flat straightaway. She would have been here in time to interrupt those ruffians' plans, or at least join forces with Salter against them. She loosened his cravat and his waistcoat to let him breathe better.

Salter drifted out of consciousness again, and Mina's heart skipped a beat. She watched his chest as it rose and fell. Gradually, her heart returned to a steady rhythm.

It seemed an eternity before the surgeon arrived. Mr. Havelock was a man in his fifties, short but trim. His hair was tousled—evidence he had been awakened from slumber—but he was alert and concerned. With just a cursory nod at Mina, he knelt beside Salter's prostrate body and looked him over thoroughly.

Mina surrounded the doctor with candles, as many as she could find. While he looked Salter over, Mina righted the settee. "Could we move him here, so he could be more comfortable?"

The doctor frowned. "He has no broken bones, but his ribs are badly bruised. If we move him, there will be pain, but I expect it would be better to move him now that he's unconscious than when he's awake enough to feel it. Is there a man around that can help me?"

"I'm strong enough."

Mr. Havelock glanced at Mina's servant's clothes and nodded. "You take his legs, and I'll lift his torso. On the count of three."

The two of them hoisted Salter onto the settee. He groaned insensibly, but never woke up.

"Right," said Mr. Havelock, panting from the exertion. "We'll need to clean his wounds. Boil us some water and fetch fresh linens. We'll need at least five yards."

Mina turned to the older woman. "Mrs. Tilbury, would you?"

"Young lady," said the doctor, "I asked you to go. I have to remove this man's shirt."

"Then remove it. This is no time for proprieties."

"But—"

"I'm not leaving his side again." The doctor met her stubborn gaze, then shrugged.

"Very well, then. Mrs. Tilbury?"

"Yes, sir," she said, and left to do his bidding.

The doctor removed Salter's shirt, and Mina saw the bashing his body had taken. As the doctor had said, there was a large red swath across his midsection—just over the spot where she herself had hit him with a plank—where they could see his ribs had been pummeled repeatedly. There were the beginnings of bruises on his shoulders and forearms. Tomorrow, his beautiful body would look ghastly. If he made it to tomorrow.

"Is he going to live?" Mina asked tremulously, afraid of hearing the wrong answer.

"He'll live. But he'll wish he was dead." The doctor made quick work of bandaging Salter's ribs. He went about it with such relaxed practice that Mina surmised it was not the first time Salter had needed his services. While Mr. Havelock worked, Mina stole a few minutes with Mrs. Tilbury.

"I don't know what to do," she said, her arms crossed pensively. "I can't leave him here. What if those men come back?"

"Oh, don't say that! Do you think they might?"

"It's a distinct possibility. I must remove Salter to safety. But where can we go?"

The woman raised a bony finger. "Mr. Lambrick knows a family in Norwood. His father was a stable man to Lord Bennett Saltyre. Mr. Lambrick remains a good friend of the family. They'll receive him there. Take him to Pemberton Manor."

"Yes," Mina said slowly. "That will do nicely. Pack some things. We'll spend a few days in the country."

"Heavens, no. I need to stay. Someone needs to clean this mess up."

"Leave it. I'm not sure if those blackguards have found what they were looking for. And if they haven't, they'll be back."

Mrs. Tilbury pursed her lips. "I know for certain that they haven't found what they were looking for. Mr. Lambrick gave them to me for safekeeping."

Mina's eyes widened. "You have the jewels?"

She nodded, then lowered her voice to a whisper. "They're in my flour canister."

Mina shoved the errant tendrils that had escaped her mobcap behind her ears. "All the more reason why you must go. They'll come looking in your rooms next."

"Heaven forbid! I don't mind telling you that it's been no end of worry knowing they're there. I think about those baubles all the time, fretting that I might lose them, or forget them, or . . . cook them! I could go to my sister's in Surrey for a few days, but I don't want to take those things with me. I should like to give them back to Mr. Lambrick so that he can hide them at Pemberton Manor."

A voice from the couch drew their attention. "Ouch! Damn you!"

Mina flew to Salter's side. "You're awake! How are you? How do you feel?"

"I'd feel a lot better if this damned sawbones would leave me in peace."

Mr. Havelock pushed his hands away. "Lambrick, stay still, or I shall tie you up!"

"Enough of this nonsense. Let me up from here." Salter tried to rise. He winced, the pain driving him back down.

"There, you see? You pigheaded fool. You've been badly hurt. Lie back until your body recovers."

Salter grimaced from the simple act of breathing.

"Who did this to you?" Mina asked.

"I didn't see their faces," Salter managed. "But when I get my hands on them, I'll make them wish they had never seen mine."

"You're not getting your hands on anyone right now," Mina scolded. "First you must get back your strength. What happened?"

Salter inhaled sharply as he ran his hand gingerly along the gash at his brow. "They completely surprised me. I must have dozed off in my chair by the fire. I never heard them come until the floorboards creaked as they crept into the bedroom. I woke up then, and that's when one of them seized my neck from behind. Another drove his fist into my gut. He got off one punch before I kicked him in the face. The one behind me, he had bony arms. He loosened his grip long enough for me to stand. But the remaining two came at me at once. They took turns swinging at me." Unconsciously, his tongue darted repeatedly to the cut on his lip.

"Oh, the miserable cowards!" exclaimed Mina. "Four against one!"

Salter smiled wanly. "Well, I don't think sportsmanship was foremost in their minds. In fact, neither was it in mine. I suspect the tall one will be unable to sire any more children after tonight."

"Ah! That must be the one I heard cry out!" applauded Mrs. Tilbury.

"I fought them off for a while, but one of them picked something up and hit me across the face with it. I fell to the floor. The last thing I remember is them kicking me."

Unable to resist, Mina ran her hand across his hair. "You might have been killed."

The dimple in his bruised cheek deepened. "Would you have missed me?"

"Not in the least," she said, though her words carried no credibility.

Mr. Havelock started to pack his instruments and bottles into his case. "What you need now is a few days of rest. Your cuts and bruises should heal in no time, but it will take a few weeks for your bones to mend fully."

"I haven't got a few weeks. The first thing I'm going to do is reinforce that damned lock on the front door."

Now Mina was the one who pushed him down. "You're doing nothing of the kind. Now sit back and do as the doctor tells you."

While Mrs. Tilbury gave Salter a sip of wine, Mina pulled the doctor to one side and told him her plans to relocate him to the country. The doctor understood her alarm, but cautioned her that it would be too painful a journey for him to make at this time. "The jarring motion of the carriage will be agony for him. The only way he'd make it there is if I gave him a sleeping draught."

"That sounds like a good idea. But do you think we

could do it without telling him? I'm afraid he wouldn't
take kindly to being treated like an invalid."

The doctor chuckled. "Him? He'd strap on the har-
ness and pull the carriage, just to prove us wrong." The
doctor handed her a small vial. "Here's the draught. Mix
it into a glass of brandy and he'll never suspect a thing.
It'll make him sleep for a good six or seven hours."

"That's more than enough time. Thank you, Mr.
Havelock."

The doctor wished him a speedy recovery and left.
Mina sent Mrs. Tilbury downstairs to bring up the
gems, then sat facing Salter on a chair next to the settee.

She shook her head. "I don't know what to say. You
were so incredibly—" She struggled for the right word.

"Brave?" he offered.

"Stupid! Have you any idea what might have happened? They could have killed you."

"You haven't much faith in me."

"Of course I do, but four against one . . . You should
have handed over the jewels from the start. They're not
worth your life."

Salter grinned mischievously. "You've changed your
tune. As I recall, you once tried to do me in for those
colored rocks."

Mina blushed, and smiled in spite of her worry.
"You know what I mean."

Salter shook his head. "Those bastards had no intention of leaving me alive. Had they found the jewels, or
had I turned them over as you suggest, you and I would
not be having this conversation right now. And Bensonhurst would have set those dogs on you next. I
could never let that happen."

"Bensonhurst? You think he hired those men?"

"No doubt. He's trying to get the stones back to protect himself. Given all you know, I've no doubt you are going to be his next target. And I'm not going to let him take even a step in your direction."

A curious elation welled up within her. He wanted to protect her. But just as quickly, she heard the insidious voice of doubt. *He's a constable. He's sworn to protect everyone.* Shaking her head, she ignored it. If he went through all of this to protect her, she must do the same for him.

She rose and went to the sideboard, where Salter kept a bottle of brandy upon a shelf. "It's late. Let's get you a nice drink of brandy to settle you down for the night." Surreptitiously, she poured in the sleeping powder from the vial Mr. Havelock gave her.

"No, thank you. I can't settle down just yet. I've got to wedge something against the door, in case they decide to come back to finish the job." He made a move to rise, and groaned when he found he could not do so unaided.

"You mustn't move yet."

"Minnow, I must secure this house."

"Very well, but first have the brandy. It will give you the burst of strength you need to get up."

Salter rolled his eyes as he took the cup. "Well, make up your mind. Is it going to make me leap off the couch or ease me into a nice slumber?"

"Both. Either."

Salter downed the glass and exhaled loudly. "Right. Now help me get up."

"Not yet. You must rest a bit first."

"Mina, stop bossing me around like a damned hospital ward nurse. Give me your hand so I can stand."

Mina put both hands on his bare chest. "I said no! Now you stay there until I say."

Salter looked at her incredulously. "Or what?"

"Or else I shall sit upon you. And stop blustering as if you can stop me. You're in no position to defend yourself against me."

"Stop you? Minnow, I *encourage* you. If you want to sit upon me, I have just the place that is sure to make us both more comfortable."

Mina blushed, but put on an angry demeanor. "Just like a man. Sitting back, letting a woman do all the work. If you want to indulge in illicit passions with me, then you're going to have to do it when you're strong enough to show me what you're made of. I'll worry about the front door, and I will look after Mrs. Tilbury. For now, sit back and remain quiet."

He raised up bruised hands. "Yes, ma'am. Now I see why the word 'domination' has your name in it." Although he sat in reproved silence watching her right the overturned furniture, his knowing smile showed he was amused by her assumption of superiority. "May I have leave to speak?"

She sighed, annoyance evident in her voice. "Yes?"

"Would my mistress deign to do her wretched servant a small service, for which he shall be eternally grateful?"

She pursed her lips. "What is it?"

"Fetch my pistol from the bedroom."

Mina saw no harm in giving him that measure of

comfort. "Very well. But only if you promise to remain very quiet and very still the rest of the night."

Mina brought him the entire holster. She watched him as he borrowed the light of a candle to check the barrel, then assured himself he had enough ammunition, gunpowder, and wadding for more shots. Meanwhile, Mr. Havelock's sleeping draught began to take effect. Salter's yawns became deeper and more frequent.

Finally, he dozed off altogether. Mina went to his bedroom and threw some of his clothes in the traveling case she found above his wardrobe. She grabbed his blanket, which was wedged under the upturned mattress on the floor, and went back to the parlor. Downstairs, Mrs. Tilbury already had her bags in the entrance hall.

"Here, my dear," she said, handing her the small pouch, now dusted with flour. "Take these jewels. They've brought nothing but trouble to this home, and I hope to the Good Lord never again to see them."

Mina dropped them in the pocket of her apron, silently agreeing. "Wait for me here. I'm going to get us a carriage."

A dense fog had settled upon the city. Salter's street was still and quiet, undisturbed by traffic. In the distance, Mina heard the sound of people talking. Rubbing her arms to ward off the cold, she walked two blocks down to the square. There she saw vendors setting up their stalls, their practiced commotion dispelling the fog so that it merely hovered above them. Tomorrow was market day, and the street had begun to line with people laying out tables with fruits, vegetables, flowers, and spices. As she walked down the middle of the square, the smell of baked bread and meat pies rose from one of the stalls. Two stalls down, a woman shoved complaining chickens back into a wooden crate. A fishmonger was arranging the morning's catch on his table, its aroma stinging her nose. No one paid her any mind because customers weren't expected until daylight broke.

Her eyes scanned the square. She was looking for a carriage she could hire to take Salter to Norwood. There was a phaeton parked along the edge of the street, but she could hardly expect to prop up a sleeping, injured man in the cramped cab. Mrs. Tilbury could use it, though, so she sent the cab to Salter's home. Finally, her gaze landed upon a vegetable cart.

A burly man with a thick mustache that wound to the middle of his round cheeks was unloading cabbages from the bed of the cart onto a wooden stall in the market square.

"Excuse me," she said.

"Evenin'. What can I do for you?"

"I wonder if I may hire your conveyance."

"What for?"

Not wanting to reveal too much, she said, "I need to take my friend home to Pemberton Manor in Norwood. He got drunk and stupidly picked a fight with a man much bigger, and now he's out cold. Can you help me?"

"Norwood, eh? That's a bit out of my way, miss. I've got orders to fill."

"I'll pay you five shillings."

He cocked his head. "Make it ten."

Mina scoffed. "You're daft. It's a vegetable cart, not the Royal State Coach. Six. Half now, half when we get there."

"Done. Hop on."

They drove to Salter's home. Jasper moved the vegetables to one side, and Mina laid a thick quilt on the cart bed. Salter was sound asleep when they got to the room, and Mina reluctantly woke him up. Jasper helped him to stand, and, draping one arm over his own shoulder, walked Salter down the stairs and onto the back of the cart. Mina brushed off his drugged questions, and threw a blanket over him. Finally, she threw their bags onto the cart. Once Mrs. Tilbury had left on the phaeton, Mina hopped on the seat of the cart and they drove away.

Though relieved to finally be leaving London, Mina knew better. They were not free from danger. An enemy left unvanquished is merely catastrophe postponed.

Chapter Fourteen

Dawn had crept upon them, illuminating their way to Norwood. Salter slept soundly the entire journey, which took about an hour and a half. Mina was not quite so fortunate. Her adventurous but sleepless night had left her feeling shredded. Pemberton Manor seemed like heaven when it finally loomed over the horizon.

Though the house was large, the façade was rather plain. Its most exceptional feature was the surrounding lands, which stretched miles in each direction. They had passed orchards of apples and pears, farms growing all sorts of vegetables, and meadows full of sheep and cattle.

She asked Jasper to drive them round to the servants' entrance, for she knew they'd be up at this early hour. She knocked briskly on the door, and a bewildered butler opened the door.

"Good morning. My name is Mina Halliday. I'm a friend of Mr. Salter Lambrick. He's been injured. May we come in?"

The butler, Forbish, immediately sent two footmen to gently move Salter to a guest room. Mina explained exactly what had happened—how he had surprised a gang of roughs that had come to burgle his home, but omitting any mention of jewels. The footmen and the maids efficiently and quickly dressed and warmed his room, for which Mina was grateful. They tsked over Salter's battered condition, their concern for him evident in the way they made sure he had every comfort.

As the maids disappeared from the room one by one, Mina observed Salter's sleeping form lying comfortably in the bed. Bathed in relief that he was finally safe, she felt the strain of her mind finally uncoiling, leaving her debilitated and unable to think.

"You all right, miss?"

Mina stared glassily at the young maid who had spoken. "I'm fine," she answered automatically.

"You look as if you're about to topple over. We should get you to a bed. You can sleep with Harriet. The other side of her bed is empty."

The girl's words weren't registering. It took great mental effort to follow the maid's logic. Mina realized that she was still wearing her barmaid's dress, giving the appearance she was Salter's servant, so the maid was therefore sending her to sleep in the servants' quarters. "No, thank you. I must look after Mr. Lambrick."

"We'll look after him," she said gently. "You get some rest."

"No, I won't leave his side. Just let me nap here, in this chair. I'll be right as rain in no time."

The maid regarded her uncertainly. "Very well, miss. I'll get you a blanket."

The sun grew brighter behind the curtains. Salter did not stir, and all was quiet in the room. Mina sat down in the plush upholstered chair, a welcome respite from the rickety sway of the wooden vegetable cart, and within seconds, fell fast asleep.

⌒Voices. They were saying things she didn't understand. She was going to ignore them and focus on another dream.

But the voices were real. Someone was in the room.

Instinctively, she bolted from the chair, foggy from sleep but braced to protect Salter. Her impulsive action startled an older couple at the foot of Salter's bed, and they recoiled from her aggressive stance.

Her addled mind finally allowed her to register that they were the lord and lady of the house. "I do beg your pardon. I thought you were . . . someone else."

The lady's hand slid from her chest. "Who are you?"

Mina rubbed her face weakly. "My name is Wilhemina Halliday. I'm a friend of Mr. Lambrick's. He was hurt."

The gentleman was robust and handsome, with gray hair at his temples. "Forbish told us that he had been beaten and that you found him and rendered him aid. Is this true?"

"That's right. I was told he could find sanctuary here, to give him a chance to recuperate. I hope that's all right?"

"Of course it is, my dear. Salter is the son of one of my most loyal retainers. We will be happy to tend to him here."

"Thank you. I'm so relieved. I didn't know what else to do."

"You did the right thing," Lady Saltyre said, her

elegant face radiating sympathy. "Darling, perhaps we should send for a doctor. He's still unconscious."

"He's not unconscious," Mina supplied. "He's asleep. The doctor who saw him in London gave him a sleeping draught. That's how I was able to bring him here without him feeling any pain."

Lord Saltyre chuckled. "That explains it. He had to be drugged for him to come visit us." His wife nodded.

Mina felt awkward, as if she had somehow gotten Salter into trouble. "His bones aren't broken," she offered, "but his ribs are bruised. Movement will be difficult. Breathing is a labor for him too."

"The poor thing," said Lady Saltyre, the fine creases in her forehead deepening. Despite her years, she was a singularly lovely woman. Her high cheekbones and languid eyes gave her an air of gentle nobility. That, coupled with her graceful shoulders and perfect posture, made Lady Saltyre appear as if she were posing for a painting.

"Did they catch the blackguards who did this to him?" asked Lord Saltyre.

Mina shook her head. "Salter doesn't know who they are."

"Hmm. Well, whoever they are, they knew what they were doing. Having disabled a chief constable, they've effectively crippled the force. I'd like to send some of my men over there to search for the scoundrels who did this."

Lady Saltyre placed a hand on her husband's arm. "Let's give him a chance to recover before we go off willy-nilly in search of his attackers. In the meantime, my dear," she said, turning to Mina, "why don't you get some rest? I'm certain Forbish can find you a more suitable place to sleep. Celeste can come and look after him for a while."

"No, thank you," she said, uncertain about having an overworked housemaid see to his needs. "I'd like to be here when he wakes up."

"As you wish," she said with a dreamy smile.

After they both left, Mina was grateful that she had found a hospitable place for Salter to heal. Lord and Lady Saltyre seemed like generous and considerate people, even if they were a trifle aloof. It was to be expected, she thought. Salter was, after all, only the son of a servant.

Mina sat gingerly on the bed and stared down at Salter. He was such a beautiful man. Never mind the discoloration on his cheek, the swelling at his brow and lip, and the dried blood that had crusted around the cuts in his skin. He was kind and chivalrous, proven when he helped her nurse the broken wings of her confidence after Underwood's careless insult. He was principled and noble, because he wouldn't let a killer go unpunished. He had an electric intelligence, with piercing eyes that saw too much. He was brave and strong, fighting off four brutal attackers. He was intensely alluring, a boy's playful charm with a man's rugged face. He was sexy and daring, a great lion of a man in complete control of his splendid body.

And to think that he liked *her*. His attentions made her feel so good about herself, it was impossible to imagine her world without him. She ran her fingers lightly along his broad hands and battered knuckles. These hands had made real her fantasies of erotic touch—and of the simple affection of one soul for another.

She made herself a vow then and there. She would become the woman he deserved, no matter what it took. If he loved her, she would make sure that she became the woman he seemed to be able to glimpse inside her.

The door opened, and a young woman gusted in. She wore the same elegant beauty as the lady of the house, only hers was younger and fresher. Her hair was immaculately arranged, with silky strawberry-blond curls framing her luminous face. She wore a charming morning dress of pale yellow with tiny white flowers embroidered along the hems, a satin ribbon of white cinching the high, narrow waist.

"What are you doing?"

Mina was surprised by the question. She wasn't doing anything except sitting by Salter's side. She looked down and noticed that she had been caressing his hand as it lay limply in her lap. "Nothing."

"I would very much appreciate it if you would do 'nothing' over there," she said with pique, pointing to the chair.

Not wanting to cause trouble with her hosts, Mina went over to the upholstered chair and sat down.

"Thank you." The beautiful woman glided to Salter's bedside and stared down at him. A look of revulsion came over her lovely features. "He looks as if he's been run over by a herd of horses."

Mina nodded wistfully. "On balance, I'd rather that he would have been. Those men beat him mercilessly."

The young woman grunted, as if she had just gotten a whiff of something foul. "Is he all right?"

"He's in a great deal of pain, though he won't admit to it. It will take him a while to heal completely."

"When will his face return to normal?"

"His face?"

"Yes, his face. I can't bear to look at him like that. He's ghastly. Did the doctor say when he'd look himself again?"

Mina was astonished. She didn't like to look at him either, but only because she couldn't abide the fact that he was hurt. "Eventually, I expect."

The lady's look of distaste deepened. "Can't you clean him up or something?"

Mina grew indignant. "He isn't painted like that. Bruises don't wash off, you know."

"Govern your tongue, girl!" she said imperiously. "Who are you, anyway?"

Her lofty attitude didn't scare Mina. "My name is Mina. And I'm his friend. Who are you?"

"What impertinence! I am Lady Celeste. Salter's fiancée."

Fiancée. The word was like a punch to Mina's gut, leaving her bewildered and gasping. No offensive name, no derogatory comment—nothing at all—could wound her more than that one.

"His . . . fian—" She couldn't bring herself to repeat it. Saying it out loud would deepen the gash in her heart. "Salter never told me he was engaged to be married."

Celeste snorted prettily. "Apparently, you're not that close of a friend."

Apparently not. Suddenly, Mina felt the consummate fool. How eagerly she had played into his hands. The Madame had been right. Salter had bought her heart with a single kiss. It was the only price she asked, because it was the only thing she treasured. But to him, it was worth no more than a small coin one would toss to a beggar. His real riches were stored here. With another woman.

Mina was shattered, but she couldn't let Celeste see her disillusionment. "I expect you never came up. In fact," she added for effect, "I don't believe I ever mentioned my own fiancé to him. Perhaps now that he's laid up, we'll get round to it. Excuse me, won't you? Now that you're here, I think I'm going to get some fresh air."

Mina walked out before her eyes started to blur with tears.

༺SWIMMING IN MOLASSES.

That's what it felt like. He tried to climb his way out of the syrupy sleep, but his body wasn't responding.

Blurry voices penetrated his consciousness. Familiar yet confounding, as if he recognized the sounds but couldn't connect them to a face.

". . . set those down on the bed. If I have to be here, I might as well get something accomplished."

His mind grew increasingly alert, but his body wasn't coming alive. He would call out, if only his mouth would open. There was a slight pressure against his legs.

"Four yards of this one. This one's too dark, it'd look like I was in mourning. This one matches the shoes perfectly but those squiggles all over it are ghastly."

Inside his head, connections were being forged. It was as if his mind were a broken jigsaw puzzle, and now it was slowly being reassembled.

"He's waking up. Quick, get all this out of here."

He moaned, and he heard the sound. He felt himself ascending into reality. His eyes blinked open, and he beheld a stunningly beautiful face.

"Celeste?" he murmured.

"Yes, my love?"

"What are you . . . what are you doing here in London?" He glanced beyond her and his eyes scanned the room. "Wait . . . where am I?"

"You're here at Pemberton Manor. We're looking after you, dearest."

Some pieces still didn't fit together. "When . . . how did I get here?"

"No matter. You're safe now."

There were too many questions screaming for his attention. He inhaled deeply, and pain exploded in his body. He ground his teeth, remembering the events that had put him in this position. It hadn't been a nightmare after all.

With much difficulty, he pushed himself up to a sitting position. Each bruise made itself known, acquainting him with a vivid reminder of every blow. The morning after a fight was always the worst.

"Where's Mina?"

"Who?" Celeste asked.

"Mina," he repeated. There was no other way to describe her.

Celeste's full lips contracted. "I don't know."

Gingerly, he peeled off the blanket. "I have to go find her."

"No, you mustn't move. You must mean that servant girl. Don't worry, she's here in the house somewhere. Where on earth did you dig her up?"

He breathed a sigh of relief. She was safe. But his physical exertions brought to the fore another pressing need.

"Celeste, hand me the chamber pot."

Her green eyes grew round as saucers. "Good heavens! Let me ring for a servant."

He groaned. "There isn't time. Just hand it to me, will you?"

"Dearest, I couldn't possibly touch that. Wait here. I'll run and get a footman for you." Celeste ran out the door, leaving him in agony.

Not wanting to disgrace himself, he slid off the bed, landing on the floor on all fours. The pain in his side was excruciating, but he had to get to the chamber pot under the bed before it was too late. Though his arms and hands were sore, he tore at the buttons on his trousers with lightning speed. He emptied himself into the chamber pot, and his body flooded with relief.

From his dog's-eye perspective, he looked around the room. He had never been inside the guest rooms at the manor before. His mother had been a lady's maid for her ladyship before she married his father, who was back then a groom in his lordship's stable. After they had children, his mother devoted herself to the care of her family, and to the keeping of their cottage on the edge of the estate. But Salter himself had never been allowed inside the manor. That is, until Celeste had taken an interest in him.

Celeste. The pain worsened as he tried to climb back onto the bed. She was a beauty, much like her gracious mother. Celeste's beauty was widely celebrated throughout the town, and everyone called him the luckiest man on earth when she had set her cap for him. It was an honor, to be sure, to have her trail him around the paddock as he helped his father tend to the horses. The lord and lady were none too pleased about it. In fact, her persistent crush upon him nearly cost his father his job. But her parents soon realized that she was chasing a servant only to goad them. Celeste rebelled against the idea of an "excellent match" with wealthy but unattractive gentlemen, all of whom came to court her when she came of age. Salter had once pitied her for that beauty of hers, as it drew men to her like flies to honey, and she often tired of brushing them away. But when she chose to, she could use that beauty as a weapon or as an inducement to getting her way, and that's what disenchanted Salter.

Celeste had never truly loved him. But she wanted him in the same way a spoiled child cries for the shiny red toy it sees. He was the one man she bedded who didn't pant after her, and that made her fixate upon him all the more. When he married Veronica, Celeste was inconsolable. She became recalcitrant, refusing every man's suit. Her parents became alarmed as she grew older, stubbornly choosing spinsterhood over marriage.

It was not for want of good offers. Although she would enjoy the pleasures of the marriage bed with any handsome man she liked, she refused to give her heart, or her hand, to anyone. Now, her parents wanted Celeste—thirty, unmarried, and shamefully promiscuous—to be wed to anyone, nobleman or no. And apparently, the only one she would have was Salter. Her parents asked him to propose.

Their arguments were compelling. It was true that he was her first crush. It was true that she liked him still. It was true that he would stand to inherit their entire fortune as the husband of their only daughter. But he was not inclined to enter into a marriage with another faithless woman. He had recovered from Veronica's death, but not from her betrayal. When Lord and Lady Saltyre realized that he was not going to accept, no matter what they offered, they brought out the trump card: his father.

Thomas Lambrick had served the family for forty years, and had become an expert horse trainer and breeder. He remained in the Saltyre family employ until his arthritic hands and back no longer let him work. Rather than turn him out, Lord and Lady Saltyre had allowed him to live in the cottage gratis, and provided for his care and maintenance, including a hired nurse who tended to his needs. They reminded Salter, ever so subtly, of their generosity toward his ailing father, and made him see that Salter was beholden to them for their kindness. If they had assumed the care of one of his relatives, they said, he should do as much for them.

That was almost a year ago. Celeste remained at the

manor to make arrangements for the wedding, and Salter returned to London and his post as chief constable.

His eyes alighted on the luggage in the corner. One of the cases was his own valise. The other one he recognized as Mina's.

Mina.

Like Celeste, Mina was a woman of contradictions. But she was as different from Celeste as anyone could be. She believed herself plain, though she was far from it. Not with those expressive eyes that revealed every emotion. She mistook men's disregard to be a result of her own lack of beauty, but that was not the case. It wasn't ugliness keeping Mina alone. It was fear. The way she worked so hard to hide what was extraordinary about her. She was so busy yearning to be *like* other women that she was missing out on the glory of being *above* other women.

She was promiscuous, too, but only in her own mind. She was such a fascinating paradox . . . a woman so knowledgeable about sex and lovemaking, but completely inexperienced at it, like knowing the recipe for creating an elaborate dish but never having set foot inside a kitchen. This combination of innocence and intelligence magnetized him to her. He couldn't help wondering what it would be like when she finally crossed the divide into experience. What a splendid lover she would make.

To another man, he thought, irritated by the painful stab of jealousy. He rubbed his face to wipe it away, and he was given a painful reminder of the beating he took. Those bruises would go away, he thought. But the ones he wore inside would not. He felt those bruises every time he thought of Celeste. And being here in this room made the sensations all the more vivid. With great difficulty, he pulled on his boots, and without his coat, left the room in search of Mina.

Salter hobbled through the halls of Pemberton Manor, stopping every servant to ask about her. They either didn't know who she was or where she was. Reining in his frustration, he paused to use a technique he'd picked up working on the constabulary force. He had caught many criminals by simply putting himself in their place, and by extrapolating from what he knew about their character and habits, he was able to determine what their logical course of action would be. So, if he were Mina, where would he go?

Alone. She would find a way to be alone.

Outside. There were too many people inside the house.

The morning room had a door that led to the gardens in the rear. He stepped out onto the expansive terrace and headed toward the stone steps at the far end that led out onto a knot garden. He didn't see her there amid the intricate greenery of the boxwood shrubs, but the garden was edged on all four sides by a covered walkway canopied with ivy. He determined which side was cast in the darkest shadow, and limped toward it.

There, on a bench, was Mina, her hands folded in front of her as she looked out at the horizon.

"You poisoned me," he said.

Mina turned her head in surprise.

"That brandy you gave me last night rendered me insensible. Laudanum?"

"I don't know. Mr. Havelock gave it to me. You should be in bed."

He hobbled over to the bench and sat down next to her. "You can't stop bossing me around, can you? If you want me in bed, come in there with me."

His playful jibe didn't elicit the response he expected. She lowered her head.

"Ah. You must have met Celeste."

Her name on his lips made Mina flinch. Slowly, she lifted her gaze to meet his. "You're engaged."

"Yes." There was nothing more to say.

They sat in an awkward silence.

"Congratulations."

He heaved a profound sigh. "I wish you hadn't brought me here, Mina. I wish my circumstances were different. I wish—"

"Mr. Havelock also gave me this medicine for you," she said, pulling a bottle out of the pocket of her dress.

"Mina—"

"He says I'm to put this on you as soon as you waken." She pulled a strip of fabric out of her pocket.

"Mina, stop. I'm trying to tell you something."

"Don't worry. It's not another sleeping draught. An American colleague of his brought it over to England. It's called witch hazel, and he says it's excellent for healing cuts and bruises." She leaned over and dabbed some of it on the dark patch on his jaw.

Salter sighed, regarding her thoughtfully. "This feels strange."

Mina stopped. "Does it sting?"

"No, I mean this. You ministering to me in this place." He regarded her as she dabbed the liquid onto his face. She never met his eyes. "It's nice having you for my second."

His second. That's all she was to him. A knot of angry tears tightened in her throat. "Well, try not to get yourself involved in another brawl. I don't know if I would be so disposed again after the way you deceived me."

"I never deceived you."

"Oh, no? Did I or did I not ask you if it would be a colossal mistake on my part to fall in love with you? Why didn't you tell me about Celeste then? I'll tell you why. Because you just wanted my help to solve your precious murder case. It was my own fault for believing you. You got what you wanted. You won't be needing me any longer."

"Mina, don't say that. I do need you."

"Ha! Like a lion needs his lunch." She made a move to rise, but he yanked her back down on the bench.

The extent of his strength took her by surprise. He gripped her arms in both hands, drawing her face close to his.

"I don't want this marriage to Celeste. I never have. But I have an obligation to her family, and it must be fulfilled. And I will not let you accuse me of taking advantage of you. I never intended to hurt you."

Angry tears stung her eyes. "You led me to believe . . . I thought that you—"

"I'm sorry you had to find out this way. I do care for you very deeply."

The tepid answer made her cringe. "Oh, you men

are all alike! It doesn't matter to you, I suppose, how many women you say that to. The more females you have trailing behind you, the better. Well, I'll not be one of your admirers. I'll leave that to your gorgeous Celeste." She tried to wrench herself free, but he held her fast.

"Minnow, she's not the one I find gorgeous . . ." His hand released her arm and caressed her face, sending invisible sparks skipping across her chest.

"Stop that," she said, her breathing quickening.

"Why?"

The truthful answer came out before she had a chance to alter it. "Because I like it."

Salter smiled. He dipped his head and let their lips unite. She resisted, but the surprising softness of the kiss quelled her reaction. Her hands splayed across his open shirt, trying to push him away. Instead, her fingers brushed the warm skin taut over the hard muscle of his chest. Black sandpaper surrounded his lips, and though it scratched her own soft ones, it reminded her how deliciously masculine he was. His hold on her arms softened to an embrace, which tightened around her.

Stop, came an unbidden voice. *What are you doing? He's going to marry Celeste and forget he even knew you. Is this how you want to be treated?*

"No!" she cried, pushing him away.

Confusion clouded his face. "What's wrong?"

"This. All of it. Let me go." She tried to untangle herself from his grasp, but he had firmly latched on to her.

"Mina, wait. I want to tell you that I l—"

"I said, leave me alone!" Deliberately, she dug into his ribs where she knew he was most tender. It was all she needed to do. He clutched his side, a grimace twisting his features. He released his hold on her, and she slithered out of his embrace and stomped out of the garden and ran back into the house.

Sobs tore at Mina's throat. When she reached the door of the room she had been given, she finally gave over to the tears that demanded release. She cried for over an hour, and when she was thoroughly wrung out, she collapsed into a deep sleep.

*MANY HOURS LATER, A maid came to the door of her bedroom. As Salter's rescuer, Mina was being invited by Lady Saltyre to join them for dinner. At first, she was tempted to decline. She had no wish to see Salter—or Celeste, for that matter—and she had nothing presentable to wear. But she regretted her moment of weakness in the garden earlier, and she wanted an opportunity to show Salter, and herself, that she was over him. She requested a bath.

As the hall clock chimed six, Mina descended the stairs in her only evening dress, a coral-colored frock her father had given her when she turned twenty. She had sold her other clothes a long time ago to pay her rent after her father was arrested, but she couldn't bear to part with this dress.

Lord and Lady Saltyre were already chatting in the library when the butler ushered her in.

"Miss Halliday! How refreshed you look," said Lord Saltyre jovially. "Please come and have a drink with us. I trust you were able to rest after last night's ordeal."

"Yes. Thank you for your hospitality."

"Nonsense, child," said Lady Saltyre, smiling as she

patted the seat next to her. "Come and sit down beside me. I've been simply aching to know the details of what happened last night."

Mina started to answer, but Forbish opened the door. "Miss Celeste, milady."

Celeste breezed in wearing the most enchanting confection. The neckline was square cut, which accentuated the gentle slope of her breasts above it. The white bodice was embroidered with shiny thread, like a silver vine blossoming from the silver-colored ribbon at the high waist. But the real stunner was the unusual fabric overskirt. Mina had never seen a fabric like this one, a shimmery gossamer layer that whispered over the white silk skirt like rays of moonlight.

"Hello, Mama. Father. And . . . Mina, was it? Will you be dining with us too?"

"Yes. Her ladyship was kind enough to ask me."

"How thoughtful, Mama. Now Mina can entertain us."

It was a polite jab, but Mina overlooked it in favor of another question that became uppermost in her mind. "If you're here," she asked, "who is minding Salter?"

"I conscripted Owens to valet him. There was only so much I could do. How would it seem for a unmarried woman to nurse a single gentleman?"

"Seem? I hardly think you need to concern yourself with appearances here in your very own house. Salter needs help."

"I need nothing of the kind," Salter said, as he walked in. "Stop trying to turn me into a bloody invalid."

Mina was astonished. Though his left brow was still swollen and there was a violet splotch on his left cheek, he seemed quite himself again. In fact, his face had taken on a much harder and more lethal edge. And those clothes . . . she was sure she hadn't packed anything that looked like that.

Lord Saltyre stood up. "I say! What a grand surprise. How do you feel?"

"I'll pull through." He glared at Mina. "With greater speed if some people would keep their hands to themselves."

Mina felt her cheeks color, but she mirrored his steely gaze. "I'm entirely inclined to agree with you."

"Celeste, ring for Forbish. Tell him to set another place at table. How about a smash of port, my boy?"

"Splendid. Thanks."

Lady Saltyre smiled placidly. "I'm certainly happy to see you about, Mr. Lambrick. In spite of your injuries, I must say you're looking quite the picture."

Celeste sat upon the arm of the chair next to Salter. "Doesn't he, Mama? I bought these clothes for him as a wedding present, but I daresay he needed something decent to wear right away. Doesn't he look dashing?"

Mina had to admit that he did. Navy blue superfine and a snowy cravat, with a cream-colored silk waistcoat, and skintight buckskin breeches. He looked like a wealthy nobleman, very much like he did the first time she laid eyes on him.

"The suit suits you, Mr. Lambrick." Everyone chuckled at her ladyship's play on words. Everyone except Mina. The sight of Salter and Celeste in such proximity was difficult to bear.

"Do you really like it, dearest?" said Celeste.

"It's excellent, Celeste. I can't lie."

"Ha!" Mina exclaimed. "That's a new failing in you." She gave him a pointed look and he shot back a warning glare.

"Well, tell us what happened," said Lord Saltyre, holding out a glass. "Those thugs that came upon you, what were they after?"

"It's difficult to say," Salter replied, measuring his words. "Nothing was stolen, though they left behind a monumental mess. I am certain, however, that it was no random act of violence. They knew precisely whom they were attacking."

"Oh, my!" said Lady Saltyre. "Do you mean to tell us that these four men had singled you out especially?"

"Yes, I do."

"To what end?"

"That I can't say," he said in all honesty.

"Set upon by four men all at once. Weren't you afraid they were going to kill you?"

"I have no doubt that it was their intention."

"That's dreadful. How did you manage to stop them?"

"I didn't. Mina did."

All eyes turned to her.

"Her arrival at the flat must have startled them," Salter continued, "and they took off."

Celeste straightened. "What an astonishing effect you have on men, Mina. They take one look at you and bolt."

Lady Saltyre swung a blistering gaze at her. "Celeste! That was very rude."

Celeste's face became blank. "I'm sure I didn't mean to be."

Lord Saltyre gave a beleaguered sigh. "Miss Mina, it appears that we have you to thank for saving our future son-in-law's life."

"Well, my lord," Mina said with a shrug, "we all make mistakes."

Lord Saltyre glanced at his wife. It seemed there were unspoken conversations taking place among the three younger people in the room. "Well, my boy, despite Mina's intervention, from the look of your knuckles it seems as if they didn't escape unscathed."

Unconsciously, Salter squeezed his hand into a fist, but released it as soon as he felt pain. "I got a few of my own in."

Forbish opened the double doors. "With your permission, milord. Dinner is served."

Oh, no. The procession into dinner. Two couples and her, a leftover carriage wheel.

"Allow me," said Lord Saltyre, and held out his arm for her. Lady Saltyre took the other one, and all three of them strode to the dining room together. Mina felt conspicuously single, but at least she wasn't alone.

He held out Lady Saltyre's chair, and then held out hers before taking his place at the head of the table. Salter seated Celeste adjacent to her father, and then sat next to her. Directly opposite Mina.

"So, Mina," Celeste began, "when is your wedding?"

"Wedding?" Salter's brows knit together. "What wedding?"

"Oh, I'm sorry, Mina," she said innocently. "I spoiled your surprise. You see, dearest, when we met, Mina began to tell me about her fiancé."

"Did she?" he said, in stark amusement.

Mina wished she could hide her colored face in her napkin.

"I hadn't heard that happy news," he said. "Who's the fortunate fellow?"

She began to study her soup. "You don't know him. Someone I met."

"Clearly. It seems I'm not the only one with failings around here. What's his name?"

She glowered at him. He knew that she knew it was a lie, and he was deriving to a great deal of satisfaction in exposing her. She wished she could slap that broad smile right off his face. "Roderick."

He chuckled. "Roderick? Not Roderick Prescott, the Lord Mayor's aide? I hate to be the one to tell you, Mina, but he's dead."

"No, not Roderick Prescott, the Lord Mayor's aide."

"That's a relief. I would have hated to see you a widow before you became a bride."

Mina spoke through clenched teeth. "Let's hope for your sake Celeste doesn't come to that very end."

Salter laughed, and despite her irritation, it pleased her he did so. He became so very handsome when he smiled.

"Shameful what happened to Prescott," Lord Saltyre said as he carved the large baron of beef. "I wonder if Lord Bensonhurst will make any sort of tribute to Prescott at the Easter Banquet tomorrow night."

Celeste turned to Salter. "It's such great fun. Each year, the Lord Mayor holds a fête for the diplomatic corps. Papa goes because he's an envoy to India. Since you're here, you can come as my escort. You will accompany me, won't you, dearest?"

Salter looked with regret at Mina. "Of course I shall."

Lord Saltyre cleared his throat. "As I was saying, Prescott and I weren't terribly close friends, but we all felt his loss. Has anything turned up on the blackguard who murdered him?"

"Although I'm not at liberty to discuss the details of the case, sir, I can tell you that we are very close to apprehending the criminal."

"Bravo. I knew you'd put your best men on the case. Prescott was a good fellow, and he deserves to have justice."

"Ha!" Mina exclaimed, indignant over the wrongs her own father was suffering at Prescott's hand.

Lord Saltyre set down his fork. "I beg your pardon?"

"Oh, I'm sorry," Mina said innocently. "Did I say that out loud?"

Lord Saltyre frowned. "Don't tell me you wish to give an opinion to the contrary?"

"As a matter of fact, I do. I happen to know a thing or two about Lord Prescott that may just scandalize you."

"What Mina means," growled Salter, the warning in his tone unmistakable, "is that Lord Prescott may have had certain bad habits, such as gambling to excess, which of course points to a weakness in character. But who among us has no bad habits?"

"What I mean," Mina said, her eyes sparring with Salter's, "is that this man for whom you cry justice is a reprobate and a pervert, a man who likes to whip women into subservience."

Salter glared at Mina. "At this moment, I know precisely why."

She ignored him. "And that was just the least of his so-called bad habits."

"My dear girl," said Lord Saltyre, "it is quite shameful to speak ill of the deceased."

"You'll have to forgive her," Salter jumped in. "She doesn't seem to understand that what a man does behind closed doors is entirely his own business. Mina is extremely priggish about things of that nature."

Her mouth dropped open. "Priggish?"

"Yes, priggish."

"Well, I'd rather be a prig than a pig."

Celeste clutched Salter's hand. "Dearest, how can you stand for this sort of talk from your own servant?"

"I've told you, I'm not his servant."

"Then what could he possibly want with you?"

"Nothing." Her anger batted away the heartache of that answer. "And I want nothing to do with him."

Salter looked at her like a bull about to charge. "Mina, stop acting childishly."

"Childishly! First priggish and now childish. Are these the kind of words one would apply to a person in my profession?"

"Mina . . ." Salter warned.

"Profession?" Lord Saltyre asked. "What profession is that?"

"I work, Lord Saltyre, at the Pleasure Emporium."

Lady Saltyre looked at her husband in confusion. "The what?"

"It's a bordello, my dear," he said somberly.

Celeste snickered. "Do you mean to say that *you* are some sort of courtesan? What man would pay for someone like you?"

"Celeste!" Lady Saltyre cried.

"Would you really like to know how many men want me?"

Celeste made no answer, but her blond eyebrow arched in inquiry.

"All of them." Mina watched Celeste's vanity being shaken, and her eyes narrowed with wicked glee. "I present an invitation that no man can refuse. It was I who lured Salter there. He, and many others, came at *my* summons. I write men letters detailing precisely what they could expect when they step through the doors of the Pleasure Emporium. I give men fantasies. And when they come to our door, it's *me* they want. When I call, Celeste, no one turns the other way."

If Mina had reached out and slapped Celeste, she could not have looked more affronted.

"I see," huffed Lord Saltyre. "You're nothing more than a Siren. Leading a man to his destruction."

Mina smiled at that. It made her feel powerful and alluring. "That's right. Take care I don't call upon you next."

"That's enough!" Salter bellowed, rising from his chair. "My lord, I apologize for Mina's behavior. She's not like this usually, and I can't imagine what's gotten into her. My lady, Celeste, our presence here tonight has scandalized you, and for that, I'm sorry. We will trouble you no more tonight." Salter came round the table and pulled Mina's chair out, with her in it, making her squeal involuntarily. He grabbed her by the elbow, and with a strength that surprised her, jerked her out of the chair.

"Take your hands off me, you brutish ass!"

"One more dirty word and I'll put the branks on you."

"I'll keel over dead before I let you touch me again."

"Good. I'll make that your epitaph."

Salter dragged her all the way up the stairs to her room, and then slammed the door shut behind them.

"What the bloody hell was that about? You insulted everyone sitting at that table, including yourself."

"Don't you reprimand me. You haven't the right. There are no rings on *my* fingers."

"I doubt you'd obey me even if there were. I can't think of a reason why you would offend our hosts in such a sordid manner."

"Hardly priggish behavior, wouldn't you say?"

"Is that what this is all about? Because I called you a prig?"

"No. It's because you called me anything at all. How dare you fling demeaning names at me! I'm no Celeste, it's true, but I won't be put upon by anyone. Least of all by you."

"I know you're not Celeste. I thank God for it."

"What?"

Salter rubbed his forehead. "That's not what I meant. Look, I know Celeste was goading you. I know she was being petty and vindictive. But is that any reason to offend her entire family?"

"I wouldn't have done if you had said one word to defend me."

Salter sighed. "You're right. I shouldn't have let her say those things to you. But I didn't think you'd give her any credence. Mina, don't you know it isn't important what people call you? It only matters what you answer to."

He brushed his thumb against her face, and Mina's anger diminished. His face was so close, his lips so tantalizingly near. It was the ultimate unfairness that such a man could belong to someone like Celeste.

She let him touch her face, relishing the feel of his fingers. She breathed in that scent of him she liked so much, woodsy and masculine, embellished by his shaving soap. He caressed one arm, and she delighted in the pleasurable sensation climbing her body. He brought his lips to a spot just behind her ear, and a soft moan escaped her lips.

He isn't yours. And you're not his. Roughly, she pushed him away.

"You can stop all your lovemaking. You're not getting the jewels back."

His thick brows drew together in puzzlement. "What's gotten into you?"

She didn't know, but it made her stronger and she liked it. "I'm not your little moonstruck calf anymore. I know what you're all about. You want to use me to get what you want. Well, I'll not be your pawn. You're not even a constable anymore. You've no authority over me. From now on, I do things my own way. I don't need you. And I don't want you. So just go."

"No. Not until we—"

"Go!" she bellowed, startling even herself.

Slowly, he backed away from her. He looked so wounded that it nearly broke her heart. She was nasty to him, and some part of her wished she could take it back. But to do that would mean that she would have to go back to being the lovesick spinster, and she wasn't about to let herself do that. His gaze lingered on her a moment longer before he turned away and walked out the door.

Chapter Fifteen

Salter wiped his bleary eyes and sat up in bed. The restless night had left his head aching. He swung his feet to the floor, hunching over his knees, and gave in to the idea that there would not be any more sleep.

He rubbed the sandpapery beard that had thickened overnight, and noticed the bruise on his cheek wasn't as sore as it was yesterday. Yesterday's pain had become today's soreness. He had always been blessed with a quickly healing body, which had come in handy on the battlefield and on the force. But now, there was a new pain to contend with, one he suspected would not heal at all.

He deserved it. He had let Mina fall in love with him, and he shouldn't have. He knew that she was especially vulnerable. At first, he had used that weakness to his advantage. But the more he came to know her, the more he began to see her inner strength, the unbreaking resilience that kept her proud and independent. He hadn't counted on being drawn in by it. And he never imagined she would use it to rise up against him.

He looked back on each day since he met her. There were so many things he should have done differently. Starting with his very first kiss. She had finally fallen asleep after they spent the whole night talking. She looked so beautiful there on the pillow. She always had that look about her, like she was waiting for something. Even when she talked, there were always unspoken questions in her eyes. It had pleased him to think he was the answer to those questions. He couldn't resist. He bent over and placed a soft kiss on her cheek.

As a man who dealt in hard evidence and cold reality, he was not given to fancies. But in the moment of that innocent kiss, something happened to him, something he couldn't explain. He had turned it over many times in his mind, the sense of connection that gave him renewed hope.

Grunting, he propelled himself off the bed. It was time he put Mina out of his mind. She'd already done as much for him. He dressed and went down to breakfast.

Celeste and her father were already there, deep in conversation. When he stepped through the doors of the dining room, the conversation deadened to silence.

"Good morning."

The family mumbled a response.

He went to the sideboard and served himself some coffee and sat down.

"Won't you help yourself to some eggs and sausages, Lambrick?"

"No, thank you, Lord Saltyre. I'm not especially hungry this morning. Please enjoy your breakfast. Our behavior last night surely must have put you off your supper."

Lord Saltyre dabbed at his mouth. "I must say, Lambrick, that your friend Mina left an indelible impression on my wife and daughter. Is it true what she said about you being a patron of that establishment?"

Salter heaved a sigh. "Yes, sir. I was a client."

Celeste pressed her lips together. "You mean to tell me that she really did lure you to her?"

Salter thought back to the letter she wrote to Lord Prescott. "It was all part of a case I was on, but I must confess, yes."

"I see," she said. "Was it business or pleasure?"

"Celeste—" It was Lord Saltyre's exhausted plea to change the subject.

"I want to know," she insisted petulantly.

Salter sighed. "It was business . . . and pleasure."

Lord Salter put his hands in the air. "I don't think there's a need for him to elaborate, Celeste. I think, as mature adults, we can all surmise what their relationship has comprised. Though I must say, Lambrick, that I never had reason to question your character until now. Dalliances with a scarlet woman have never done a man any good."

"She's not a scarlet woman, sir. A bit pink, perhaps, but only in the thinking, not in the doing." At Lord Saltyre's questioning look, Salter decided to change the subject. "With your permission, I'd like to borrow a conveyance to drive down to London. I'd like to take Mina back right after breakfast. There's some business I need to see to."

"And pleasure," jabbed Celeste.

He couldn't deny the truth of Celeste's words. As angry as Mina made him, there was never a time when he didn't feel pleasure at being around her. The realization made it all the more painful when he stared across the table at Celeste.

"I'd better see what's keeping Mina."

"Dearest, let her be. Some servant probably took her a tray. I must say I credit her with tactfulness for remaining upstairs after last night's debacle."

"Nevertheless, I'd like to be off to London without delay, and she should pack her things with haste. Excuse me, I'll be back in just a moment."

As he stepped outside the dining room, he felt immediate relief. He took the stairs two at a time and knocked on her door.

There was no answer.

"Mina, it's me, Salter. Open the door."

Still no answer.

"Mina? I'm coming in." He turned the knob.

The door flew back all the way, and so did the curtains over the open window. Her bed had not been slept in, and her clothes were gone. He went to the window and looked down. The little monkey had jumped onto a nearby branch and shimmied down the tree to escape from the second-story bedroom.

He cursed colorfully.

IT WAS ABOUT EIGHT o'clock in the morning when Mina finally made it to the Pleasure Emporium. The streets of Whitechapel were buzzing with activity, but all was quiet behind the door of the bordello.

Mina crept round the back to the kitchen door. It was often left unlocked by someone making a trip to the outhouse in the middle of the night. She tried the door, and the knob turned.

The main rooms were deserted. She wended her way up the stairs, down the hall, and stopped in front of one of the bedrooms. With the stealth of a burglar, she slowly turned the knob and crept inside.

"Serafina," she whispered softly. "Serafina."

The Spanish beauty looked even more ethereal in sleep. In the darkened room, her milky complexion glowed against the contrast of her raven's-wing hair and finely arched brows. Serafina stirred, fluttered open her eyes, and sat up in surprise.

"Mina! What are you doing here? Where have you been?"

"It's a long story. I'll tell you some other time. I don't want Madame Fynch to discover me here. Have you had any word from Lollie?"

She wiped the sleep from her dark eyes. "She sent you a letter. The Madame opened it and threw it into the fire."

"Oh, no. Now I'll never know where she went."

"No, no," she emphasized. "I know where she ces. She went to live with her constable man."

"Yes, but where does *he* live?"

"In Stepney. Twenty-four Walden Lane."

Mina was so relieved she embraced Serafina. "You've no idea how good that news sounds to me. I was afraid I'd never see her again."

"Oh, Mina. We were all so worried about you. Madame wouldn't say why you'd been dismissed. First Lollie and then you. We had no idea what had happened to either of you. Where did you go?"

After all Mina had been through, she needed a friend now more than ever. Someone who could navigate her through the sinister, overgrown trails and back into the clear light of day. She told Serafina everything that had happened since she set eyes on Salter Lambrick. It felt so wonderful to be able to unburden herself of all her heartache and troubles. If there was one thing that Serafina and Mina had in common, it was the private way they carried around their exquisite sadness.

When Mina had finished, Serafina grasped her hands. "Mina, it ees a pity you had to fall in love with thees man. But it ees the same for all of us. When a quill ees very kind, very handsome, and he treats us well, it feels like he ees romancing us, and so he ees. It ees easy to fall in love with such a man. We want to believe in hees devotion, because we crave it so much. But this kind of love . . . ees only temporary. An illusion meant only to enhance the act of passion. The heart-love goes the moment he ees finished. He may still feel tenderness for us, but it eesn't the same thing. You cannot expect *amor verdadero*—true love—from caresses and kisses."

Tears of self-pity pooled in Mina's eyes. "But how can we know when a man has this for us? How can we tell the difference between true love and temporary love?"

Her beautiful face became serious and serene at the same time, like a goddess about to impart wisdom. "True love does not just come from the heart. It comes from the head. It ees a decision . . . a resolve to be with thees person whether the time ees right or not, whether the sex ees there or not, if the road will be easy or not. He would risk everything he has—even hees own life—if it would mean your happiness and security.

Such love is not easy to discover among men. And it cannot be sought or demanded, only received."

Salter didn't have true love for her. She could see that now.

The ache in her heart was screaming, but she silenced it. There was something she had to accomplish, and it required all her wits. Later, she would give her pain its voice. For now, a mission lay before her.

"Serafina," Mina began, "I have a favor to ask of you."

"Of course," she answered. "What ees it?"

Mina thought carefully before she put her dangerous plan into words, thus making it real. "I want you to turn me into you."

"What?"

"Just for tonight. I need to become a courtesan, a beautiful one. Not a painted-up one, like before. I need to be as resplendent as you can make me." If Serafina could make a beauty out of her, she would bring the rest—the heart and the balls of a lady of the evening. "Can you transform me into Aphrodite?"

"Whatever for?"

"Because," she said, steeling her heart for war, "I need to get my father back."

Chapter Sixteen

Salter reined in his horse in front of the Pleasure Emporium. He slid off the beast and landed on both his feet. He marched up the steps to the door, and turned the knob. The bloody thing was locked even though it was already three in the afternoon.

Time to change that. Salter knocked on the door, but there was no answer. Then he pounded on it.

Voices buzzed inside. The Madame came to the door and threw it open.

"We are closed at present . . . to the public, that is. To you, we are always closed. Good day."

She tried to close it, but Salter stopped it with his powerful forearm. "Correction. You are never closed to the constabulary. Stand aside." He didn't wait for her to move before stepping over the threshold.

The other ladies were in the parlor. Some were still in their sleeping gowns. He addressed them all at once.

"I'm here for Mina. Where is she?"

The ladies looked at one another, then over at Madame Fynch.

"She's not here," offered Charlotte.

"Where is she?"

Charlotte looked nervously at the Madame.

"She's no longer in my employ," Madame Fynch responded, her hands clasped at her waist. "I dismissed her two days ago."

"Why?"

"For entertaining men I didn't approve of."

Salter's heart skipped a beat. "Who?"

The Madame looked him squarely in the eye. "You."

His fingers curled but he stifled the urge to seize the woman. "Tell me where she is!"

"You persist. I told you, she's not here. I haven't seen her since the day I terminated her."

"Fine. Since you won't get her for me, I'll find her myself."

He pushed his way past Madame Fynch to the rear of the salon. The rest of the girls opened a path for him as he stomped toward the stairwell leading up to the bedrooms.

Affronted, the Madame chased after him like an angry goose. "Evie! Fetch the constabulary!"

"But Madame, he's already here!"

Salter barged through the upstairs corridor like a loosed bull. He flung open every door, shouting Mina's name. The women flocked behind him.

He went up to the third floor, where Mina's bedroom was. He tried the door. It was locked.

He banged on the door. "Mina, open the door."

There was no answer. He hammered louder. "Mina! Open up this instant!"

He waited for an answer, but none was forthcoming.

"All right, then. You asked for this." He lifted his leg into the air and kicked the door. It made a loud noise, and he heard a yelp. The door, however, didn't budge. He took better aim, and, cocking his leg, drove it onto a spot nearest the doorknob. The door flew back on its hinges, and a woman shrieked inside. Salter barely got a chance to see her face as she scurried out screaming, but it was clear that the plump middle-aged woman was not Mina.

"Who was that?" he asked.

"The new barmaid." Evie bit her lip as the woman continued to scream down the stairs. "That is, the former barmaid."

"Evie, be quiet," snapped the Madame. "Mr. Lambrick," she drawled, "perhaps you'll believe me now. As I told you —repeatedly—Mina is not here. And if she ever did set foot inside this establishment, I would have her thrown out as a trespasser. Are you satisfied?"

No, he wasn't. His heart plunged deep in his chest as he realized he had no idea where Mina was. She was not at his flat, she was not here. He had to tell her that he was sorry, that Celeste was not his choice of wife. Even though he could not marry Mina, he wanted to assure her that no one on earth was more beautiful to him than she was. On the inside, on the outside. The totality of her was altogether lovely to him. Above all, he wanted her to know that.

"Now, if you would be so kind as to remove yourself from this establishment. After you've paid for the damages to my house, that is."

He looked around the room. Her secret cache of erotic books was not in that drawer, her father's painting was not on that wall, her blue paper and ink were not on that table. The room was painfully familiar, and yet without her, it was absent of heart.

He turned to the gaggle of women at the door. Someone must know where she was.

"Wait. There are only ten of you here. Where's the other one?"

The girls looked around at each other. "Serafina," they concluded.

"You." He jabbed his finger in Charlotte's direction. "Go bring Serafina to me."

Charlotte's dress fluttered as she dashed off to do as he ordered.

Salter made his way through the throng of women, ignoring the Madame's angry tirade at him for ordering her girls around. He went downstairs to return to the salon, but just as he made it to the second floor, Charlotte came rushing back.

"She's gone," she told Salter, holding out a sealed letter.

The Madame snatched it away, tore it open, and read it. "I'll kill her."

"Let me see that," said Salter, reading the note. It said she'd gone to see an old friend and would return before the house opened for business.

"No one leaves my house without permission. She knows that. I shall terminate her at once."

"Madame, no," cried Charlotte. "Serafina has never disobeyed you. She must have had a very good reason to go."

The Madame would not listen, but Salter did. And he strongly suspected Mina had had something to do with why Serafina was gone. But he still didn't know what it was, or where they had gone.

He had to find them.

LOLLIE HANDED MINA A cup of hot tea. "Cor, it's good to see you again," she said for the third time.

Lollie was dressed in a pretty frock of pale blue muslin. With her blond curls in a bonnie coif, she looked a girl of fifteen. Only her generous bosom gave away her true age of twenty-four.

Mina took the tea and looked around. It was a humble flat, but a clean one, and Mina began to recognize Lollie's decorative touches. Her favorite pink satin ribbon was tied around a settee pillow and her Indian silk shawl was draped along a hall table.

"Where's your constable friend?" Serafina asked Lollie.

"He's at work, in't he?"

"At work?" Mina asked. "One would think he would stay at home, what with a beautiful courtesan here who's madly in love with him."

"Ees he a good lover?"

Lollie made a slight shrug. "I wouldn't know. We haven't done it yet. He treats me real good and we have a grand time together. It's funny . . . I guess I'm not used to bein' treated like a real lady."

Mina smiled. "You were right, Loll. He really *is* a prince."

They talked until the tea in the pot grew cold. Finally, Mina glanced at the clock. "It's getting late, Serafina. Help me get dressed."

"You still mean to do thees?"

"Do what?" asked Lollie.

Mina hesitated, considering once more the danger of what she was about to do.

"Go on, tell her," Serafina insisted.

She lifted her head. "I'm going to get my father back by bringing down the man who had him imprisoned."

"You know who he is?" asked Lollie.

She nodded. "Alexander Bensonhurst. Lord Mayor of London."

"You're joking. You're going up against one of the most powerful men in England? What can you do to a man like Bensonhurst?"

"I can hit him where he would hurt the most."

"His balls?"

Mina pursed her lips. "His reputation. If he doesn't have my father released, I'm going to humiliate him in such a way that he would never recover." Mina explained her plan to bring about Bensonhurst's downfall.

Lollie laughed mirthlessly. "A kick in the crotch would get you further. Mina, you can't seriously think he would be afraid of someone like you. A man like Bensonhurst don't get to his position in life without knowing how to deal with his enemies."

"Like he dealt with my father?"

"Exactly. That should show you what he is capable of. And if you're not careful, he'll dispose of you too."

"He's not going to get away with what he did to my father. I won't let him."

Lollie sighed. "What does Salter say about all of this?"

Mina looked away. "He doesn't know. He would try to stop me."

"Too bloody right! It's a barmy idea."

"I have to do it. Salter can do nothing legally. By fair means or foul, it falls to me to get justice."

"Didn't Salter promise you he would see to it? Why can't you trust the man you love?"

"Because he isn't mine to love. He never was. Clearly, I was in love all by myself. I was feeding my heart on airy nothings."

"Mina, thees doesn't sound right. If you truly love heem—"

"Enough," Mina interrupted. "I don't want to hear any more of your observations. And I definitely don't want to talk about Salter. Just do me up, nice and proper like you promised. I'll deal with the grief later." Tonight, Mina's mind was set on a different man altogether.

⌒IN JUST OVER AN hour, Mina was dressed for the Lord Mayor's Easter Banquet.

Serafina had taken Mina's straight, lifeless hair and clasped it tightly into a bun at the back of her head as the Spanish ladies do. Serafina then inserted crimson feathers directly into Mina's hair, forming a scandalous coif. The pull of her hair backward slanted Mina's eyes, giving her face an exotic, catlike quality. Then Serafina took some Moorish blacking and lined the edges of Mina's lids. The effect made Mina's dark eyes look smoky and powerfully seductive. The powder she dabbed on Mina's face was not at all like the alabaster one Lollie, Charlotte, and Evie had put on her; this one illuminated her natural skin tone. And the lip rouge that she dabbed on Mina's lips was not the rose-red the ladies had put on her when she went out with Salter, but a subtle soft pink. The cosmetics gave her an air of sophistication and flair.

As she looked at herself in the mirror, Wilhemina Halliday marveled at her appearance. She did not look like a streetwalker, as she realized she must have done when she was sent to meet with Salter. Now she looked like a lady of quality. She looked exotic, alluring, dangerous . . . everything she had wanted to be all of her life, but especially tonight when she encountered Lord Bensonhurst. The woman looking back from the glass was not Mina. Tonight, she was Willa.

In a flash of recollection, she remembered how the steward at White's took notice of her when she pushed her way into his world, upsetting the order of things. Well, it was time to upset the order of things yet again.

Willa would most definitely be noticed tonight.

Chapter Seventeen

Salter shoved his right foot into the gleaming new Hessian boots. He winced as the stiff leather squeezed his arch unmercifully.

Just his luck. It seemed he was under pressure from all sides. Why should his footwear be any different?

The truth was, Salter was one giant knot. Every time he thought about Lord Bensonhurst, his jaw clenched. After thirteen years in the constabulary, Salter had the measure of criminals now. And Lord Bensonhurst was among the worst kind, both intelligent and powerful. He was a player on the world political stage, a man who dined with kings and potentates. He had authority over much and command over many. And while his influence and power might insulate him from detection and capture, Salter suspected they might also be his Achilles' heel.

He straightened in front of the mirror, now cracked by the thugs that had ransacked his flat, and took a look at himself. Though it was tight around the shoulders and arms, he found he could still fit into the coat. But it brought back painful memories he'd rather not remember. The last time he had worn this coat, Veronica came down the aisle and he put a ring on her finger.

He shrugged the memories off. It did no good to dwell on the past.

Not that his future looked any less bleak. When he
thought of Celeste, he got that sickening feeling of knowing precisely what the future held. Like the days when, as
a boy, he'd come home and the cottage smelled of cooking liver. He knew at that moment that the evening would
be miserable, because his mother would not let him up
from the table until he had finished his plate.

Mina wouldn't make him miserable.

The thought came unbidden and unwanted. She was
so warm and tenderhearted. Each facet of her character
sparkled in the light of his gaze. The more he thought
about her, the graver his demeanor grew. Mad with
worry, he had spent the entire afternoon looking for
her, and he hadn't a clue where she'd gone. But he was
certain that she would go after Bensonhurst, so he had
to get to the man before she did.

Tonight, he would bring Alexander Bensonhurst to
justice for the murder of Roderick Prescott. And he had
to be at Mansion House in time to surprise the Lord
Mayor with the evidence of his crime.

&A LINE OF CARRIAGES paraded in front of Mansion
House as the social and political elite poured into the
swelling residence. More than four hundred guests
would soon fill the Lord Mayor's receiving rooms,
where the champagne flowed as smoothly as the conversation that changed the course of nations.

Salter walked up the steps behind Lord and Lady
Saltyre, with Celeste hanging on his arm. Once atop the
portico, they waited patiently as the guests ahead of
them made their way through the receiving line.

"Isn't this exciting?" bubbled Celeste.

"Thrilling," he responded stoically, his eyes focused on the man poised at the head of the receiving line. Bensonhurst had on his public face—smiling eyes, a charming *bon mot* on his lips, and a ready laugh. It was this face Salter had grown leery of, the one that hid his true nature from the public eye.

"Lord and Lady Saltyre, milord," announced the steward.

"Bennett, Elizabeth!" Lord Bensonhurst said, gripping Lord Saltyre by the hand. "So glad you could come. I see India's sunny climate has quite overpowered you, Bennett."

"Quite," he responded. "Elizabeth's always reprimanding me for returning from overseas as brown as a nut. What is it you're always telling me?"

Lady Saltyre smiled. "Only that you may blend in among the locals in Calcutta, but here in London, people are likely to confuse you for the dustman."

Bensonhurst gave a robust laugh.

"Alexander, you remember my daughter, Celeste. And this is her fiancé, Salter Lambrick."

His gaze swung over to Salter's, and the smile disappeared from his face. "Lambrick."

"Do you two know each other?"

"Yes, we've met," said Salter.

"Of course," Lord Saltyre responded. "You're investigating the death of Alexander's aide."

"I was," he replied as he shook Bensonhurst's hand. "But I think I have my man now." Salter gave it a vicious squeeze.

"All the more reason to celebrate, eh, Alexander?" said Lord Saltyre.

Bensonhurst's pallor now matched the hue of his cream-colored waistcoat. "So it would seem. Let us discuss your findings over a glass of champagne, Lambrick."

"I look forward to it, Bensonhurst."

Salter relished the look on the man's face. He left him to welcome his remaining guests in a distinctly less jovial mood.

The four of them proceeded into the lofty receiving room, where they accepted drinks from liveried servants. While Lord and Lady Saltyre renewed their acquaintance with the ambassador to Italy, Salter took a look around. Mansion House was different from when he had visited it earlier. By night, the sunlit splendor of the Parthenon was replaced by the shimmering dazzle of Mount Olympus. The enormous chandeliers burst with twinkling candles, radiating light into every corner. The gilded capitals above the columns blazed with reflected light. It was a place fitting to entertain statesmen and orators, those who considered themselves human gods.

And that's when he saw her. The goddess.

Standing atop the half-moon-shaped balcony, surveying the sea of humanity below her, was Mina.

He took a step forward, unsure of what his eyes told him. Though it didn't look like Mina, his instincts told him it was her.

He drew closer, staring at her unseen. Her dress appeared to be made of silver, for it reflected in the light of the chandelier, making each contour gleam. It was cut daringly low, allowing her delicate breasts to curve over the décolletage. Her hair was drawn back from her face, and an array of scarlet feathers fanned the back of her head. The face was hers, but not, colored in such a way as to heighten her natural loveliness. Something about her took his breath away. Hers had always been a beauty that shimmered. But now, she dazzled.

And she was here. Safe and sound and beautiful.

He'd kill her.

He put down his champagne flute on a servant's passing salver and stormed out of the hall toward the adjacent room, where a grand staircase led up to the balcony.

When he reached the balcony, he regarded her from behind, and his steps slowed. Something inside him unfurled, and the relief of seeing her again made him breathless.

"Mina."

She spun around, and looked up into his face. Her warm brown eyes blinked back at him.

"Salter! What a disagreeable surprise."

"Disa—" He reined in his temper. "Have you any idea—any idea—what I've been through today?"

"On my account?"

His lips pressed together in irritation. "Why didn't you tell me you were discharged from the Pleasure Emporium?"

She laughed mirthlessly. "Between the two of us, I did not think *I* would be the one accused of harboring secrets."

"How did you get in here? I know you weren't invited."

"Neither, I'll wager, were you."

"Don't play games with me. Why are you here?"

"No doubt, for the same reason as you. To get Bensonhurst."

"Dammit, Mina! I told you this was a constabulary affair. I don't want you involved."

"I've got nothing to do with your constabulary affair. Go on, do your worst to Lord Bensonhurst. Leave me to do mine."

"What are you scheming? Out with it."

She picked up her skirts. "It is none of your concern."

She walked past him but his hand curled around her arm before she could get too far. "Like hell it's not. I warned you before against interfering with my investigations."

"Oh, yes, I remember. You threatened to lock me up. Well, you're not a constable anymore. You have no power over me."

His hand tightened around her arm. "Don't count on that." A servant came by with a tray of shrimp canapés. Salter turned to him. "Would you please have someone fetch Miss Mina a hansom? She is leaving."

"No, *she* is not," Mina bit back.

"Minnow, when I tell you to do something, it's not a conversation. You do as I say."

"And just who do you think you are? You're not my husband. You're not even my betrothed. You're nothing to me. You can go to blazes for all I care."

Like an angry goddess, she turned her back on him and left him to burn in mortal helplessness.

MINA FLEW DOWN THE stairs, weaving through the throng of people. How dare he speak to her like that! He had done nothing but distract her from her mission since the moment she set eyes on him. And here he was again, not to help but to hinder.

She stood against the Greek statue of Athena, and wondered if she herself possessed any wisdom at all. She pressed her burning forehead against the cold marble statue. She had underestimated the force of the blow at seeing him again, and she scrambled to recover both her confidence and her callousness.

She looked up into the crowd and saw Lady Celeste. To her credit, she was as beautiful as any woman could hope to be. Dressed in a white evening gown and royal-blue gloves, with her strawberry-blond hair done up in springy curls, she looked stunning. The man in the British Army uniform, whom she was speaking to, was in thrall to her.

Mina turned away, dejected. What on earth could Mina offer that would even come close to competing with Celeste?

YOU'RE NOTHING TO ME.

The words pummeled Salter, and he found it hard to recover. He had been unprepared for her anger, though he richly deserved it.

A bell sounded, announcing dinner. He wended through the crowd in search of Celeste, in order to escort her into the dining hall, but she was not amid the throng. A few guests were still outside on the portico, so he went to one of the windows along the front wall of Mansion House. It was there he found her, speaking to a man in uniform. Salter recognized him right away— Lord Preston Endicott, an army officer on leave from abroad. And Celeste's former lover.

The portico emptied of guests, leaving only them between the massive columns. Lord Endicott leaned his bronzed face against Celeste's ear, and she smiled. But when he put his hand on her behind, Salter knew.

He was nothing to Celeste either.

❧THE NIGHT SEEMED INTERMINABLE to Salter.

Dinner was a grand affair. Lord Bensonhurst and a few guests were seated at the head table at one end of the long hall, while four long rows of tables stemmed from his like the tines of Neptune's fork. Scores of servants attended to each table, and all seven courses were delicious. Or at least they would have been, had Salter been able to find his appetite.

Nothing had turned out as planned. Chase was supposed to have arrived over an hour ago with a witness who could place Lord Bensonhurst at the scene on the night of Lord Prescott's murder. Celeste had clung to him all evening, showing him off to her friends like a prize bull. And Mina was not supposed to be here.

She was now seated directly opposite him on the next row of tables. He could see her, but not hear her. He watched her gaily laughing at the intimacies the man next to her was sharing, and it kindled the fires of jealousy in him.

Next to him at the table, Celeste was easily the most beautiful woman at the ball. Any man would feel proud to have her on her arm. She was droning on about her plans to honeymoon in Italy, where she said some of her dearest friends lived. He chuckled inwardly. He could read her thoughts as clearly as if she had them printed on her forehead. It didn't take a leap of the imagination to picture her flitting away with one of those oily young Italian charmers, men of ordinary birth and dilapidated villas, who made a competitive sport of bedding English women.

Yet he didn't get jealous over Celeste.

Mina would never give her body or her heart carelessly. Hers was a loftier challenge for a man—to be deserving of her devotion.

He was immersed in thought when Celeste took his arm for the hundredth time that night. "Dearest, why don't you answer me?"

"Hmm?"

She rolled her pretty green eyes. "Greece."

"Greece?"

"I'd like to extend our trip to Greece. I know some people in Corinth and Athens. We could spend a month or two there as well. I'd like to do the entire Mediterranean before coming home."

I bet you would. "Celeste, I think we need to have a talk. Let's go someplace quiet."

Now that the banquet was over, the guests began to stream up the stairs to the hall. "Not now, dearest. The dance is about to start."

"This is important, Celeste."

"Dearest, so is the dance. There are a number of people who simply must see us together."

"There will be no dance."

Celeste's eyes rounded in surprise. "What?"

"I'm not so certain that I am enough to make you happy."

"Whatever do you mean?"

"After Veronica died, I thought the spark we had could

be kindled back into a flame. But I am not the same man you fell in love with. I don't want to marry you, Celeste. I'm sorry."

"You can't cancel our wedding plans now! What will people say about me?"

"Tell them what you like. Tell them that you had second thoughts about marrying a constable. Tell them that I've disappointed you. Tell them that you decided to do as your parents have always wanted and marry a nobleman. That sounds true enough."

Her eyes grew flinty and her nostrils flared. "The truth is that I presumed that you were a good match because you were a superb lover. But you won't be so for long. Pretty soon you'll be forty, and I have no intention of wasting myself on nursing an old man. I'm glad your true feelings come out now, while I still have a chance to find someone younger."

Salter snickered. "At least we enjoyed each other in our prime."

"I can't believe that's all I meant to you. Are you saying I was just your bit of fluff?"

"No. I'm saying that I was yours."

"How dare you speak that way to me! You're nothing but the son of a servant! How dare you think me beneath you?"

"Not me. It's the countless others you're beneath that bothers me."

Celeste gasped, grabbed her reticule, and stormed away. And for the first time, Salter felt free of the oppressive stranglehold his life had become. He would find some other way to repay the Saltyres for their kindness to his father while he was alive. But for now, the first and only person he wanted to tell about his newfound freedom was Mina.

He looked around, but he could no longer find her in the emptying room. He followed the throng to the dance hall. Quadrilles were forming on the floor, allowing Salter to scan the hall for Mina. But she was not in the dance hall either. His instincts started to warn him of danger. He scanned the room again, this time for Lord Bensonhurst, without success.

Dread crawled up his arms.

Chapter Eighteen

"You have got a bloody nerve coming here."

The Lord Mayor of London paced up and down the center of his courtroom. Mina rubbed her sore wrist where he had grabbed her and pulled her into the empty justice chamber. He was taller than Mina remembered, and his florid face contrasted sharply with the white of his hair.

"The choice is yours, Lord Bensonhurst. If you don't want this entire gathering to know that I am your mistress, you will do precisely as I say."

An angry scowl towered over her. "How dare you show up at *my* house to *my* banquet and threaten to spread lies about *me*?"

Mina would not be intimidated today. "Oh, but you and I don't reckon truth the same way, do we, Lord Bensonhurst? You've been known to tell a fib or two in your time, especially about an innocent man you saw to it was punished for a crime he didn't commit. All so you could silence him for a crime that *you* committed!"

"Not this drivel about your felonious father again."

"I know you used your power and influence to convict my father and then send him to prison." She took a step toward him. "And you are going to bring him back again."

"Who do you think you're speaking to? You can't dictate to me what you will have me do."

"Get my father acquitted. Do it, and no one need suspect you of any wrongdoing. Don't do it, and a few well-placed words in a few well-connected ears will leave your saintly reputation in tatters before midnight."

His voice dropped to an ominous whisper. "Miss Halliday, I have absolutely no tolerance for people who try to blackmail me."

Mina quaked inwardly, but she steeled herself. "The choice is yours."

He chuckled hollowly. "Do you honestly think that my life will be ruined because of a supposed dalliance with a courtesan? Half the men out there have mistresses of their own."

"They're not the ones you need to be afraid of. But I doubt Lady Bensonhurst will be as forgiving."

A shadow passed over his enigmatic expression.

Mina took a step toward him. "I know that she is the source of all of your wealth. She's bankrolled your political career. And these friends of yours outside have whispered to me that she's been tightening the purse strings on you for some time. No doubt this is why you stole the tiara in the first place, to have a little capital of your own, free of her control. If she found out you'd been cuckolding her, it would sew those purse strings shut permanently."

Lord Bensonhurst nodded slowly. "I must credit you with cunning, Miss Halliday. Yours is a vicious but promising stratagem. Alas, the answer is no."

Mina looked up into his eyes, silently swearing all

kinds of retribution. "Have a care, Lord Bensonhurst. I'm in no mood for flippancy."

"I don't care for being strong-armed. By you or anyone else. So off with you. Do your worst."

"I want my father back, you son of a bitch!"

With lightning speed, he closed the distance between them, and seized her by the arms. He pushed her backward, and Mina fell painfully onto one of the long wooden benches in the gallery. She hit the back of her head and winced.

"But before you make good on your threat, let's replace lies with the truth." He threw her to the floor, seized her wrists, and pinned them above her head. He pressed his weight on top of her, flattening her painfully to the unyielding wooden floor.

"You want to be my mistress?" he said, his eyes capable of drawing blood. "Now's your chance."

A cold dread smothered her as she realized what he was about to do. With ruthless hands, he lifted her skirt above her hips and ripped at the pantalettes she was wearing. A blind panic seized her, and she screamed. The man clenched his fingers tightly around her throat.

"Make one more sound, and it'll be the last breath you ever take."

She couldn't breathe now, so she froze until he released her throat. His finely lined face became deeply wrinkled as he hovered above her. Finally, his fingers unclenched, and she could take a breath. She felt him trying to unbutton his trousers, and tears sprang to her eyes. What a fool she'd been. Why hadn't she let Salter help her deal with him? Why hadn't she trusted him?

Lord Bensonhurst positioned himself between her thighs, and she shut her eyes against the impending violation.

With a loud grunt, Lord Bensonhurst grimaced and arched his back, but Mina felt no penetration. Then she saw something. Over Lord Bensonhurst's shoulder was Salter's face. He cocked his fist back and drove another blow into Bensonhurst's kidney.

The man scrambled off Mina, and staggered away from Salter. Salter advanced upon him and let his fist fly into Bensonhurst's mouth. Mina rushed to her feet and hid behind Salter.

"Are you hurt?" Salter asked her, concern etched into his face.

Mina shook her head.

His expression transformed into one of sheer rage as it swung back to Lord Bensonhurst. "That's the only reason you're still alive."

"I can't say the same for you," Lord Bensonhurst responded between ragged breaths. "By the time I'm through with you, you'll be hanging from your neck six feet off the ground." He hobbled toward the door.

"The guard you posted won't be any use to you, at least not for another five minutes. He's out cold."

The remark made Lord Bensonhurst slow his steps, but he continued toward the door.

"And if you're going to fetch constabulary help, they're going to hear what I have to say. All of it."

"And just what is that?"

"I know all about your conspiracy with Lord Prescott to defraud the Queen."

"What?"

"You heard me. You accepted a gift on behalf of Her Majesty from the Siamese King, a tiara meant to grace her brow. But you knew the bauble would probably not even be looked at by the Queen, let alone worn by her. So instead of handing it to Queen Charlotte, you turned it over to Lord Prescott so he could purloin the valuable jewels out of it before it was placed unseen into the Queen's coffers."

"What a load of rubbish," he said, blood darkening his lips.

"But what you hadn't counted on was Lord Prescott's own greed. He kept the jewels and ransomed them for more than you two had bargained. And that's when you killed him."

"Lambrick, I'm warning you. Don't even try to blame me. I'll crush you."

"I've no doubt you could. And I've no doubt I will."

"Don't be absurd," he said. "Your own report stated that a prostitute's letter was found in his possession, a letter that you later admitted *she* had written. If anyone appears guilty, it's her."

"It's not about appearances, Bensonhurst. It's about the truth. She didn't kill him. You did."

"You can't prove that."

"Oh, but I can. I have a witness that can place you at the scene of the crime, five minutes after the inquest stated Prescott died."

The sweat began to run down Bensonhurst's face. "Who?"

"The hansom cab driver who picked you up shortly after four in the morning, and deposited you at this very residence."

Lord Bensonhurst laughed again, revealing blood-stained teeth. "Evidence like that has a tremulous relationship to the truth. Take it from me, that'll never hold up in a court of law."

"Not in this one, surely. But I wonder if the Chief Justices will be as blind to the sum total of facts as you are when they also collect into evidence that counterfeit crown and subpoena King Rama's emissary to scrutinize it."

"Don't rattle your sabers at me. Do you honestly think that Their Majesties want the international scandal that this will ignite? There's not going to be any trial for me. You two, on the other hand, are another matter. Assault on a representative of the Crown, slander, prostitution, enticement, trespassing. You'll be lucky to avoid a capital sentence. On the bright side, Miss Halliday, you may get sent to the same penal colony as your father."

Mina looked down. There was once a lonely time when she would have welcomed that opportunity. Now, as she clutched the back of Salter's coat in her balled fists, she could no longer give up the man she held for the father she longed to hold.

Salter did not let her answer. "A constable is on his way now with the witness in his protective custody. He will be given the opportunity to identify you as the man who hired him that night. Confess all now, and it may go better for you in the end."

Lord Bensonhurst's bravado began to crumble. "What's gotten into you, Lambrick? Ever since you laid eyes on this woman, there's been no end to the destruction in your life. If you want her, keep her. To each his own. Let's not have any more of this unpleasantness. You can even have your job back. We'll call it a gentleman's agreement. But don't try to defame my good name with a lot of baseless accusations and unsubstantiated rumor. I can promise you that it's a very steep and slippery hill, and the fall will kill you."

The door flew back on its hinges. Four footmen ran in and surrounded Lord Bensonhurst protectively.

"What do you say, Lambrick?" he asked urgently.

"It's no good, Bensonhurst. I already know your next move. Whether I remain silent about my accusations or shout them out, you're going to try to kill me. Let's not play games by pretending we're going to become friends."

"I'm sorry that you feel that way. Men," he shouted to the servants, "please escort Mr. Lambrick to the holding cell. Let's give him a taste of the other side of justice. Maybe some time spent with the criminals he helped apprehend will temper his stubbornness." Salter didn't take his eyes off Lord Bensonhurst as the footmen seized him.

"Wait." Mina's voice was soft, but it silenced everyone in the room. She looked up at Lord Bensonhurst with eyes that showed a gentle desperation. "The jewels. You can have them. They're the only real evidence in this case. And they're yours. I was going to hold them until you released my father, but you can have them now. Just let Salter go."

The footmen turned to Lord Bensonhurst, awaiting further instructions.

She exchanged a look with Salter. In that instant, she told him how much he meant to her. She would sacrifice everything for him, just as he had done for her. No price on earth was too great to pay for his happiness.

"Men, wait for me outside."

The footmen unhanded Salter, and stepped away from the exchange. They did as he asked, closing the door behind them.

"Let's have them."

Mina reached down into her corset and pulled out a small pouch that was once the end of a silk stocking. She held it out to him.

Lord Bensonhurst looked inside the pouch and smiled. "Prescott was a fool for keeping these from me. For all the good it did him. In the end he learned that I wasn't a man to be trifled with."

"Can we go, now?" Mina asked.

Lord Bensonhurst shoved the pouch into his pocket, and removed a handkerchief to dab at his lip. "I don't believe for one moment that you'll keep quiet about this, Miss Halliday. Or you, Lambrick. But I know one way to ensure that you do." He walked to the door and opened it, and the footmen came back in.

"Take these two criminals down to the holding cells. I intend to arrange a swift trial for them."

A voice from behind Lord Bensonhurst answered. "That won't be necessary."

Bensonhurst turned around. From the darkened witness box stepped Sir Giles Mornay. The Home Secretary walked down to the middle of the gathering and spoke to the footmen. "Please release them. On my authority, they are free to go."

"Giles," Bensonhurst stammered. "What are you doing here?"

"Alexander," he said, shaking his head. His eyes were barely visible from behind the thick glasses, but it was clear that his duty weighed heavily upon him. "I was astonished when Lambrick asked me to accompany him here to confront you with a crime. I would never have believed him. But by remaining hidden, I have let your own actions and words confirm his report."

Lord Bensonhurst put on his smiling mask, the one he used for the public. "You misunderstand. There's an entire story to this you don't know about."

"I'm in no mood for stories, Alexander. We've known each other a very long time. You've had a career that most men would envy. I always suspected your ambition has been your greatest attribute, because it took you so incredibly far. But I never thought you would stoop to this. Chief Constable Lambrick, please take the young lady outside and wait for me there. We now have a public crisis on our hands, and I'll need your help to sort things out."

"Yes, sir. Come, Mina."

The moment they stepped outside of that awful place, Mina threw herself into Salter's arms.

"I'm so sorry, I'm so sorry, I'm so sorry." It was all she could say.

He chuckled into her neck. "For what?"

"For not trusting you. For not seeing how much you cared. I knew you were up to something, but I suppose I was too blind with jealousy to see it."

"I should be the one apologizing. I should have told you sooner about Celeste."

"I was only angry because she has everything I've ever wanted. Including you."

"Well, she's not the one in my arms. You are."

She pulled away, questions written on her face.

"Minnow," he said, stroking her hair, now erratically free of its coiffure. "I called off the wedding."

"Why?"

"Because I don't love her. I love you."

"You do?"

He smiled then—a broad, adoring smile. "I do."

Footsteps pounded toward them, and Chase Alcott came to a halt in front of him. "There you are, gov. Beg your pardon, Miss Mina." He slid his hat off his head.

"Where in blazes have you been? You're two hours late. Where's the driver of the hansom?"

"Didn't bring him."

"You what?"

"Couldn't help it, gov. The poor chap broke his ankle. What was I to do?"

"Threaten to break the other one."

"Gov—"

"Never mind. Bensonhurst's in custody. You just better make sure that bloke is fully mended by the trial."

Sir Giles came out to the foyer. "There isn't going to be any trial."

Salter's brows drew together. "Sir?"

"I'm not going to broadcast this scandal to the world. This situation is going to remain between us and Their Majesties. No one else must know. I'll ask the Prime Minister to make an announcement tomorrow at the opening of Parliament. He will explain that the Lord Mayor has been feeling the burden of his position, and he has agreed with his physician's advice to step down from his seat."

"But, sir, he must be brought to justice."

"He will, Chief Constable. Justice of a sort. I shall consult the matter with Their Majesties, but my recommendation is that he be sent to a fine institution with plenty of vigorous exercise and fresh air. The same institution, Miss Halliday, where your father is serving out his wrongful sentence."

Mina smiled hopefully. "And my father? Will he get a new trial?"

Light twinkled in Sir Giles's small eyes. "There will be no need. He will be released as soon as I can dispatch a message to the Governor of Australia."

Happiness welled up inside her, and the only person she wanted to share the overflow with was Salter. She turned around, and threw her arms around him. And his embrace was tighter than hers could ever be.

Chapter Nineteen

Mina stood before the full-length mirror. The brocade fabric was embroidered with a chain of white rosebuds, and it was cinched around her rib cage with a pale pink ribbon. The short sleeves fell in multi-tiered scallops, and the square neckline accented the curve of her breasts. It was the most beautiful dress she'd ever owned.

Beautiful. Although her hair was collected in a chignon and decorated with pink rosebuds, a voice inside her whispered that she herself was not beautiful. But with a practiced stamp of her slippered foot, she silenced the voice and took a second look at herself in the mirror.

The image in the glass changed. Now she was spectacular.

She opened the door and went outside. The man who sat in the chair in the hall didn't hear her approach, and just kept staring off into the distance. He was heavy in memories. His sun-darkened skin looked more weathered, and it clung to his much thinner frame. Leathery hands clutched the brim of his hat on his lap. And although his short brown hair had grown a shade lighter and a touch grayer, he looked impeccable in the dark green swallowtail coat and crisp white cravat.

"It's time now, Father," she said.

Emmett Halliday turned his head in her direction, and he rose.

"Wilhemina," he said, beaming at her. "You look a picture."

"Do you really think so?"

He nodded. "If only your mother could have lived to see what a beauty you turned out to be."

Mina blushed to the color of her dress.

"And to think," he continued, placing his bony hands on her shoulders, "how close I came to missing out on this moment. I thought I'd never see you again."

"Don't, Father. You'll make me cry all over again."

"No. Not today. The only tears I want to see are those of happiness." He stood there, staring at Mina, warmth emanating from his soft brown eyes. "Oh, Wilhemina. I knew this day would come for you, even though you never thought it would. And now you're going to get a chance to show every guest out there exactly what I have always known to be true. That you are beautiful. And I love you." He placed a kiss on her cheek just as a tear fell down it.

Mina gave a wet chuckle as she wrapped her arms around him. "So does he, Father. He never lets me forget how much."

"Well, then. Take your bouquet, and my arm. Let's get you to that altar."

Finally, it was quiet. After the nervousness of the wedding, the jubilation of the reception, and the jarring rattle of the carriage ride into Hampstead, Mina found herself relishing the silence.

She stood at one of the windows overlooking the garden. They had made it to the house just as dusk had fallen, but before the rains had come. Though clouds began to gather around it, the moon still beamed its light onto her face.

Mina stared down at the ring on her finger. It was a simple silver band with two smaller diamonds on each side of a large glittering diamond. As she gazed upon it, it returned a blue wink at her. Her father had made it for this occasion at Salter's request. It was a spectacular piece, created by the two men she loved most.

"Do you like it?" Salter asked, leaning over her left shoulder as he wrapped his arms around her.

"It's beautiful. I've never seen its equal."

"Nor I yours," he said, placing a soft kiss on her left ear.

She smiled. "But Salter, it's far too dear. You must have spent a fortune on it."

"That, Minnow, is none of your concern." He began to light the candles on a candelabra that the new house-keeper had put out for them. "Besides, there is nothing as dear to me as you."

Mina sat down on the upholstered settee in the draw-ing room, one of the few furnished rooms in the house. "Salter, really, you must be more circumspect. Their Majesties have bestowed their gratitude on you with this beautiful house and its lands, but there are so many things to purchase for it still. You mustn't lavish such ex-pensive things on me."

"They're but worthless stones. You are my treasure." He crouched down in front of her.

Mina offered him a smile, but it hid a jumble of emotions. Here they were, in their new home, on the first night of their life together. Just beneath the surface of her joy, her nerves began to roil like a restless ocean.

He stayed in that position, staring at her, which made her anxious. Could he see what she was feeling?

She could take no more of his silence. Without thinking, she said the only thing that was on her mind, the very subject she had been trying to avoid since they arrived at Buckley House. "So, what happens now?"

"I thought we'd do a bit of light reading. From this." He pulled a small volume from his coat pocket, and placed it on her lap. She recognized the nondescript, damaged spine and dog-eared pages instantly. It was her copy of *Memoirs of a French Lover*.

"It's . . . my book," she said, making no move to open it.

He handed her a glass of wine, and sat down next to her on the settee. "Yes. I thought we'd start with page twenty-seven."

Mina choked on her wine, almost spilling the liquid from her glass. She took a breath and coughed loudly.

"Your enthusiasm pleases me."

The spasms subsided, but her eyes watered. "Page twenty-seven?" Her voice was wet. "Gosh, I was hoping we could, well, lead up to page twenty-seven."

He laughed, and she could tell he was amusing himself at her expense. "Here." He opened the book to the page in question. There, at the bottom of page twenty-seven, was a little blue heart drawn in the margin. "Read it, and tell me why you desire it."

It wasn't the wine or the coughing that made her

flush now. It was the shame that he knew what she wanted. She read the paragraph.

It was early in the story, before the French lover, Léandre, had become a profligate. He was still a young man, and he had finally persuaded his first love, Abrielle, to accompany him to the lake. He took her by the hand, overjoyed at the sensation of finally holding her, and together, they walked.

She had forgotten about this paragraph. Throughout the book, she had marked many lewd passages recounting bawdy acts and describing nude bodies. This one, however, was innocuous and sweet.

"You told me before that you had put little hearts in the places describing things you wanted to try," he said. "Why is this one so special to you?"

"I—I can't remember."

"No," he said sternly. "No lies. Not tonight."

Her eyelashes fanned her cheeks. "Very well. I wanted . . . to know how it felt to be wanted." She took a deep breath, and it came out in a quiver. "The other acts in this book, they obviously give pleasure. But this was only about affection. This man shows her how much he wants to just *be* with her by holding her hand. And I wanted to know that from a man."

He leaned over, and took the book from her. He took both her hands in his, and kissed each one in turn. "I want to be with you, Mrs. Salter Lambrick, for the rest of my life and yours. And you are wanted, Mina, above all things. There is no one else in the whole world I want beside me. You have become a part of me, the very best part. I rejoice at your happiness, and your sadness becomes my own. And now that you've chosen to give yourself to me, you have become my reason for living. Nothing, but nothing, can take away my love for you."

Mina could see the depth of his love in his eyes. She opened her arms and enfolded him in them. His strong arms wound around her, lifted her out of her seat and onto his lap.

She felt the hard length of his thigh underneath her behind, and it caused a stir in her. His right arm wound around her back, and his left rested over her thighs. There was hardly any part of each of them that wasn't touching the other. Except for one.

He tilted his head, and gently pressed his mouth against hers. It was a soft, unhurried kiss. She loved the texture of his lips, so smooth and so strong, and yet so gentle with her.

But his kisses began to stray, and she had no intention of confining them. A chain of kisses wended down her neck, and she mewed. And when his warm lips began to dance upon the soft spot behind her earlobe, all memory prior to that moment vanished.

He brought his hand to the side of her face as he deepened the kiss. A curious tongue slowly poked into her mouth, and she opened herself to his exploration. His lips began a seductive dance that ignited her passion. With his fingertips, he stroked the column of her neck, right over the line where the blood raced, making her entire body thrum in anticipation.

She heard him moan, a deep, throaty, gratified sound, and it excited her. Her coiffure had come loose in his hand, and wisps of her hair tickled her shoulders. His hand traveled downward, the backs of his fingers drifting across the top of her breasts, sending shivers running rampant all over her body. She had felt the blaze of sexual excitement many times by herself. All alone, once the erotic words in her contraband books had seeded in her fevered brain, she would allow her passion to swell into large red blooms of lust, and she would stroke herself to the full measure of ecstasy. But this was altogether different, and she reveled in the sensation of another person driving her to pleasure.

She felt his hand reach down and gather up her skirt, and it jolted her out of her reverie. There was yet another presence in the room that she had done a good job of ignoring until now. Fear.

"Here," he said, his hand on her hair. "Let me deflower you."

The fear that she had held at bay now came rushing at her full force. She bolted out of his lap. "No! Please! I can't—"

Her hair was still tangled in his fingers. She grasped his hand, which had taken hold of something, and pulled it away from her head. There, in his fingers, was one of the pink rosebuds that had been clinging to her loosening chignon.

Embarrassed by her overreaction, she laughed sheepishly. "Oh, yes, I see. You've 'deflowered' me. How witty."

Salter got that suspicious look in his eye again, a look she began to dread whenever she was hiding something. "Are you all right?"

How could she explain it? Her body was not like other women's. She knew from the naughty books, and from seeing courtesans' bodies at the Pleasure Emporium, that her body was not up to snuff. "Of course I am. Why wouldn't I be?"

"You seem rather agitated. You know, it's natural to be a bit nervous. Would you like me to tell you about my first time?"

"No!" She walked to the far end of the room. Hearing how he made love to another woman would only amplify her anxiety.

"I'm sorry, Minnow. That was an indelicate suggestion. Forgive me."

She became angry now, not at him, but at the situation. Still, anger was better than fear.

He stood up and walked over to her. He placed his strong hands on her shoulders. "Come to bed. Let me show you just how pleasurable it can be."

Since Salter came into her life and showed her how beautiful he thought her to be, she'd worked hard to banish the self-doubt that had always plagued her. But it was useless. Faced with the reality before her, she knew she'd only been fooling herself—and Salter would find out soon enough.

"No, Salter," she said. "I'm not all right. I'm not even satisfactory. I'm completely unacceptable."

"What?"

"I know what you're thinking. You think I'm being silly. You think I've got wedding-night jitters. It's neither of those things. I just . . . can't let you see me . . . with no clothes on."

"Why?"

"Because . . . because I'm not as lovely as other women." If her naked body failed to arouse his passion, she would never live down the humiliation. "And I don't want to lose you."

"I see," he said thoughtfully, but Mina wondered if he truly understood.

He stood, collected the candelabra, and held his hand out to Mina. "Come with me."

Uncertainly, she slid her hand in his and let him lead her out into the hallway. The house was dark and still, as he hadn't yet hired any servants but the housekeeper, and they proceeded up the stairs to the bedchamber.

The bedroom was beautiful, newly wallpapered and tastefully furnished. The bed was immense, twice the size of the one in her room at the bordello. The bedposts, wardrobe, and washstand were all made of cherry mahogany. A gold brocade canopy streamed down from the ceiling in a fabric that echoed the ones draping the walls and the spread across the bed. Vases frothing with flowers stood on every surface. As elegant and clean as everything was, it inspired a feeling of dread in her.

Salter set the candelabra down on the table, creating a sphere of yellow light around them. She watched him light the wood in the fireplace. There was an upholstered chair on each side of the hearth, and he dragged them together until they touched. He sat her down in one, and began to pour out two glasses of wine from the decanter in the room.

"Tonight, I want you to talk to me."

"Talk? What about?"

"I want to know precisely what it is you find so displeasing about yourself."

"What?"

"I want you to tell me everything that you hate about your body."

"Why?"

"Because this is what is keeping you from being my wife. So out with it."

"I'm not going to play this game." She rose from the chair.

A hand shot out and pulled her back down into it. "It's not a game. And I'm not letting you leave until you do."

Mina looked at his hand on her elbow as if it were a monster's claw. "Do you honestly expect me to sit here and confess my ugliness to you? Just . . . bleed for your amusement?"

"That is precisely what I expect."

"Salter, if this is your way of seducing me, it isn't working."

He shook his head, his eyes never leaving hers. "No seduction, no fantasies, no lies. The real you. The real me."

Mina swallowed hard. "I can't do this."

"Start at the top and work your way down."

"Salter, we'll be here all night."

"We've got all night. And tomorrow. And the next day. Take as much time as you need." He took a sip of his wine . . . and waited.

She waited too. The silence between them filled the room, interrupted only by the soft crackle of the fire in the fireplace, but only she seemed to be made uncomfortable by it. Occasionally, she glanced over at him. He sat back in the chair, his legs open in a relaxed posture.

She took a swallow of wine. Her shoulders were

hunched, her legs tightly closed, and her breathing was erratic. She felt like a goldfish trapped in a bowl. The mantel clock ticked in long, slow intervals, but her heart raced inside her like a runaway stagecoach.

"Hair," she breathed.

"Pardon?"

She took a deep breath. "M-my hair. I've always hated it. So brown and lifeless. Never responded to curling irons, much as I tried to make it."

He nodded thoughtfully. "Go on."

She focused on a spot on the carpet. "My eyes . . . they aren't sapphire or emerald, or any other pretty color. Just plain earth brown."

"And?"

She rolled her eyes, but returned them to the spot on the carpet. "My face. It never seemed to draw a man's attentions. Beauty attracts the eye, but my face never did. I would have liked to have been more becoming."

"Continue."

There was nothing more to add that he didn't already know. The rest of her flaws were hidden underneath her clothes.

"My b-breasts. They're too small. And oddly shaped. They're nothing like other women's. If that's your main interest, well, then you may be disappointed."

There was that resonant chuckle again, only now she didn't much care for it. Still, she could not bring herself to look into his face.

"I'm listening."

In for a penny, in for a pound. "My waist isn't narrow enough. And my hips should be fuller. And I have little dimples on my bottom and thighs. Lollie says many women have them, but she doesn't. None of the courtesans at the Pleasure Emporium do. Just me. The wrinkly grape in the bunch." Her breath caught. "So there. That's a foretaste of what you can expect to see without all these clothes on me." She shut her eyes against the embarrassment. "You don't have to stay. I won't blame you if you decide to go."

She heard the chair creak and then his footfalls on the floor. Could he have left that quickly? She opened her eyes, and he was crouching right in front of her.

"I'm still here," he said, and his face became a blur as the tears fell over her lids. "And I'll never leave your side. Ever."

She smiled hesitantly and wiped a trail of hot tears away.

"Are you finished?" he asked. "Are there any reservations about your knees? Your ankles? Your pinkie toes?"

"Don't make fun of me, Salter."

"I can't help it. You haven't mentioned a single thing that rang of truth, let alone something that carried any importance. I give you my name, my earthly provisions, and my eternal love. But of all the things I have, the thing I want most to give you are my eyes, these eyes that see how magnificently beautiful you are."

Her lip trembled inside the lattice of his hands on her cheeks.

"But since I can't do that, I'll have to show you. Here, this is what I think of your hair."

He lifted himself off his haunches, bent over, and placed a kiss on her brown, lifeless hair.

"And this is what I think of your eyes." He lifted her chin, and brought his lips onto each of her eyelids.

"Salter—"

"And as for your face . . ." She felt the soft press of his lips upon her mouth. They smoothed over her lips as if they were tasting a succulent fruit. He turned his head, showing her all the ways their mouths fit together. His lips opened and closed over her mouth, as if he were mouthing her name over her lips. Oh, how she loved the sensation.

Without breaking the kiss, he pulled her to a standing position, and wrapped his thick arms around her. As he pressed against her, her skin was warmed by his heat. His mouth slid down to her jaw, and she lifted her head to receive it. His tongue darted out and pressed against her flesh, and she nearly shuddered from the steam of it. The sensitive skin at the base of her neck ignited from the new sensations.

Behind her she felt him undoing the buttons on her dress. Reflexively, she put a hand on a muscled shoulder and pushed. He didn't let her go.

"Mina," he said, his voice soothing but his tone firm. "Trust me."

She felt like a cat being forced toward a barrel of water. What if he was repulsed by her? What if he compared her with Celeste, Veronica, or any other beautiful woman he may have been with? What if he regretted his decision to be with her? What if she lost him forever? What if—

She closed her eyes on all those frightening thoughts, and a rogue memory from her youth flashed in her mind. Two kittens, abandoned by their mother. She had adopted them both. One was affectionate and trusting. The other shrank from the very sound of her approach. She fed them both and cared for them equally, and loved them just the same. But only one accepted her caresses, only one allowed himself to be blessed by her love and kisses. The other one missed out.

Mina drew fresh wisdom from that memory. She knew she would be loved by Salter no matter what. But it was up to her to determine how much love she would allow herself to receive. It was up to her to trust his love for her. And it was up to her to let herself reach out and touch the source of her happiness.

She softened the hand on his shoulder, and instead pressed her cheek against it. A sigh quivered out. "I love you, Salter."

Salter smiled down at her. "And I love you."

The last stronghold of fear vanished. And Salter was there waiting for her. She embraced him tightly, and he reciprocated. As he unhooked the last of the buttons, she inhaled his scent deeply.

The dress slid off her and puddled around her feet. He pulled at the knot of her corset and loosened her stays, freeing her from their prison. The hard casing opened enough to let her step out of it, and she did. All that was left was the thin chemise.

He enfolded her in his arms, and she relished the warmth he gave her. He bent his head and placed a kiss on her shoulder. His glossy hair tickled her cheek. Her arms entwined around his neck, she hung on his shoulders as his hands outlined the body she had described in detail.

Balling her chemise in his hands, he began to pull up the fabric from her body. Up and up it went, and by degrees she felt the air connect with her skin. Finally, he held it just under her shoulders. All she had to do was let go.

She let go.

He pulled the underdress through her arms, and it fell on the floor next to her.

She stood before him in complete nakedness. The shell of her bashful reserve had cracked and fallen away, and she lay panting within it like a chick thrust into a new world.

His eyes took their full measure of her, resting on each of her much-maligned parts. She might have shrunk from the intensity of his stare, or covered her body in shame. But it would not have done any good. She had bared, he had seen. She had trusted —and the rest was up to him.

Finally, his gaze met hers again. "Oh, Minnow." He took her in his arms and gave her a passionate kiss.

Such powerful hands. They could crush her with the softest of squeezes, and yet they opened gently to caress her. And that mouth . . . the urgency of his kiss sparked something wanton inside her. She felt a warm sensation between her thighs, a river of desire flowing through her body. And when she felt his manhood rise against her, she knew it. She wasn't ugly. Or repulsive. Or invisible.

She was magnificent.

Smiling, she pushed off his coat, and a warm musky scent greeted her nose. It was so wonderful, so intoxicating, more than the wine had been. Next, she began to unbutton his waistcoat, the silky texture of it making her fingers slip. She had done this before, back at the

Roman bath at the Pleasure Emporium, but this time, it was different. Back then, she had had no intention of arousing him. Now, it was what she most desired.

Mina let her hands stroke his stomach and chest through the linen shirt. It was a glorious sensation, all hard and ridged, and he inhaled sharply as she did that. His hips leaned into her, and she could see his manhood rising, despite the confines of his trousers. She passed her hand over the hardening organ, and delighted in the groan rumbling inside Salter's chest. She looked up at his face, and his eyes had closed to experience the pleasure.

She pulled his shirt from out of his trousers, and threw the voluminous fabric over his head. He now stood before her, undressed from the waist up, his beautiful masculine torso illuminated in the dim candlelight. Mina couldn't help but place a kiss on the wide expanse of his smooth chest. With his sculpted chest served up to her eyes, rising and falling with unmet need, and his trousers hanging from his chiseled hips, teasing her with their barely covered secret, he looked more naked than if he had had no clothes on. The look of him, the feel of him, the smell of him—it was arousing her beyond measure.

He picked her up and laid her on the bed. He knelt beside her, lowering his hot mouth over her breast. The breasts she had been so ashamed of came to life suddenly, and as if to punish her for withholding this pleasure, they spread a flame of sexual need to her womanhood, making it ache like never before.

His hands flattened against her waist. The heat of his touch against her cool skin melted feeling into her, as if her whole body had been covered with an invisible layer of frost. His mouth planted a trail of kisses down the middle of her torso, and each kiss blossomed into a vine of pleasure that weaved throughout her body.

The voracious mouth moved down, farther and farther, until it connected with one of her thighs. Her breathing came faster as her womanhood throbbed like a raw nerve. It seemed to be straining toward him.

He lifted her thigh in the air, exposing her sex to his gaze.

"Oh, no, Salter. Not there," she said, as her hands covered her mons. That had been her private playground, known only to the touch of her fingers. It seemed silly to think it, but having him look at her seemed an invasion of privacy.

"There isn't any part of you I don't want to taste."

Taste? "You've kissed every part of me already."

He smiled wickedly at her. "Something tells me you're going to like this kiss the best." Kneeling down on the floor, he twined his thick forearms under each knee, and gave her thighs a firm yank until her body was at the edge of the bed.

This ignoble position was too much to endure. She raised herself on her elbows and tried to push his head away. But when that magical tongue made the first contact with her humming sex, all trace of embarrassment vanished. Myriad new sensations astounded her. As his tongue slowly danced around her pearl, her whole body thrummed like a plucked harp string. "Oh," she exclaimed softly, and closed her eyes to the spark he set off within her. She recognized the commencement of her sexual crescendo, a slow burn of gathering heat. In minutes, it would burst into a flame that would not be extinguished until she had her release.

She had no idea what he was doing to her, but blessed his amazing expertise at doing it. His tongue circled her sensitive nub in a motion she had never before tried. How could he know the way she liked to be touched? She was one raw nerve, each part of her close to the edge. Even if she wanted to, she couldn't stop him. Her pleasure had taken on a life of its own, and she was merely a passenger on the journey to ecstasy. Her breathing grew labored as his tongue reached a thrilling rhythm. But just as she began that ascent to her release, he stopped.

"No," she whined weakly, and reluctantly opened her eyes. He stood up between her legs, a powerful erection straining the limits of his breeches. With a look of determination, he ripped his breeches apart and let them fall to the ground, revealing a great and glorious cock. He strode to the side of the bed, lifted her effortlessly to the top of it, and knelt over her.

"This may hurt," he said, his voice gravelly, "but I'll go slowly."

She wanted him, and she would take any amount of pain to be able to achieve her release. He positioned himself over her and poised his manhood at her moist opening. As he eased in, there was no pain. Yet.

He pushed farther in, and her tightness was forced to cede to his girth. The stretching brought pain, but he didn't move out of her, giving her body a chance to accommodate him. Inch by inch he slid inside her, and her face contorted into a grimace. Finally, he was buried to the hilt, his body resting on hers as he waited until the hurt passed.

The pain soon diminished, replaced by a stinging ache that was not much different than when her body yearned for him moments ago. Still silky from his kisses, her sex eased his movements inside her, though each thrust elicited a twist of her features. The muscles on his backside contracted with each lunge. She held on to his muscled back, which massaged her fingers with his motions. Her hands curved round to his buttocks, and her touch tightened his cock even more. Anything she did, anywhere she touched, his response intensified.

In time, his movements rekindled the flame from his intimate kisses, and she closed her eyes to allow that bliss to snake through her body once more. It was a strange mixture of pleasure and pain, and the sweet torture increased with each stroke until Mina reached the pinnacle of her orgasm and she convulsed for the first time with a man inside her. The spasms seemed to suck on his member, swallowing him further inside her, until he, too, exploded with contentment.

They stayed conjoined for a while, bathing in their mutual pleasure, her pulsations slowly diminishing. Mina found that although the pleasure of her body had ebbed, there was still an exhilarating thrill that remained, and she knew it had something to do with the man in her arms. He lifted his head and placed a tender kiss on her smiling mouth, and then rolled to her side.

She turned to him as he lay in the spent posture of a

sated lion, and smiled. It gave her great satisfaction that she had given him such pleasure.

Stroking her cheek, Salter gazed lovingly at Mina. "I knew you were going to be an audacious bedmate. Now I love everything about you."

They lay together for a long time. Whispered words and hummed kisses made music against the rhythmic snap of the rain against the window.

As midnight approached, everything they said seemed to make them laugh. He lifted an arm and wrapped it around her shoulder, squeezing her tightly. "Thank you," he said.

"For what?"

"For being my wife."

"Whose but yours? You branded every part of me with your kisses."

He smiled lazily. "I wanted to make sure you'd be only mine."

"Of course," she began, "you forgot something."

He cracked open his eyes. "What?"

"My bottom. You going to kiss my arse too?"

His surprised look dissolved into a look of irritation. "Certainly. Here's a wet smack for you." His hand slapped her backside.

She yelped in surprise, but broke out into giggles. He tightened his grip on her, and pulled her on top of him.

"What are you going to show me next?"

He laughed, his chest vibrating as he did. "How to sleep between bouts of ecstasy."

"Oh, no you don't. There will be no sleeping in this

bed. I have a lot of catching up to do. Let's move on to page forty-nine."

"Are you trying to kill me?"

She nodded, liking the sound of it. "Death by a thousand orgasms."

Chapter Twenty

"Over my dead body," Mina shouted, setting her cup down on the table with such force that the liquid spilled over the edge.

"Calm yourself," said Salter, putting a hand on her arm.

"Absolutely not." Mina whirled her gaze back on Lollie. "Whoever heard of such a thing? Having your honeymoon in Catford? You'll have it here at Buckley House."

Lollie shook her head, bending over to dab at the tea with her napkin before it made a stain on the blond wood. "We couldn't do that. We'd be a bother."

"Nonsense. We'd hardly even see each other in this big old house."

"Thanks all the same, Mina," said Chase. "But you two are barely out of your own honeymoon. Besides, Mum will look after us in her flat in Catford."

Salter chuckled at the mere thought of it. "A mother-in-law and a daughter-in-law in the same house are like two cats in a bag. Mina's right, Alcott. There's plenty of room here. We don't have many servants yet, or even enough furniture. But Mina's been seeing to the gardens, restoring them to what they must have looked like when the earl was in residence. You two can ride, take walks to the stream, and the local town is very pleasant. Buckley House isn't exactly Blackheath Manor, but it's a damn sight nicer than Catford."

The words were having a seductive effect on Chase. He put his hand on Lollie's. "What do you think?"

Lollie smiled at him, her blond curls bouncing as she nodded.

"Looks like the future missus is keen on the idea."

The two girls beamed at each other.

"Excellent!" exclaimed Mina. "Then it's all settled. After your wedding next month, you'll come and stay with us."

Lollie poured Mina more tea. "Ye wouldn't sound so thrilled if you knew what Chase is like. He eats like a horse, only faster."

Chase swung a withering gaze at Lollie. "Which is surprising, considering that Lollie's cooking is only slightly preferable to hunger."

"Is that so? Well, how'd you like a goose for supper tonight?"

"I'd love it."

She reached over and pinched him on the bottom. "There. Made it early for you. Feast on that."

Chase rolled his eyes in Salter's direction. "How'd you like that. She gets more and more like a shrewish alewife every day."

Lollie perched a hand on her hip. "Alewife?"

Salter's laughter rolled across the room. "If you fight like this before you're married, I'd hate to see you after."

Mina smiled. "We'll see soon enough. After next month, that is."

Chase lifted Lollie's hand to his mouth. "Naw. Everything'll change once Lollie becomes mine forever. There won't be a discontented day in the lot."

Lollie's face softened. "You can't let me stay cross with you, can you?"

He shook his head forcefully. "I don't want you to ever look at me with anything less than that expression there."

"You always know just what to say."

"That's right," he said proudly. "'Cause I'm a gentleman."

"Yes, you are. My Cockney gentleman." She leaned over and squished her full lips upon his. "Even Serafina recognized that about you."

That name brought a host of nostalgic memories back for Mina. "How is Serafina? I heard Madame Fynch never did sack her for leaving the house to help me."

"Naow. Even the Madame wasn't stupid enough to let two of her girls go at once. She kept her on, but it was Serafina who grew restless. She wrote to her husband in Spain, begging him for his forgiveness for leaving him as she did. He wrote back, quick as you like, telling her he'd been heartsick over her, and that he missed her dreadfully, and that of course he'd forgive her. So off she went, on the first ship back to Alameda."

Mina glowed. "I'm so glad. She had the biggest heart of anyone I knew. I'm so happy her husband recognized it."

"Too bad the Madame never did. It ticked her off good and proper. First time a girl ever quit on her."

"Serves her right," Mina said.

"I've given a lot of thought to that place," Salter remarked. "I think it's time that we shut Madame Fynch down permanently."

Mina and Lollie looked at each other, concern etched on their faces.

"But Salter," began Lollie. "We've got friends there too. What'll happen to 'em? If you close the place down, they'll have to go to work on the streets. Some of them there were brought up proper . . . they'll never make it as streetwalkers."

Chase squeezed her hand. "You did."

"I'm different than what they are."

Mina turned to face Salter. "Lollie's right. I don't condone what they do, but they oughtn't to be turned out all at once. There are lots of other bordellos in London, but none of them are better than Madame Fynch's. If they get put out, I promise you, they'll be forced into worse circumstances than before. I agree that the vice should be stopped, but closing the place down will do nothing to reach that aim."

Salter's chest expanded as he considered the quandary. "You're right, of course. But the law is the law, Minnow. Running a bordello is a violation. Tell you what. I'll let you give them advance notice. This way, they'll have ample opportunity to find respectable employment."

"Well, it's time we were off," said Chase, rising. "Thanks for lunch, Mina. It was splendid. Gov," he said, extending his hand to Salter, "thanks for the invitation to stay at your home. You're a toff."

Mina beamed at her husband. "Actually, Chase,

you're more right than you know. Salter's being knighted next week."

"Go on!" said Chase.

Salter expelled a beleaguered breath. "The Home Secretary wants to make me Superintendent of Police. Apparently, that carries with it a knighthood."

"Ha! Wait till I tell them at the station!"

"Don't you dare, Alcott. Or it's back to scrubbing out the riverboats."

Chase was undeterred. "Does that mean we all have to call you 'Sir Salter'?"

"Not if you want to keep your job."

Lollie furrowed her brow. "Why not? It'd be nothing less than you deserve."

"I won't be called Sir Salter or anything that even closely approximates it."

"Why not?"

"In the first place, it makes whoever says it sound like he's got a stutter. I won't be able to keep a straight face. And in the second place, I don't want any of that snobbery."

"Sir Salter . . ." repeated Chase. "I quite like the sound of that."

Salter smiled in spite of himself. "Go on, get out. While you still can."

Lollie gave Mina a kiss on the cheek. "Guess that'll make you a 'lady,' won't it?"

"She's already a lady," said Salter, wrapping his arm around her.

Hand in hand, they saw Chase and Lollie to the door. When their phaeton rolled down the graveled path to the main road, Salter turned to Mina.

"You know, a thought occurred to me just now. We do need to staff the house. Why don't you bring one or two of those girls at the Pleasure Emporium here as servants?"

"Not on your life."

"Why not?"

"I'm not bringing any of those beautiful women into this house."

Salter wrapped his arms around her possessively. "Minnow, don't you know by now that you're all the woman—the only woman—I desire?"

She squeezed him back, her ear pressed against his chest. Yes, she knew that. She wouldn't have believed that she would ever be so to any man, let alone this wonderful, noble, perfect man. But he had proven it to her time and again, and she would trust him to continue to do so for the rest of her life.

"I love you."

"And I love you," he said, the sound reverberating in his chest.

The meaning and the vibration of those words set off a tremor that awakened every nerve within her. A rogue fantasy, one from a long time ago, materialized in her mind. She couldn't remember if she had read about it or if her own naughty mind had spawned it, but she was certain it would be something he had never even heard of before, let alone experienced. A wicked smile cut across her face, and she decided to show him precisely what would happen whenever he said those words to her and meant them.

"And now, my darling husband, if you'd care to follow

mc to our bedroom, I'd like to demonstrate something from an as-yet-unpublished erotic book."

A groove deepened in his forehead, even as the corners of his mouth lifted. "What 'as-yet-unpublished' erotic book?' "

"I think it shall be called *Memoirs of an English Lady*."

A knowing smile spread across his face. "Memoirs of an 'English Lady,' ch? Anyone I know?"

"Mm-hmm," she agreed. "And provided your stamina is up to par, you can know her again, and again, and again."

Acknowledgments

I want to thank God, my loving Father, and Jesus, my Lord and Savior, who has a special place in His heart for bad girls like me.

To my parents, Lino and Juana Marcos, and my siblings, Marilyn, Miriela, Mabel, Lino Jr., and Marlene, I love you all. You are my greatest blessing.

I owe a debt of gratitude to Rose Hilliard, my editor, and all the other brilliant and talented people at St. Martin's Press. Thanks for your enthusiastic partnership.

Finally, I wish to thank the readers. Your messages of encouragement and friendship always bring me joy. It is a privilege to know people who share my passion for romance.

Wickedly Ever After

Marshall Hawkesworth jerked on the reins, forcing his horse to an awkward stop. He curled his gloved hand around the pommel and flung himself off the stallion.

His scowl blackened as he looked up at the redbrick structure. The door was painted a cheery blue, and geraniums lined the windows beneath lace curtains. But he had just been made aware of the house's sordid past, and irritation threatened to choke him all over again. This was no place for his sister to be *seen* in, let alone *taught* in.

He took the stairs two at a time, and rapped on the door with his riding crop. A diminutive maid opened the door and curtseyed. "May I help you, sir?"

"I'm here to see the headmistress." He gave her his crop, hat, and gloves.

Marshall followed behind the maid, but he was more inclined to jump over the girl's head and charge ahead of her. But as he didn't know where the headmistress was, he thought it best to school his temper. Until, of course, he met the woman responsible for giving his sister a scandalous education that had rendered her unmarriageable to a most advantageous prospect.

They came to a door at the far end of a grand salon, and the maid knocked on it. "One moment, sir. I'll announce you."

"There'll be no need," he said, and opened the door himself.

Sunlight streamed in through the windows at the far end of the room, casting squares of light onto the green carpet. The walls were papered in a light green silk frothing with tiny pink and blue blooms. A cherrywood table sat in the middle of the room, its legs curving down to the floor. Sitting behind the desk was a red-headed young woman who looked up from her ledgers to frown at him.

"You're late," she said, placing her quill into its stand. "I was expecting applicants at noon."

"I'm here to see the headmistress."

"Then it is a happy coincidence that you've found her. I am Lady Athena."

Marshall blinked in surprise. "You? You're in charge of this school?" He had expected a bookish lady, wizened in face and feature, her curves disfigured by the ravages of time. Not someone like—

"Yes, I am. Now kindly close your mouth and take a seat."

He flinched at her impudence. "Young woman, I am here on a matter of great importance, with nothing less at stake than family honor."

Her posture stiffened. "In the first place, you may call me 'Lady Athena' or 'Miss McAllister.' I'll thank you to remember to whom you are speaking. And in the second place, I know precisely why you are here."

An angry retort died on his lips. "You do?" he said

slowly, wondering how she could possibly ascertain his intentions.

"Of course," she replied, rising from her chair. The fabric of her blue dress cascaded to the floor. "You are not the first man to step over our threshold who has found himself experiencing some degree of financial embarrassment. You might even say that gentlemen who have fallen on hard times provide our stock in trade."

His eyes narrowed suspiciously. "Do they?"

"There's no shame in earning an honest wage. A good hard day's work would do many gentlemen a world of good. Including you, I daresay."

The affront was almost more than he could stand. It was bad enough that the saucy woman had mistaken him for someone other than the Marquis of Warrington. But to upbraid his character without the benefit of even a formal introduction was beyond tolerable.

"Nevertheless," she continued, crossing her arms at her chest, "we, more than anyone, appreciate the importance of tact. After all, modeling has been a much maligned profession."

He almost laughed. Tact was something this girl knew nothing of. As he debated how best to put her in her place, something she'd said buzzed in his head like an angry hornet. *Modeling?*

"You will find that at this school, educational candor is valued above all else. These young ladies are taught a broad range of subjects, without capitulating to what is deemed acceptable for members of our sex. To the outside world, however, our curriculum may raise a few eyebrows. Your involvement in our program will be treated with discretion for as long as we have yours."

Marshall had not ascended to the rank of captain in the Royal Navy without learning how to deal with an adversary. And something told him that it would be far more effectual to get the information he sought by concealing his intent rather than disclosing it.

"Indeed. That had been a concern of mine."

"What is your name?"

"Marshall."

The woman returned to the desk and pulled out a fresh piece of paper from a box of stationery. "Well, Mr. Marshall, have you ever done any modeling before?"

"I can't say that I have, no. But I have been told that I'm not too hard on the eyes."

"Hmm. I suppose if the room were dark enough."

He chuckled in spite of himself. This girl seemed to make a habit of insulting people.

She scribbled something down. "Your hair is flaxen, your eyes are blue . . . how tall are you?"

"Six feet, three inches."

"A large fellow."

"I come from good Oxfordshire stock."

She glanced up from the sheet. "I've no wish to discuss your relatives. No matter what manner of farm-yard species they came from."

Marshall smothered a laugh. This girl was a complete surprise to him. Proper ladies of his acquaintance rarely disagreed with him, let alone offended him. She had a nerve—no, bloody cheek—to treat him this way. He looked around the room. There were paintings hanging on the wall, each with curious images—an idyllic countryside with a darkened wood to one side, a woman cradling a locked box, two people at a ball wearing masks. All of them seemed to be painted by the same hand.

"Will you be the one I shall be posing for?"

"Not exclusively. I lead a class on art, and I will need a model for our next lesson. Seeing as you're the only applicant who has presented himself, I expect you may have to do."

He pursed his lips. "Please don't flatter me. It goes to my head."

She smirked, and it lent her face a wicked charm. Her skin was lovely . . . fair and luminous, offset by her striking red hair. Her eyes were like cut emeralds, sparkling with a lively intelligence. Her mouth was like a rosebud, pink and kissable, and he experienced a rogue desire to make that mouth moan instead of smirk. This meeting had completely veered off his intended course, but he was intrigued by the prospect of the fresh adventure. This woman warranted exploration.

"The job pays a shilling an hour. If I engage you, I'll want you to pose for no more than two hours at a time."

It was a generous wage. Clearly, this woman had no idea that anyone off the street would pose for a twentieth that price.

"When shall I start?"

"I said *if* I engage you. You haven't been given the position yet."

He couldn't help but smile. He was beginning to understand how her mind worked. There was another volley of mortar fire coming, and he had to let her launch her attack. She wasn't about to give an inch without taking a foot.

"What must I do to be hired?"

"I'll need a proper look at you. Stand up."

He pursed his lips at her commanding manner. She could do with a lesson in civility.

"Over there, in the light." She strolled up to him and took a closer look. She walked around him, examining him from all angles. The top of her chignon came to just below his shoulder.

"Well, Admiral?" he quipped. "Do I pass muster?"

"I haven't even begun my inspection yet. Take off your clothes."

The sardonic grin was torn from his face. "I beg your pardon?"

She looked him squarely in the face. "Take off your clothes so that I can get a better look at you. You can't expect me to hire you on the basis of a smile."

"You want me to model *nude*?"

"Why should you appear so surprised? My advertisement called for a male model to pose *a la française*. Did you think that meant I would serve you up with croutons?"

Marshall shook his head in amazement. "Lady Athena, aren't you afraid of what this compromising situation will do to your reputation? Or that of the school?"

She walked over to the window and untethered the curtain next to the window. The fabric swished over the window, muting the light in the room. "There is no one else watching."

His rational judgment began to dissolve in the rising tide of his fascination. What an audacious woman this was. And yet, as he began to tug at the knot of his cravat, her eyes drifted to the floor.

His studied her intently as he pulled off his coat. A muscle in her throat tensed, and color suffused her face.

He pulled the linen shirt over his head and dropped it on the chair with the rest of his clothes. Naked to the waist, he waited for her to look up at him, but her gaze was riveted to the floor. His hands went to unbutton his trousers when a soft voice stopped him.

"That'll do for now," she said. Finally, she looked up at him.

Marshall watched as her eyes traveled nervously across his broad chest. She was too uneasy to assess him properly, and he wondered briefly if this exercise was just a childish display of power. But she was visibly shaken by what she saw, and despite her bravado, he wondered if she had ever before beheld a man in a state of undress.

He watched in growing amusement as she timidly inspected him from different angles. Her rushed, unsteady breathing betrayed her nervousness. Though her crossed arms attempted to communicate a distant reserve, her whole body was as tight as a manrope knot. It was as clear as daylight. She wasn't necessarily an innocent—she was *attracted* to him.

"You may have the job," she said finally from behind him.

"Thank you."

"On one condition."

He turned around to face her. "Yes?"

"You must tell me how you acquired those scars."

"Perhaps."

She blinked up at him.

"If you ask me nicely."

The haughty expression returned, and her full lips thinned. "You may get dressed now. I shall open the drapes."

As she walked past him, he reached out and grabbed her forearm. Her body jerked back and collided with his. "Just a moment," he said, snaking his arm around her waist. She looked up at him in equal parts panic and fascination. She tried to push away, but everywhere her hands touched his bare flesh. In the hollow of her throat, her heartbeat fluttered like a trapped bird.

He lowered his head to within inches of hers. "I have a condition or two of my own."